JUDY MAYS

A BREATH OF HEAT

D0191669

ELLORA'S CAVE
ROMANTICA PUBLISHING

An Ellora's Cave Romantica Publication

www.ellorascave.com

A Breath of Heat

ISBN 9781419954993
ALL RIGHTS RESERVED.
A Midsummer Night's Heat Copyright © 2004 Judy Mays
Solstice Heat Copyright© 2005 Judy Mays
Edited by Raelene Gorlinsky
Cover art by Syneca.

Trade paperback Publication June 2006

Excerpt from Sheala Copyright © Judy Mays, 2006

Content Advisory:

S – ENSUOUS
E – ROTIC
X – TREME

Ellora's Cave Publishing offers three levels of Romantica™ reading entertainment: S (S-ensuous), E (E-rotic), and X (X-treme).

The following material contains graphic sexual content meant for mature readers. This story has been rated E-rotic.

S-*ensuous* love scenes are explicit and leave nothing to the imagination.

E-*rotic* love scenes are explicit, leave nothing to the imagination, and are high in volume per the overall word count. E-rated titles might contain material that some readers find objectionable – in other words, almost anything goes, sexually. E-rated titles are the most graphic titles we carry in terms of both sexual language and descriptiveness in these works of literature.

X-*treme* titles differ from E-rated titles only in plot premise and storyline execution. Stories designated with the letter X tend to contain difficult or controversial subject matter not for the faint of heart.

Also by Judy Mays

෨

A Touch of Heat
Celestial Passions: Brianna
Celestial Passions: Sheala
In the Heat of the Night
Nibbles 'n' Bits *(anthology)*
Perfumed Heat

About the Author

෨

Foxier than a Hollywood starlette! More buxom than a Vegas show girl! Able to undangle participles with a single key stroke!

Look! At the computer!

It's a programer!

It's a computer nerd!

No! It's - Judy Mays!

Yes, Judy Mays - romantica writer extraordinaire who came to Earth with powers and ablilities far beyond those of mortal writers. Judy Mays! Who can write wild, wanton werewolves, assertive, alluring aliens and vexing, vivacious vamps. Who, desguised as a mild-mannered English teacher in a small Pennsylvania high school, fights a never ending battle for Heroic Hunks, Hot Heroines, and Sexy Sensuality!

Judy welcomes comments from readers. You can find her website and email address on her author bio page at www.ellorascave.com.

Solstice Heat

"Ms. Mays continues one of my favorite shape shifter series with SOLSTICE HEAT, and she doesn't disappoint...Not only are the main characters enjoyable, but the secondary characters are a real treat. The ribbing between the pack members and the family members is humorous and shows a deep affection. However, my favorite secondary character is Belle's smart-mouthed cat, Callie. I love Callie! I highly recommend SOLSTICE HEAT to the reader of shape shifter, erotic romance and can't wait for the next installment of this series." ~ *The Best Reviews*

"Solstice Heat by Judy Mays is sure to leave you panting for more as well as panting from the heat it generates. Ms. Mays just proves that some series get even better as they go along with this installment in her Heat series.... All in all, Ms. Mays deigns to bless us with her talent for creating a masterpiece capable of making you forget that dinner is burning in the oven despite the smoke-alarm going off over your head." ~ *eCataromance*

"...This is a must for any Mays fan, particularly followers of the *Heat* series. If you haven't read a Judy Mays tale before, I suggest you do so. You will soon find yourself a Judy Mays convert and will be looking with eager eyes towards her next novel – as I am." ~ *Fallen Angel Reviews*

"This is an excellent story with many interesting characters. If you have been following Ms Mays' werewolf family, the Greys, as I have, this is a must have book. My only complaint with the story is that some threads were clearly left dangling for the next Grey werewolf story and I hate to wait!" ~ *Just Erotic Romance Reviews*

What the critics are saying…

ဆာ

A Midsummer's Night Heat

4 ½ Stars "This story of lust remarkably achieves a great amount of romanticism. Both Alex and Belle are strong, attractive and heartwarming characters. Part of a series, the overall story continues to grow and remain interesting." ~ *Romantic Times Magazine*

"This is the third book in Ms. Mays' fabulous werewolf series "A Touch of Heat"…You'll definitely need some cooling down after this story. If you love werewolves, this is a must read!" ~ *eCataRomance Reviews*

"Judy Mays has a way of creating characters that grab you from the very beginning. *A Midsummer Night's Heat* starts and ends with action that will keep you interested. I loved this book. Like all of Judy May's books it was enthralling. Her attention to detail really shows in this well crafted story that you are sure to enjoy." ~ *Enchanted Romance*

"Judy May's has created a beautiful story of a couple who must overcome prejudice and age old beliefs in order to find happiness. She has created a world of werewolves that have the same problems as us: infidelity, prejudice, greed and the desire for love. I really enjoyed the fact that both characters are equals and complement each other perfectly." ~ *Romance Junkies*

Contents

Dedication

❦

*A Breath of Heat is dedicated to my most devoted fans,
the members of my Judy Mays' group.
The support of you ladies and gentlemen
means the world to me.*

A Midsummer Night's Heat

ɞ

Chapter One

೫

Finally, I'm free. Belle braced her hands against the porch railing, closed her eyes, and breathed deeply. The freshly washed scent of rain-soaked pine trees teased her senses. A fox yipped somewhere behind the cabin. An owl hooted.

She inhaled more clean air. A vacation! Her first vacation on her own! She could read books without being interrupted, paint without being interrupted, do anything without being interrupted. Shoot, if she wanted, she didn't have to do a damn thing but lie in the sun all day. Coming to this cabin deep in the woods, away from the hustle and bustle of the company and city life, was the smartest thing she'd ever done. With her father focusing all of his attention on Moira and their newborn twin daughters, she didn't have to worry about him anymore. And the business could certainly survive without her for a couple of weeks — or months.

Belle threw back her head and shouted, "And I don't care! I don't care if Dad doesn't need me anymore. I can finally stop worrying about him and do what I want to do! Who knows, maybe I'll never go back! I love being alone!"

As her voice echoed back off the mountain, a wolf howled.

Concentrating on the howl's direction, Belle grinned. A forest brother. How long had it been since she'd even talked to a wolf, let alone run through the woods with one? This vacation kept getting better and better! She kicked off her sneakers then stripped off the tee shirt and bike shorts. Naked, she jogged away from the cabin toward the forest.

Smiling, Belle lengthened her stride when she reached the path that disappeared into the forest. Again she took a deep breath. How she missed running free though a fresh, rain-washed forest.

Dark mist swirled and a lithe, black wolf loped along the path.

Belle was barely a mile from the cabin when a shot from a high-powered rifle shattered the peace of the forest.

Skidding to a halt, she cocked her ears and raised her nose to the wind. Who was shooting? At what? In spring? Hunting season wasn't until fall.

She bared her teeth and snarled. Those two yuppies in the new Hummer she'd seen at the gas station in town yesterday would probably shoot at anything that moved. She'd glanced in the open window and seen a rifle stock sticking out from beneath a coat lying on the backseat. Idiot survivalist wannabes. They had to go into the woods and prove they were real men by shooting at defenseless animals.

Belle snarled again and shook her head. No exercise for her tonight. No way could she go running through the woods if those two idiots were taking potshots at whatever moved.

She'd just turned back toward the cabin when a second shot reverberated down the valley.

Her sensitive ears registered the agonized howl of a wolf.

Without thinking twice, she leaped forward. A forest brother wounded—maybe dead? That settled it. No way was she going to let those two morons get their hands on a wounded or dead wolf.

* * * * *

"Damn it, Sam, go back to your wife and kids and forget about this other woman."

A belligerent glare in his eyes, the short man shook his head. "My old lady's a shrew. All she does is nag. Marjorie is *nice* to me. Why shouldn't I divorce the bitch for a woman who treats me with respect? Last time I checked, divorce was legal in this state."

Alex stared at the scruffy man in front of him and wrinkled his nose. Sam needed a shave — and a shower. "Your wife didn't start nagging until you started spending every night in a bar and coming home drunk. And she wouldn't keep nagging if you'd stop blowing your paycheck on booze and spend time with your kids. Besides, *we* mate for life. We don't get *divorced*."

Eyes narrowed, Sam drew himself up to his full height. He still had to look up to his Alpha. "Easy for you to say, Alex, with no woman badgering you because you work in a sawmill and don't make enough money to suit her. Oh wait, your woman ran away, didn't she? Didn't want anything to do with the high and mighty Alex Whitehorse when he started ordering her around. What the hell do you know about women anyway? You couldn't keep one."

Sam never saw the hand that shot out and grabbed him by the throat.

As he hoisted the smaller man up to eye level, Alex fisted his other hand.

"Problem, Alex?"

Alex gritted his teeth. *Damn Omega.* "Nothing I can't handle, Dave."

The blond man leaned against the doorframe. "You might want to handle it more quickly then. Sam's eyes are starting to bug out. I don't think he can breathe either."

"Fuck!" Alex opened his hand, and Sam fell gasping to the floor.

"Frickin' asshole!" Sam sputtered between huge gasps. "I'll get you for this. I'll bring you up before the Council. You had no right to grab me like that. I didn't do nothing to you."

Alex turned his back and rested his fists on his desk. "Get out, Sam. Just get out. Go home to your wife."

"Fuck you." Pushing himself to his feet, Sam staggered to the door. "Get out of my way, fucking pussy Omega."

13

Dave dipped his head to hide his slight smile and stepped back.

Sam clomped across the porch and down the steps. Both men heard the door of his pickup slam. The engine coughed and sputtered but caught after a couple of backfires. Gravel bounced up onto the porch as the truck tore down the driveway.

Alex buried his face in his hands, then finger-combed his long hair back off his forehead. He really needed to get a haircut. "I'm sorry, Dave. That insult…"

"…was from Sam Irons. Do you really think I'll let it bother me?" the blond man answered with a wide grin. "Nothing I haven't heard before."

Alex shook his head. "You don't deserve to be treated like a second-class citizen…"

"…because I'm an Omega?" Dave finished, grin still firmly on his face. "All Alphas need an Omega to be successful. I'm the one who heads off the most volatile problems, defuses the explosive situations before they get to you. Besides, anybody else would suck at this job. You know me, I get along with everybody. I have since we were kids together. Why do you think I volunteered for this job? I don't have to work my ass off at the mill or in some other back-breaking job. What more could I want?"

Refusing to rise to Dave's humorous baiting, Alex turned and crossed his arms over his chest. "And the one who gets treated like shit by everyone else."

Dave's bark of laughter had Alex frowning.

"Who treats me like shit, Alex? A few assholes like Sam. Nobody else. That's it. Now, what did Sam want? Another fight with his wife or another advance from the Pack bank so he can buy food for his kids?"

Alex walked around his desk and sat down. "He wants to get a divorce so he can marry a human woman."

Dave stiffened. "Is he crazy?"

Alex raised an eyebrow.

Dave smiled ruefully. "Okay, point taken. What are you going to do?"

Again, Alex raked both hands through his hair. "What can I do? I can forbid him to divorce her, but how can I stop him if he really goes through with it? It's the twenty-first century, Dave. Pack Law isn't as cut and dried anymore. Let's face it, a lot of pack members ignore the rules that don't suit them."

Dave sighed. "Sam's wife isn't going to take this very well. She's a real pain in the ass. If he does leave, she'll be at your door every day."

Alex leaned his elbows on his desk and buried his face in his hands again. Ever since Serena left, it seemed as if anything that could go wrong had. Why wasn't he good enough for her? How could she have chosen that...that half-breed over him?

Dave strode across the room, grabbed Alex's shoulder and shook him. "Damn it, Alex, you're thinking about Serena again, aren't you? Forget her already. She made her choice, and it wasn't you. Move on. There are plenty of females out there who would throw themselves at your feet if you let them."

Alex lifted his head and pushed himself up out of his chair. He jerked his tee shirt over his head and stripped off his jeans "I'm going for a run—a long run. Don't be surprised if I don't come back for a day or two, so if anything comes up, tell Josh he's in charge."

Swirling and dipping, dark mist surrounded Alex. When it finally dissipated, a large black wolf loped across the room and out the door.

Snorting, Dave crossed his arms over his chest. "Run all you want, Alex, but until you accept the fact that Serena didn't love you, you won't have any peace."

* * * * *

Lengthening his stride, Alex ran. Nostrils flared, and he sucked in the scents of the night. Thousands of odors both fragrant and foul teased his senses. He opened his mouth and let his tongue loll out as he ran. Rotting leaves and damp mold caressed the hard pads of his paws while soft ferns and small branches grazed his sides. He sucked in a huge breath. All his cares and problems melted away when he ran. Why couldn't managing the affairs of the pack be this uncomplicated?

A deer leaped through the pines before him and, with a quick flick of his tail, Alex changed direction. The heady thrill of the hunt and the thought of hot blood flowing down his throat if he were successful would go a long way toward calming the disquiet in his soul. Yes. The hunt. Exactly what he needed. Veering more to the left, he increased his speed and chased after the buck, pushing himself to the limits of his endurance. Exhaustion and hot blood would push everything from his mind—Sam, the pack...Serena.

He hurdled a fallen tree, and the velvet-antlered buck's white tail bobbed before him. It leaped right then left, zigzagging in a vain attempt to lose him.

The lust for hot blood pulsing through his veins, Alex drew closer. When the deer bounded into a small clearing, he didn't hesitate.

The boom from a high-powered rifle echoed, and a fiery pain lanced across his shoulders.

Yelping, Alex rolled head over heels. As he struggled to his feet, another shot echoed. Searing agony exploded in his head. He fell and didn't move.

Chapter Two

೫ා

Her lungs laboring, Belle ran faster than she had ever run.

Off in the distance, she could hear two men holler to each other about wolf pelts.

Eyes narrowed against the wind streaming into her face, she veered toward the shouts. Damn assholes. Stupid asshole yuppies. They don't give a damn that wolves were practically endangered a couple of years ago. They were just interested in another trophy to prove how macho they were.

The scent of fresh blood teased her nostrils, and she slid to a halt at the edge of a small clearing. Beams of moonlight danced across the small opening in the forest to illuminate a dark mass lying in its center—a dead wolf. Off to the left, an owl hooted and took wing. The sound of branches snapping was followed by human curses. The yuppies were drawing steadily nearer.

Belle looked at the prone wolf. No way was she going to allow those lamebrains to skin it. The forest brother deserved a proper burial. The two hunters struggling through the underbrush were still far enough away so that they wouldn't see her. They'd never know what happened.

Shifting back to her human form, she strode into the clearing and knelt at the wolf's side. The long bloody furrow that ran across its back from one shoulder to the other seeped dark blood. More blood trickled from an ugly gouge on the back of his head.

Its rib cage rose and fell with slow, shallow breaths.

Belle caressed its soft fur. "You're still alive. Good thing for you those guys are lousy shots."

After one last glance over her shoulder, Belle wrapped her arms around the wolf and hoisted it over her shoulder with a grunt. "Damn, brother, but you're a lot heavier than you look. Lucky for you I'm stronger than I look. Now, let's get back to the cabin so I can fix you up. You'll be back with your pack in no time at all."

Shifting the wolf's weight across her shoulders, Belle took one step, staggered a bit, regained her balance, and headed back into the forest. The return trip to the cabin would be far slower than the run out. Ducking a low branch, she headed for the small stream she'd hurdled. Walking down through that thin strip of water for a while was a good idea just in case those yuppies were better trackers than they were shots.

Sucking air into her straining lungs, Belle staggered up the steps and into the cabin. One last effort got her into the bedroom on wobbly knees where she carefully dropped the wolf onto the bed. Groaning, she sank to the floor. Crossing her arms on the bed, she closed her eyes and dropped her head onto her arms. The wolf had gotten heavier and heavier with every mile. The last ten had been pure torture.

A sharp claw dragged across her bare thigh penetrated Belle's exhaustion. *Where have you been? I was worried about you.*

Belle lifted her head and stared at the half-grown calico kitten she'd found alongside the road yesterday. "Did you say something?"

The kitten sat, wrapped her tail around her forepaws, and stared at Belle.

Shaking her head, Belle blinked to clear her blurry vision. She couldn't ever remember being so tired and now she was hearing things. For a minute there, she'd thought the cat had talked to her.

"Meeeooooow?"

Belle pushed the kitten away as it butted its head against her thigh.

"Scat!"

The kitten jumped and hissed.

Groaning, Belle rubbed her hand across her face. Gods, but she was tired. "Sorry, kitty."

The kitten jumped up on the bed and sniffed the unconscious wolf and hissed again.

Belle chuckled—weakly. "Never expected to find yourself in this position, did you? Rescued by a werewolf who then brings a wolf home. I'm sorry if your cat sensibilities are offended, but he's still alive. I couldn't leave him out in the woods to die any more than I could just leave you at the side of the road."

She glanced back over her shoulder, then with a small moan, pushed herself to her feet. "I still need to clean his wounds."

She got as far as the leather armchair on the other side of the room. "I just need to sit down and rest a little first." She sank onto the soft leather and was asleep almost before she curled her legs on the seat.

The kitten stared first at the wolf then at the woman. After a disgruntled meow, she trotted across the room and jumped up onto the back of Belle's chair. With a little nudging and clawing, she was able to push the woolen afghan that lay there down onto Belle, more or less. Then she jumped back to the floor and headed to the bed. Leaping up, she sniffed the wolf. Curling back her lips, she hissed. After a grumbling growl, she began licking its wounds.

Hissing between licks, the kitten continued to clean the wolf's wounds. The things a cat would do for a human—even one that wasn't completely human. Bad enough she'd attached herself to a Were. Pulling her lips back, she grimaced and spat out a chunk of dirt. After another hiss, she continued to wash the wound, a low growl vibrating in her throat. Ministering to a wolf. Her ancestors would be snarling and hissing in their afterlives.

Oh well, at least it wasn't a dog.

A wet nose in her face woke Belle.

She pushed the kitten away and snuggled deeper into the afghan.

The kitten didn't give up. "Meooooooooow!" *I'm hungry.*

Groaning, still half asleep, Belle uncovered her head. "Okay, okay. I'll feed you." She blinked two or three times.

Dust motes danced in the sunshine that poured through the window.

Belle glanced at the bed. The gentle rising and falling of the wolf's side told her he was still alive.

Pushing the afghan to the side, Belle uncurled her legs and stood up. Muscles on all parts of her body screamed with protest, and she crumbled back onto the chair. "Oh, gods. I've never ached so much in my entire life. Even my ass hurts."

Bracing her hands on the arms of the chair, she pushed herself to her feet. After swaying a moment, she staggered across the room to the bed. The wolf's rib cage rose and fell with deep steady breaths.

Carefully, Belle probed the wound on the back of its head and frowned. She didn't remember cleaning it, but she must have. She shrugged. She'd been so tired last night she shouldn't be surprised that she didn't remember everything.

Straightening, she turned, groaned again, and stumbled into the cabin's small kitchen where she pulled a half-empty can of tuna out of the refrigerator and set it on the floor for kitten.

The disgust on the kitten's face was obvious. *Cold tuna! You aren't going to warm it up for me?*

Belle gaped, snapped her mouth shut, and shook her head. She was hearing things.

An imperious, adolescent female voice stabbed her brain again. *Well? Are you going to warm it up?*

Belle shook her head again.

It talked. To her. "You can talk?"

The kitten settled onto her haunches, wrapped her tail around her feet, and stared up at Belle. *Of course.*

"But you're a cat!"

The kitten didn't so much as blink. *Obviously.*

"But…"

I love you. You saved my life. I choose to talk to you.

Swaying, Belle leaned back against the counter. "Can all cats talk to people?"

Of course, if they want to. But most people can't listen. You can because you're – special. You're Were.

Belle continued to stare. Not only did she have a cat, something no one else in her family had ever experienced since cats had a definite aversion to werewolves, but it talked to her. "Nobody is going to believe this. Ah, do you have a name, or do I give you one?"

My name is Callie.

"That's a pretty name." Belle closed her eyes and shook her head yet again. "I'm standing in my kitchen talking to a cat. A half dead wolf is sleeping on my bed. I need a drink. A good stiff drink."

She grimaced. "I don't have anything stronger than coffee. I'll have to settle for a bath."

Callie batted the can of tuna across the floor. *Aren't you going to warm my breakfast for me?*

Belle simply growled, stumbled to the bathroom, and turned on the hot water spigot full blast. A long, hot soak in the tub was mandatory. So what if she used every drop of water in the water heater. Nobody else here to complain. And the wolf could wait. It was still alive. She'd check it once she didn't ache so much.

After the tub was half full, Belle turned on the cold water and dumped in half a bottle of her favorite bath oil. Pushing herself to her feet, she wiped the condensation from the small medicine cabinet mirror and glared at her reflection. There were smudges of dirt on her face and twigs in her hair. Carrying a full-grown wolf through the forest at night was not something she ever wanted to do again.

Inhaling deeply, Belle glanced over her shoulder. Wisps of steam twirled and dipped above the rose-scented water in the deep, claw-footed tub. Thank all the gods that the bathtub was one of those old-fashioned varieties. She'd be able to sink her aching body up to her neck in all that lovely hot water.

After pinning her hair up on her head, Belle sank into the tub. As the steaming water surrounded them, her aching muscles screamed with protest then began to relax.

Belle leaned her head back against the round edge of the tub and moaned. "Oh, that hurts so good!"

After fifteen or twenty minutes, Belle sighed and grabbed the sponge. The water was getting cool, and her skin was starting to wrinkle.

Standing, she fished the plug out with her toe, pulled the curtain closed and turned on the shower. Unpinning her hair, she dunked her head under the water, grabbed the shampoo, and scrubbed out the dirt. After a quick rinse and condition—the water was definitely only lukewarm and getting colder—she turned off the water, squeezed the excess out of her hair, and wrapped it in a towel.

Belle was just stepping out of the tub when the door rattled then cracked open far enough for Callie to squeeze in.

You better hurry up.

Belle grabbed a thick towel. "Look, I'm sorry you had to eat cold tuna, but I wasn't in any kind of shape to give you anything else."

The kitten sat on her haunches and smiled a cat smile. *I forgive you for that.*

Wrapping the towel around her torso, Belle mumbled an obscenity under her breath. Even with mind speech, that kitten had a condescending tone. "Then what do you want? I'll be out in a minute."

Your wolf.

Belle's head snapped around. "What? Is he dead? I didn't think he was hurt that badly."

Callie's smile became a Cheshire cat grin. *No. He's alive. But he's not a wolf anymore. He's a man.*

The door banged against the wall when Belle jerked it open and sprinted into the bedroom, where she found a very large, very naked, very angry-looking man sitting up on the bed. As she skidded to a stop, he glared at her and growled, "Who the hell are you, where the hell am I, and how the hell did I get here?"

Chapter Three

৵

Stumbling to a halt, Belle fisted her hands on her hips and glared at him. "Did your mother teach you to be that rude or is that your natural disposition?"

"Damn it, woman. Answer my questions." He swung his legs over the side of the bed and stood up.

As soon as he was fully erect, his hand went to his head, he swayed, and promptly collapsed on the bed again.

Tucking the end of the towel more tightly under her arm, Belle stomped to the bed. "Stupid fool, you were shot last night. You lost too much blood to be standing up. You probably have a concussion too, considering a bullet grazed the back of your head," she snapped as she rolled him onto his stomach and threw a blanket over him. "You're lucky I didn't leave you lying out there. Those hunters were shouting something about hanging a wolf pelt on their wall. Wouldn't hurt you to show a little gratitude here. Now hold still and let me check the wounds."

Groaning as pain stabbed into the back of his head, Alex glared up at the woman who was spitting condemnations at him as she poked and prodded the fiery stripe on his back.

"Christ, woman! My back is on fire."

Another poke. "Of course it is. You got shot there, too."

Her words finally sank in, and Alex lay stunned. Shot? Wrapping his arms around a pillow, he buried his face so the woman couldn't hear his gasps of pain.

The bed shifted as she rose, and the stabbing pain became a dull ache. He inhaled deeply—and froze. It was her pillow, and the scent it held teased his senses—roses, some other herb, and something far more interesting.

Lifting his head—slowly—Alex flared his nostrils, sniffed, then inhaled again—deeply. Her scent was unmistakable. She was a werewolf.

Carefully, Alex lifted his hand and probed the wound on the back of his head. Pain radiated outward. Fuck. She was right. He had been shot. Closing his eyes, he searched his memory. He had no trouble remembering the confrontation he had with Sam and his decision to go for a long run. He remembered reveling in scents that teased his nose as he ran through the forest, in the feel of the path under his paws as he loped along, the excitement and bloodlust when the deer had jumped into his path. Then he'd leaped into that clearing, and fiery pain had burned the consciousness from his body.

A hard poke from the woman sent a fresh surge of pain radiating down his back.

"Lucky for you you're a werewolf. You'll heal fast." She poked his wound again.

"Jesus Christ, woman, stop your damn prodding and let me be!" Gathering his strength, Alex snarled, rolled over, grabbed the woman, flipped her onto her back, and settled his body on top of hers. His face only inches from hers, he gritted his teeth and glared into her face.

Not the least bit intimidated, she bared her teeth and glared back at him. She bucked her hips. "Get off of me, you ungrateful idiot."

He felt her gathering her strength.

Before he could reply, razor-sharp claws were dragged across his bare ass.

"Son of a bitch!" Rolling off of the woman, he searched for his attacker.

A calico kitten stood on the bed, back arched, fur puffed out, hissing and spitting at him.

"A cat? *You* have a cat!"

She rolled off the side of the bed and scrambled to her feet. "Of course I have a cat, moron. Why shouldn't I?"

Alex shook his head—and winced at the pain. "You're a werewolf. Cats don't like werewolves. They won't tolerate us."

The woman held out her arms and the kitten leaped into them. "I can understand why they don't like you, considering you have the manners of a pig," she snarled. "Me, I get along fine with them."

Fisting his hands in the sheets to restrain himself, Alex glared at the woman. "Fine, cats like you. I repeat, who are you, and what are you doing here?"

She bared her teeth again. "I should have left you lying in the woods."

Alex clenched his teeth against the howl of fury building in his throat. Damn it, but this woman was enough to make an Omega lose his temper. Throwing his legs over the side of the bed, he pushed himself up—and promptly sat back down, head spinning. Okay, he'd been shot. Werewolves recovered from wounds remarkably fast, but he must have lost a fair amount of blood. He needed food and liquids if he wanted to continue recovering. Aggravating this smartass woman wouldn't help.

After taking several deep breaths and swallowing his temper, he opened his eyes. "I'm sorry if I seem inconsiderate, but I don't get shot every day."

One of her eyebrows rose. "Inconsiderate? You're being downright obnoxious."

Alex gritted his teeth again. "Look, I said I'm sorry. Why do you have to be so damned contrary?"

"You're the one sitting here bitching after I saved your life, and you say I'm contrary?"

Closing his eyes, Alex took a deep breath. This woman was well on the way to becoming a bigger pain in the ass than any of the troublemakers in the pack! He took another deep breath. Pain in the ass or not, she was the only one available to help him. What did he have to lose by showing a little gratitude? She *had* probably saved his life. He opened his eyes and stuck out his hand. "Alex Whitehorse. Thank you."

Belle chewed her bottom lip as she stared at his hand. Why the sudden change in personality?

Callie rubbed her chin against Belle's. *He has no one else to help him.*

Belle stroked Callie's head. That made sense. And she had let her temper get the better of her. After all, he was hurt. With a sigh, she let Callie drop to the floor, stepped forward, and grasped his hand. "I'm Belle. You're welcome."

He dropped her hand. "Look. We got off on the wrong foot, but I don't get shot and rescued everyday."

Cocking her head to the side, Belle resumed chewing her lip and stared at him. His answer did make sense. God knows what she'd be like under these same circumstances.

Alex concentrated on the white teeth worrying her full, red lip. "So, what are you doing here? My pack didn't receive any notice of other werewolves in the area."

Her chewing stopped. "*Your* pack?"

He nodded.

Belle closed her eyes and blew some hair off her forehead. "Damn, oh damn. An Alpha. I rescued an I'm-the-one-in-charge, I'm-the-one-in-command-and-don't-you-forget-it Alpha. What do I have to do to get away from you guys?"

Alex stiffened. *Get away from.* His tone was sharp. "What pack are you running from? Are you in trouble? I'll help you if I can. I owe you for my life, but don't expect to drag me into some kind of internal pack feud."

Belle snapped her eyes open. "Pack feud? Me? Are you crazy? I'm on vacation. From New York—City. You do know what a vacation is, don't you? Or are you too far out here in the sticks to understand the concept?"

He crossed his arms over his chest and snapped, "Now you're the one being rude. I only asked a simple question, as is my right as the local Alpha. This is our territory."

Belle gritted her teeth against the expletive that wanted to escape. Damn it. Why did Alphas have to be so—alpha! "Look. I didn't know there were any other werewolves around here. I'm sorry if I screwed up on pack etiquette, but it's been a long time since I've been around any werewolves except my father and brother. Those are the Alphas I'm referring to."

"It's their responsibility to protect you."

Nostrils flaring, Belle snarled, "Protect me! From what? From whom? I'm perfectly capable of taking care of myself. I have a BA and MA from Harvard, make enough money to live a very comfortable life, and have enough friends to make that life happy and interesting."

His voice was a sneer. "Then why are you here?"

Belle threw up her hands. This guy *was* a moron. "I'm *on vacation*, idiot! Remember? Besides, if I hadn't taken this vacation, you wouldn't be alive to argue with me or anyone else."

He pushed himself to his feet and once again collapsed back onto the bed.

Belle stomped to his side. "Damn Alphas and their belief they're invincible. Look—Alex—you're as white as the sheets. You lost a lot of blood. Let's call a truce until you're feeling better. Then I won't have to worry about you dying on me when I rip your throat out because you're being such a pigheaded moron."

"I am not going to die," he growled as she pushed him back against the pillows and pulled the blanket up over him.

"Oh, sorry. Forgot about your back," she said when he gasped and rolled onto his side. "Let me go see if there's first aid cream in the medicine chest. With your metabolism and ability to heal, that should be all you need."

Belle was halfway to the bathroom when she stopped and turned. "Shouldn't we inform someone about you getting shot?"

Alex mulled over her question for a moment. He'd lost sight of the bigger picture while he was arguing with her. He'd been shot. Somebody was hunting on the pack's land. Who? He shook his head. "No. My Beta can handle things until I get back."

"Won't someone worry about you?"

He shook his head again. "I'm usually gone a few days when I decide to run."

Belle stared at him for a moment. She'd lived with Alphas too long not to recognize when one wasn't telling the complete truth. She started to say something, then stopped. Whatever his secrets were, he could keep them. She was just here on vacation for a couple of weeks.

Chapter Four

 හ

Alex stared at the empty doorway. Belle. A pretty name for a pretty woman, even if she had a more aggravating personality than any other woman he'd ever met. He closed his eyes, and another woman's face appeared in his mind. Serena. Sighing, he rolled onto his stomach and buried his face in the pillow again. Her rescuer's scent tickled his nose.

Belle's face replaced Serena's.

A few times while they'd been arguing, the towel Belle'd wrapped around her body had slipped—and she'd jerked it back up. Too bad it hadn't fallen. Her breasts were too well hidden. She did have a nice face. Small, heart-shaped, a pert nose, wide mouth with kissable red lips. Sooty, long eyelashes shading gray eyes.

Gray eyes? He searched his memory. Where had he seen gray eyes like hers?

A light thump on the side of the bed caught his attention and he turned his head. Pain stabbed from back to front.

Belle's gray eyes were completely forgotten.

He covered both eyes with his hands. "Ahhh."

You'll feel better if you don't move, stupid man.

Slowly, Alex opened his eyes.

Belle's cat sat on the side of the bed staring at him.

He swallowed. "What?"

The cat looked down her nose at him. *If you don't move, you won't hurt.*

Alex continued to stare. A cat had talked to him. Could they do that?

At that moment, Belle returned. She'd replaced the towel with a bright pink tee shirt and jeans.

Alex glared at her. "Your cat just talked to me."

Belle refused to allow her surprise to show. "She does have very good manners."

The cat smirked at him.

Alex buried his face in the pillow again. When had he ever been so not in control of a situation—one that didn't involve Serena, anyway?

The side of the bed sank as Belle sat down. "Hold still while I wash your wound and put this cream on it."

Alex grunted then gritted his teeth as she smoothed warm water over his back and patted the wound dry. Her fingers were gentle as she applied the ointment.

"It's beginning to heal already. Now let me check your head."

He buried his gasp in the pillow as she carefully probed the wound.

"It's an ugly gash, but it's scabbed over. Just let me clean the matted hair away and get a better look. You're lucky you have such a hard head."

Alex let her comment pass and concentrated on keeping his jaws locked against the groans that wanted to escape. He wasn't going to give her the satisfaction of knowing the back of his head felt like it was going to explode.

"There. That's better." She pushed his hair off his shoulders. "You really could use a haircut, you know. Go get one after you get home."

Alex sighed into the pillow. Gods, what did this woman do if she didn't have somebody to give orders to? Her father and brother were probably glad she was gone. The sooner he was healed enough to leave, the better.

"Here, I brought water. You must be thirsty, and with the blood you lost, you need fluids."

Slowly, he rolled over and pushed himself up into a sitting position. He leaned back against the headboard and, after a minute, took the glass from her hand.

She immediately began to gather up the towels, the tube of ointment, and the basin of water sitting on the table next to the bed.

Alex closed his eyes and sipped the water. Cool but not icy cold. He swallowed a mouthful then gulped the rest. Holding out the glass, he said, "More."

Belle glanced back over her shoulder and cocked an eyebrow.

Alex gritted his teeth. "Please."

She smiled, returned to the bed, and took the glass. "Now, was that so hard?"

Alex grunted. Her smile had lit up her face. She was *very* pretty.

"Don't move. You'll probably give yourself a worse headache than you already have. I'll be right back with more water and something for you to eat."

Alex kept his eyes fixed on the tight seat of her jeans as she left the room. She had a nice ass.

Why were you shot?

Alex shifted his attention to the calico kitten crouched at the bottom of the bed with her paws tucked into her chest. "I don't know, but I intend to find out."

A beeping sound came from the other room, and the cat's head snapped around. *Food!* She leaped off the bed and scampered out of the room.

Alex stared at the far wall. He had to get back to the pack. If there were poachers around, everyone was in danger.

She set a tray on the nightstand. "Here's more water, and I brought you aspirin—six should be enough considering the normal werewolf constitution—and some soup."

Frowning, he shifted his attention to Belle. "Soup? You have to have something better than soup."

She frowned. "Quit complaining and eat it. You're an invalid, and invalids get soup."

His answer came out with a growl as he tossed the pills into his mouth and washed them down with the water. "I'm no more an invalid than you are."

"Bullshit. I haven't been shot. I could hold you down with one hand tied behind my back."

"Care to try?" A picture of the pink tee shirt she was wearing ripped to shreds appeared in his mind. Were her nipples rosy pink or a gingery tan?

She planted her hands on her hips. "And hurt you even more? I don't think so. The sooner you're healed, the sooner you're out of here, and I can get on with my vacation. I didn't come all the way from New York to be a nurse."

Alex set the tray on his lap and began to spoon soup into his mouth. The two glasses of water had strengthened him, and the soup would help more. "What do you do there?" he asked between spoonfuls of soup.

"Accounting."

Alex wrinkled his nose. A numbers cruncher. Probably spent her day sitting behind a desk. How in the world could any werewolf allow itself to be stuck in a building all day? And live in one of the largest cities in the world, no less. Miles upon miles of concrete. Dirty air, millions of humans, few trees. If there really was a hell, that was it. "How can you stand it?"

"Stand what?"

"Living in a city?"

She smiled. "At first I thought I'd go crazy, but I got used to it."

"Then you haven't always lived there?"

"No, my family moved to New York when I was a teenager."

Alex finished the last of his soup and shifted the tray back to the nightstand. A yawn surged up through his lungs.

Belle smiled. He needed to sleep to heal, and she'd given him a couple of sleeping pills with the aspirin. "Why don't you lie down and try to sleep? Your body will heal faster, and you'll be able to get back to your pack."

Another yawn stretched Alex's mouth as he nodded. With a slight grimace, he pushed himself down, rolled over onto his stomach, and buried his face in her pillow.

Belle carried the tray with the empty soup bowl to the small kitchenette. He'd certainly gulped the soup down fast enough. After sleeping a while and eating a meal of rich, red meat, he'd probably be able to leave.

"And that suits me just fine. How am I supposed to get any rest and relaxation with an Alpha breathing down my neck?"

After making herself a sandwich and washing up the dishes, Belle stepped back into the bedroom to check on her patient.

He'd kicked off the light blanket.

She had a clear view of his torso and legs. After a quick survey of the bullet wound on his back, which was already closed and healing nicely, she allowed herself the time to peruse the rest of his body.

His face was half-buried in the pillow. Reaching down, she brushed some stray hairs from his copper cheek. He really needed a haircut. It brushed his shoulders.

Callie jumped up on the bed. *He's not as white as you.*

Belle nodded. "He's Native American. I wonder which tribe?"

Who cares?

Belle chuckled as the kitten tucked her paws into her chest, closed her eyes, and began to purr. No it didn't matter what tribe Alex was from. She switched her attention from the kitten back to the man. The half of his face she could see intrigued her. High cheekbones, broad forehead, thin mobile lips, a firm chin. Thick brows and curly eyelashes. His eyes were dark, almost black, she remembered—except for those golden specks that appeared when he was angry.

After a quick check of the wound on the back of his head, she brushed his hair back off of his neck and trailed her hand down over his broad shoulders. Except for the bullet's furrow, his back was smooth with well-developed muscles. His waist was trim, and his behind…

"Damn, but he has a great ass."

Belle glanced at his face. The sleeping pills she'd given him were working perfectly. With a grin, she turned her attention to his backside. She smoothed her hand down over his left cheek and cupped it. Muscular and firm. No fat on this ass. She shifted her glance. No fat on his thighs either. They were all muscle, as were his calves. She caressed the hairs on the back of his thigh and sighed. Soft, just as she'd thought. Body hair on a werewolf was far softer than that on a regular human.

Cocking her head to the side, Belle smiled. He was naked and at her mercy. True, she'd seen every inch of him already but hadn't even thought to take a really good look at him before this. She glanced up at his wound once more and sighed. If only that bullet hadn't ripped across his back from one shoulder to the other, she'd roll him over so she could get a better look at his chest—and cock. Didn't hurt to check out how well he was hung. Maybe she'd try to talk him into staying around a few days. She hadn't had a werewolf lover in years.

"Hmmmm. I wonder how well-equipped he is. Didn't really look too closely earlier. Would he wake up if I rolled him over?"

Belle pursed her lips. After staring at his ass for a moment, she shook her head. Rolling him over onto that sore back would be cruel.

Bracing her hands on the bed, she bent over and looked between his slightly spread legs. "Nice balls. Sure wish I could see his cock."

Chapter Five

ଈ

Belle dropped the book she was reading onto her lap, looked at her watch, and then glanced out the window. Shadows lengthened as the sun set.

Callie woke, yawned and stretched. *The wolfman is still sleeping.*

"I know." Belle shifted and her stomach growled. Should she start grilling the steaks before he woke? She wrinkled her nose. Better not. If he was like every other werewolf she knew, he'd want his bloody rare. Slap it on the grill for a few seconds then flip it over for a few more.

Callie cocked her head and stared at Belle. *When one hungers, one should eat.*

Belle grinned down at the kitten. "I should, but humans practice what are called manners. That means we wait and eat together."

Callie licked a paw. *How silly. What if one person isn't hungry? Does that mean the other may not eat?*

Sighing, Belle rose. Explaining human etiquette to a kitten was not how she wanted to spend the time until Alex woke up.

The sound an engine drifted in through the open window, and she frowned. Who would be coming here? Brendan? He couldn't have found her already, could he? Damn it, this vacation was supposed to be *away* from her family.

Bolting across the room, she jerked the door open, and stomped out onto the porch, her mouth open to berate her brother for being overprotective. She snapped it closed. The men climbing out of the yellow Hummer were the same two she'd seen at the gas station.

Belle took one look at the expensive sports clothing they were wearing and snorted mentally. Weekend thrill seekers from the city out in the woods to "rough" it. They probably had a trailer equipped with all the necessities—big screen TV, satellite dish, video games—parked at some campground. Stupid morons. They were probably the ones who shot Alex.

The breeze shifted. She sniffed the air and smiled to herself. Both men were wearing her father's signature Artemis Gray cologne.

The man who crawled out of the passenger side pushed his glasses back up onto the bridge of his nose and grinned. "Good evening."

Crossing her arms over her chest, she nodded her head. "Evening. What can I do for you?"

The man smiled. "Not too much. We were just wondering if you've seen a wolf around."

Belle had to grit her teeth to keep her mouth from falling open. "A wolf? Around here?"

Snapping his cell phone closed, the other man said, "Yes, we have a permit to hunt wolves. Last night we shot one, but it seems to have gotten away. You didn't see it, by chance?"

An eyebrow rose. "Why would a wounded wolf come this close to human habitation?"

Eyeglasses had a ready answer. "Why, to crawl underneath your cabin of course, where it will feel safe."

Belle snorted. "Who the hell fed you that line? And who sold you a permit to hunt wolves in the first place? There is no such thing. Wolves are *protected*. You aren't allowed to hunt them." *At least I hope you don't know wolves not on preserves are fair game.*

Cellphone looked at his companion and then back to Belle. "You're one of those tree-hugging, nature lovers who don't kill any animals we were warned about, aren't you? The guy who sold us the permit told us there'd be people who told us that."

Belle rolled her eyes. How stupid could any man be?

"Look. I'm not a 'tree-hugger' though I do have a healthy respect for nature. I'm here on vacation—from New York. I'm an accountant, but even I know that a wild animal that's hurt will get as far away from humans as it can."

Eyeglasses smiled. "From New York? Really? So are we. You must have had the same idea we did, spend some time in the great outdoors. See what all this nature stuff is about." He looked around and grinned. "You here by yourself?"

"No, she isn't."

Both men started when Alex stepped to her side—wearing nothing but a sheet wrapped around his waist.

Both men smirked. "Oh, sorry. Didn't realize there was anyone else here."

Callie leaped up onto the railing, sat, and wrapped her tail around her paws. She hissed once.

Alex crossed his arms over his chest. "Obviously not. I'm the local game warden. Care to tell *me* about this wolf?"

Cellphone stumbled back. "Game warden? Ah, we gotta go. We're meeting a couple of friends in town."

Eyeglasses yanked the door open. "Yeah. We gotta go. Friends waiting." He had the Hummer rolling down the lane before his friend had his door shut.

Belle watched until it disappeared. She didn't bother to hide the irritation in her voice. "So you're the game warden?"

Alex grinned. "No, but they don't know that."

She snorted. "I could have handled them."

He shrugged. "Maybe. Maybe not."

Belle was admiring Alex's chest. It was just as broad and muscular—and smooth—as she remembered when his remark sank in. "Maybe! What do you mean, maybe? Those two yuppie survivalist wannabes? I could have handled them with one hand tied behind my back."

Belle wrenched her gaze from his chest, looked up into his face, and froze.

Alex was grinning—and his smile transformed his face. He looked younger, more at ease. She shifted her glance to his eyes—and fell in.

As her stomach dropped to her feet and her emotions roiled in chaos, the werewolf in her soul awoke and howled with joy. *Mine!*

Gasping, Belle whirled away from Alex and grabbed the porch railing, the last conversation she'd had with Moira before she left New York leaping to the forefront of her mind.

"How could you possibly agree to marry my father after knowing him barely a week?"

Moira was relaxed in the rocking chair nursing one of the babies. Smiling contentedly, she looked up from her daughter's face and said, "It was the easiest decision I've ever made. The first time I looked into his eyes, my stomach did a complete flip-flop and my heart felt like it was going to explode. I just didn't understand what it meant. Your father knew, though. He'd experienced much the same thing with your mother. Wolves know, Belle, when they meet the male or female destined to be their mates. They don't fight their instincts. Humans, on the other hand, require logic and don't trust their instincts at all—at least most of them. Werewolves find themselves torn between both heritages. They should follow their instincts more than they do. Living with the wolves taught your father not to question himself, so when he met me, and his 'soul shifted' as he likes to say, he knew we belonged together."

Moira switched her daughter to her other breast and looked back at Belle. "You're very special, Belle, because your mother was a wolf. You're much more in tune with your instincts than the average werewolf. When it comes to men, trust your instincts. They'll never lie to you."

Staring blindly at the forest, Belle sucked in another breath and shivered. Her instincts would never lie to her? Oh, shit. A sexy, arrogant Alpha werewolf in the middle of nowhere had just rocked her world. How did this happen? Why did this happen? Why now? Why here? No! Her instincts had to be wrong. She finally reached a point in her life where she could do whatever she wanted, whenever she wanted.

Her knuckles whitened as she clenched the railing harder and shook her head. No! She would not subjugate herself to a cocky Alpha, no matter how sexy he was.

She looked back at Alex. He was frowning.

"You okay?" Grasping her upper arms, he pulled her away from the railing.

Belle turned in his arms and flattened her hands against his chest. Slowly, she outlined his pectorals with her palms. Gods, but his chest was smooth—no hair anywhere—just lots of copper skin covering hard muscles.

He flared his nostrils and inhaled.

Belle looked up at his mouth. How would it taste?

Pushing herself up onto her tiptoes, she captured Alex's mouth with hers and sucked his tongue deep into her mouth. She laced her fingers through his hair as she twirled her tongue around his. He tasted so good!

Slowly, Belle untangled her tongue from his. Her head fell back. Why fight fate? Lips parted, she stared into his eyes. "I want you—now."

Chapter Six

ꙅꙅ

Alex stared down into Belle's flushed face, into the gray eyes that smoldered with fiery sparks of gold. She wanted him? Excitement rippled through his veins as the Alpha werewolf in his soul howled with expectation. Granted, he was usually the one who propositioned the woman, but...

The tip of her tongue slid out of her mouth to trace her lips. She scissored her fingers over his nipple and squeezed.

A shudder rolled through his body. Taking a deep breath, he closed his eyes.

Her scent tickled his nostrils—hot, sweet.

Reaching up, she cupped his face in both hands. "I want you, Alex," she repeated. "Do you want me?"

Answering her with a growl, he pulled her lithe, firm body closer and captured her mouth with his.

Moaning, she reached up, grabbed two handfuls of hair, and pulled his head closer. Her mouth moved and her teeth clicked against his.

Sliding his hands down her back, Alex cupped Belle's ass and pulled her hips hard up against his now rigid cock. He deepened his kiss, sucking her tongue into his mouth, demanding that she surrender to his dominance. Gods but she was passionate. He did want her. At this moment, burying his already aching cock deep inside her mattered more to him than anything else.

As she ground her hips against Alex's erection, Belle's blood pounded in her ears and bliss wrapped itself around her. Never had she experienced such feelings of passion—and joy! Her werewolf soul sang with it.

She pulled her mouth from his and stared into his dark eyes, eyes now flecked with gold. "Kiss me more — harder, deeper."

He complied. Capturing her lips with his, he slipped his tongue between them, caressing the inside of her mouth. Then he sucked her tongue into his mouth, sliding his against it, teasing, stabbing, sucking harder.

Moaning deep in her throat, Belle allowed him to ravage her mouth.

Eventually, she had to breathe. Pulling back, she sucked in a breath. Her tone was demanding, dominant, Alpha. "Bed. Now."

Not caring that Belle was taking the lead in their lovemaking, Alex swept her up into his arms, wedged his foot between the screen door and the jamb, and toed it open.

The door slammed against the wall.

Licking her paw, Callie watched them disappear into the cabin. Not even the revered ancestors could have understood humans — even werehumans.

Sheet sliding down his hips and dragging behind him, Alex strode into the bedroom and tossed Belle onto the bed from halfway across the room. He leaped after her, intending to pin her underneath his body.

She moved at the last minute, and he landed on his stomach. Quick as only a werewolf could be, she flipped him onto his back and straddled his stomach.

Before he could complain, Belle pulled her tee shirt over her head. She wasn't wearing a bra.

Alex found himself staring at two of the loveliest breasts he'd ever seen.

Her nipples were gingery brown.

Grabbing her upper arms, Alex pulled her forward until she was sitting on his stomach, and sucked a nipple into his mouth.

Lacing her fingers through his hair, Belle shivered and pulled his head closer. "Oh, gods, yes. Your mouth is so hot! More."

His mouth left her right nipple, and he nibbled his way across her chest to her other breast. After a couple of quick laps, he nipped her left nipple, lapped it again, and sucked it into his mouth. When he finally released it, both nipples were hard and pebbled.

Releasing her arms, Alex captured a breast, which became firmer as they swelled with anticipation, in each hand. Slowly and gently, he kneaded. Her nipples became more distended.

"Your breasts are beautiful. I could suck on your nipples all night."

"Gods, yes. Please, suck on them."

Releasing her breasts, he slid his hands down her rib cage and around her slender sides to her smooth back. Firm muscles under soft skin shuddered under his caresses. He pulled her breasts to his mouth.

Arching her back, Belle moaned.

His lips were pure magic.

A quick nip on her left nipple had her stomach muscles clenching. Fire pooled low in her belly — and between her legs. She rubbed her crotch against his hard abdomen.

"I need your cock inside of me. I need you hard and deep, buried inside of me up to your balls."

Still sucking on her breast, he hooked his fingers in the seams of her shorts and ripped them apart.

As the torn cloth fell from Belle's hips, she pushed herself erect and looked down into his face. His irises were completely golden now, his nostrils were flared, his eyes hooded.

She wiggled again and felt his cock prodding her ass.

When he slid a finger between her thighs and slipped it inside of her, she arched into his hand. "Yes, oh yes. More. I want more."

He slid a second finger into her and began to twist and pump them. He thumbed her clit.

Throwing back her head, Belle ground her hips into his hand and cupped her own breasts. She pinched her nipples. Then she began to ride his fingers.

Alex's breath caught in his throat as he watched her fondle herself.

She thrust against his fingers even harder.

Hell, he'd never been with a woman who showed so much passion! "Easy," he growled as he pumped and screwed his fingers deeper. "You'll hurt yourself."

Moisture gushed over his fingers.

She slid her right hand down over her stomach, through her pubic hair, and tangled her fingers with his thumb as he fondled her clit. "More. I want more."

He pulled his fingers out. "Move back and raise yourself."

Panting, she slid back.

His cock bounced against her back, and she wiggled her ass. "Oh, yes."

Alex groaned. His balls felt ready to explode.

Grabbing her by the waist, he lifted her, positioned her above his cock, and dropped her onto it, thrusting up at the same time.

She threw her head back and howled. Throwing her hands up into the air, she arched her back, rose up on her knees then settled back onto his cock.

Hot moisture oozed around him.

Alex lifted his arms above his head and grabbed the bed railings and bucked.

Belle slid back down his cock, gripped him with her internal muscles, and swiveled her hips. She released him, rose up, and started over again.

Groaning, Alex gripped the wooden slats harder, thrust his hips upward, and watched his cock slide in and out of her, brown against her fiery red lips, her swollen clit, and black pubic hair. The werewolf in his soul howled; and the urge to roll Belle over and mount her, to watch his cock slide in and out of her as she pushed her ass back against his hips, to curl over her back and clamp his teeth into her shoulder, exploded in his soul.

Snarling, he ground his hips against hers and regained control of himself.

Belle moaned, rose up again, and grinding her hips down. "Harder. Harder. I want to feel you deep inside."

Releasing the slats, Alex grabbed her hips and pulled her down as he thrust up.

"Come for me, Belle. Come for me." As fantastic as sex with Belle was, he had to end it before he did flip her over and try to mate her. He couldn't claim a woman he'd just met. The pack would never accept her.

Nostrils flaring, she looked down into his face. "Come with me. Now!"

Sliding down his cock, she grasped with her muscles and pulling it as deeply as she could. Bending over, she suckled his nipple then nipped it—hard.

Alex howled with his release.

Belle melted around him and collapsed on his chest.

The sounds of heavy breathing filled the room as they both fought to collect their wits.

Alex lay with his eyes closed. Never, ever had he been fucked so hard and so well. Cum was still seeping out of his cock.

Soft hair tickled his shoulder.

He brushed Belle's hair out of her face. "Are you all right?"

A soft, sly smile answered him. "I've never felt better. You're a hell of a ride, Alex."

He answered her smile with one of his own. "My pleasure, ma'am."

A long, loud meow interrupted Belle's answer, followed by Callie's plaintive mind voice. *Are you finished mating? Can we eat now? I'm hungry.*

Chapter Seven

ဢ

Mating? Alex glanced from Belle to the kitten and back to Belle again. He frowned.

Chuckling, Belle rolled off the bed and grabbed a brush. "Don't worry, Alex. I'm not in heat—werewolf or human—and aconite tea to prevent conception is part of my morning regimen."

Callie leaped off the bed and galloped into the kitchen.

Grunting, Alex relaxed. He'd have noticed a heat scent no matter how hot Belle made him. More than one woman had tried to ambush him into a permanent relationship by mating with him when she was in heat. He wasn't going to fall into that trap.

As Belle dragged the brush through her hair, Alex felt his cock stir. Why was a woman brushing her hair so damn sexy?

His stomach growled.

A wide grin on her face, Belle glanced his way. "Hungry? I have a couple of steaks ready for the grill."

Alex's stomach growled even more loudly. "I like mine rare."

Belle's breasts lifted and bounced as she tied her hair into a ponytail. "Give me a second, and I'll get my tablet to take your order."

Alex didn't miss the sarcasm in her voice. He felt the heat crawl up his neck. "Sorry, but…"

She cocked an eyebrow. "Women fall all over themselves to satisfy your every whim?"

Mumbling under his breath, he sat up and swung his legs over the side of the bed. "You wouldn't happen to have an extra pair of sweatpants lying around here somewhere, would you?"

Still grinning, Belle tilted her head to the side and watched as Alex rose to his feet. "Sorry, but I don't think any of mine will fit you. I wear a small, and you — you are definitely not small."

Alex grinned back. Christ but she wasn't afraid to say what she thought. He liked it. "Okay, won't be the first time I ate in the buff. I like my steak rare."

She nodded. "Do werewolves ever eat steak any other way?" Turning, she led the way to the kitchen.

Alex followed Belle out of the bedroom, his gaze glued to her gently swaying behind. She had a great ass, the perfect size for him to hold onto as he buried himself deep inside of her.

Stretching his legs out under the table, Alex leaned back and rubbed his stomach. He hadn't lost his touch. He could still grill a mean steak.

The hard oak back of the chair rubbed against his bullet wound and he grimaced.

Belle pushed her chair back and circled the table. "Let me see that. You don't want to rub it open and start it bleeding again."

He complied with a grunt. He pushed his plate out of the way and leaned his elbows on the table.

Belle brushed his hair off his back and gently probed the angry red line. "It's closed and looks to be healing cleanly. Have it checked by your doctor or healer when you get back to your pack.

Alex grunted again. His pack. He'd been gone over twenty-four hours without contacting any of them. Even though he'd told Dave he might be gone for a couple days, he'd planned to be back by morning. He was never gone more than a night. Both Dave and Josh knew that. They'd be pissed — and worried.

Half turning, he grabbed Belle's hand and kissed her palm. "I have to get back."

She smiled. "I know. You have responsibilities. Your Beta is probably starting to worry."

He grinned. "Getting pissed off, more likely."

Belle combed some stray hairs out of his face. "Getting angry with you. Gee, now isn't that hard to believe?" She stepped behind him and parted the hair around the bullet wound on his head. "This one is closed, too. I'd take it easy for a few days, though."

Alex pushed his chair back and stood. The naked woman at his side was more appealing than any other he'd ever met, but he had responsibilities. His pack came before his personal life.

Leaning over, he kissed her forehead. "I'm glad you saved my life, Belle."

Belle smiled up into his face. "You're the first person I've ever saved. It's been interesting."

"Very," he agreed. The urge to pull her into his arms and carry her back to bed was fast becoming overwhelming. The werewolf in his soul demanded that he do so.

Alex stepped back. "I'd like to stay, but I really do have to go."

Belle's smile was gentle. "I know, but—you're welcome to visit anytime."

He cupped her face. "I'll remember that." Bending, he kissed her, long and slow.

A sigh escaped Belle when he lifted his head.

Black mist swirled, and a large black wolf stood before her. He licked her hand, turned, trotted to the door, nosed it open, and leaped off the porch.

Belle followed him across the room, leaned against the doorjamb, and watched him disappear into the forest.

Callie rubbed her head against Belle's leg. *Are you sad he's gone?*

Chuckling, Belle bent and gathered the kitten into her arms. "He'll be back."

* * * * *

The sun had just set when Alex leaped up the steps to his cabin, shifted to his human form, and strode inside.

His Beta looked up from behind the desk. "Where the hell have you been?"

"Shot."

The anger drained from Josh's face. "Shot? What the fuck?"

Alex disappeared into his bedroom only to reappear in a few minutes wearing a fresh pair of jeans and pulling a tee shirt over his head. "A couple of yuppies from New York are playing survivalist. They bought a fake hunting permit from somebody. See if you can find out who. And warn everybody. I don't need anyone else getting shot."

The door opened, and Dave walked in. "Shot? Who got shot?"

Josh rose and walked around the desk. "Alex."

Dave leaped to Alex's side and grabbed his arm. "Fuck! Where were you hit? How bad is it?"

Alex tried to shake Dave's hand off his arm. "I'm fine."

Josh grabbed his other arm. "We're going to check your wounds the easy way or the hard way. Your choice. Together, the two of us can take you."

"I'm fine! You don't have to check anything."

Dave's voice was far harder than an Omega's had the right to be. "The easy way or the hard way?"

"Fucking, pain-in-the-ass friends." Alex pulled the shirt back over his head. "Across the shoulder blades and a crease on the back of the head."

Both men started to poke and prod.

Grimacing, Alex shook them off. "Christ, it hurt less when it happened."

Josh frowned. "These were bad. You're lucky you aren't dead. And they're clean. Who took care of you?"

Alex's lips twitched. "Vacationer staying in that cabin on Spruce Creek. An accountant from New York. She was running in the woods and heard the guys who shot me talk about skinning a wolf. She found me, carried me back to her cabin, and tended my wounds. She's Were."

Josh's voice was angry, then amazed. "Running in the woods. Carried *you*! Were? Whose pack? Accountant? New York?"

Dave's voice was curious. He raised an eyebrow. "She?"

Alex pulled his tee shirt over back over his head and tied his hair in a ponytail. "Relax, Josh, she didn't know she was supposed to let us know she was in our territory."

Dave leaned back against the sofa. "How pretty is she?"

Alex shrugged. "Who said she was pretty?"

A broad grin appeared on Dave's face. "You've been gone almost thirty-six hours. With our rate of healing, you should have been home, oh, twelve hours ago. What kept you?"

Alex stepped behind his desk and began shuffling through the papers piled there. "None of your business." He glanced up.

Josh was glaring at him. "What's her name?"

Muttering under his breath, Alex stared back. No way would he get any work done until he gave them the information they wanted. "Her name is Belle."

"Belle what?"

Alex shrugged. "I didn't ask."

Josh's nostrils flared. "Didn't ask? Why not? You're the Alpha. You can't be running around with just any bitch."

"For Christ's sake, Josh," Alex snapped. "Lay off. It's not important."

Josh mumbled something under his breath.

Dave kept grinning.

Alex looked back down at the paperwork on his desk. "Anything I should know about happen while I was gone?"

Chapter Eight

ॐ

Hands clasped behind his back, Alex stared out the window at the late afternoon sun. Papers lay neglected on his desk. Every time he started going over the blueprints and estimated costs for the renovation of the old house the pack was going to turn into a bed and breakfast, Belle's smiling face appeared. Why did she haunt his memory so?

Muttering curses, he turned away from the window and strode back to his desk. These plans had to be examined and approved if they wanted to be open this autumn.

The screen door squeaked.

Dave sauntered to his side. "How are the plans? They looked good to me, but I'm no expert. And the costs seem reasonable, especially since we'll be doing most of the work."

Alex spit out another curse as he stared at the blueprints.

Dave grinned. Alex hadn't been the same ever since he'd been shot—and it wasn't the near death experience that had his brains all twisted up. "Problems?"

Alex growled something unintelligible.

"Guess you're finally over Serena, huh?"

"Shut the fuck up."

The door squeaked again when Josh walked in.

"You need to oil the screen door," Dave said. "The squeak is getting worse."

A full snarl rolled out of Alex's mouth. "I don't give a damn about the fucking door."

Josh stopped short. "Is there a problem with the blueprints?"

Dave chuckled. "No. Plans looked fine to me. Alex has a problem with his libido."

Josh frowned. "Fuck, Alex. Enough already. Serena picked someone else. Get over it."

As Alex's face darkened, Dave howled with laughter.

"Fuck you two. I'm going out for a run." Pushing between the two men, Alex slammed out the door.

It squeaked shut behind him.

Josh turned and followed.

The door squeaked again.

Alex's clothing lay on the porch, and he was sprinting toward the forest.

Josh gripped the porch railing. "Damn it, Alex! You've already been shot once, and those two yuppies are still running around with rifles playing great white hunter."

Still chuckling, Dave leaned against the doorjamb. "We've got a couple of our men watching them, Josh. Don't worry. Besides, I don't think Alex is going to do all that much running."

Josh looked back over his shoulder.

Dave grinned. "The New York accountant—Belle."

* * * * *

Belle pushed her toe against the floor and the rocking chair moved slowly. Her latest attempt at painting sat on an easel in the corner. Not bad. She was no Rembrandt, but not bad.

On her lap, Callie rose, stretched, and snuggled back down.

Belle's hand strayed over her back, and the kitten purred.

Closing her eyes, Belle sighed. What a wonderful vacation she was having.

"Are you just going to sit there and rock all night?"

Belle opened her eyes.

Naked, Alex Whitehorse leaned against the wooden pillar supporting the porch roof.

She smiled. Damn, what a man! Broad shoulders, wide chest, flat stomach, trim hips. She chuckled mentally. Though it was now flaccid, she knew just how thick and hard that dangling cock could get.

She continued to stroke Callie. "Are you asking me out?"

He grinned. "If you want to call it that."

Her gaze slid down his body. "You're a tad underdressed, don't you think?"

He straightened and stretched. "I thought you might like to go for a late-night run."

Hard muscles slid under firm skin, and Belle's mouth began to water. She swallowed. "What about those two yuppies who think they're great white hunters?"

"I have men keeping an eye on them. They're locked in their RV watching the hockey playoffs."

Belle chuckled. "Okay. A run sounds good. I've always loved the forest at night." Rising, she set Callie back on the rocking chair, pulled her tee shirt over her head, and slipped off her shorts.

Belle smiled as Alex flared his nostrils. Four days had passed since he'd disappeared into the forest. The werewolf half of her had wanted to track him down—he was her mate, no ifs, ands or buts about it. Her human half had told her to wait—he'd be back. She hadn't known if he'd show up tonight, but she was glad she'd worn her red satin thong. Her eyes never leaving Alex, she slid her thumbs under the straps hugging her hips and shimmied. It slid down her legs to her ankles. She stepped out of it and kicked it away.

His gaze fell to her crotch and stayed there.

Gotcha, wolfman. Didn't expect me to shave there, did you? Jumping from the porch, she shouted, "First one to the forest is the winner." Dark mist shimmered and a black wolf leaped toward the trees.

More mist swirled, and a second black wolf sprinted after her.

Tongue lolling out the side of her mouth, Belle allowed Alex to shoulder her to the left onto this new path. As the climb became steeper, she slowed her pace.

Alex loped along behind her.

They'd been running for half the night. Belle was both exhilarated and tired. How long had it been since she'd run through the woods with another wolf for the simple joy of running? Much longer than she wanted to remember.

Lifting her head, Belle inhaled the myriad scents on the breeze. A grouse hid beneath the pines to her left. The fresh spoor of a squirrel crossed the path just ahead. A small group of deer were upwind to the left. The fresh scent of clear water was off to her right. She licked her lips and followed her nose. Sweet water—she was thirsty.

A few minutes later she hurdled a fallen tree and leaped into a small clearing. A delicate waterfall cascaded from a small cliff into a bathtub-sized pool at its base. Crouching on the moss-covered rock, Belle lapped water until her thirst was quenched. Then she changed to her human form.

As soon as Belle moved away from the pool, Alex took her place and quenched his thirst. Then he, too, changed.

Belle was sitting on the moss smiling up at the almost full moon.

Without a word, Alex threw himself down beside her, pulled her into his arms, and covered her mouth with his. His kiss was long and hot. He stabbed his tongue into her mouth, wrestled and danced with her tongue then withdrew his and sucked hers into his mouth.

Belle moaned deep in her throat.

Alex shifted and settled himself on top of her, spreading her thighs with his knees, sliding his hard cock against her shaved mound.

When he finally released her tongue and started to nibble his way down her neck, Belle sucked in a huge gasp of air.

Alex smiled against her neck. He bet she'd never had anyone kiss the breath out of her before.

He licked a bead of sweat from her collarbone.

She was still panting. "Al...Alex?"

He switched his attention to her left nipple. He lapped it then suckled. "Hmmm."

She arched into his mouth. "What...what are you doing?"

Alex chuckled. He must really have kissed her senseless if she had to ask that question.

He switched his attention to her other nipple. "Fucking you."

She shivered beneath him.

No one had probably ever talked so bluntly to her either.

"Do you want me to stop?" He shifted again and slid his hand down over her stomach.

She raked her fingers into his long hair. "No. Don't stop. Please, don't stop."

He lapped the sweat from between her breasts. "I won't stop, but I won't fuck you until I'm ready either." He slid down her body and dipped his tongue into her navel. He trailed his fingers down over her shaved mound and between her thighs.

She was wet—so very, very wet.

Alex licked his way down over her stomach and hips, stopping at her bare mound. He kissed it. "Did you shave for me?" He slid two fingers into her and began to pump them.

She squirmed against his fingers. "Yes, oh gods, yes. Please..."

He slipped his fingers out of her and settled between her legs. "I've been dreaming of tasting you for three nights." He dipped his head and lapped the juices from between her thighs. He nipped her swollen clit then suckled it.

Moaning, Belle kept her hands fisted in Alex's hair as he lapped, laved, and licked her lips, her hairless mons, and her swollen clit. She arched into his mouth, and he nipped her clit.

Her moan became a howl as she thrust her hips against his mouth. Only his hands pinning her thighs to the ground kept her from locking her legs around his head. Never had a man driven her so wild.

"Yes! There! Again!"

He lifted his head. "Are you ready to come?"

Belle let go of his hair and cupped her breasts. She arched her back. "Yes! I want to come, Alex. I *need* to come." She looked down at him.

His face was drawn and his dark eyes glittered golden. "Good, because my balls are on fire."

Releasing her thighs, he slid up her body and settled on top of her. "Time to fuck, sweetheart." He slammed his cock into her.

She arched her hips to take all of him.

Thick, hard flesh met hot, melting fire.

Both groaned.

Alex pumped, withdrew, twisted his hips, and thrust.

Belle arched, clasped, relaxed, and clenched.

Alex pushed himself up onto his hands and watched her breasts bounce as he pumped his hips.

Belle wrapped her legs around his waist, lifted her hands, and pinched his nipples.

"Oh, baby," he growled as he twisted his hips and thrust one final time.

"Yes!" Belle moaned as she slid her hands down over his back and dug her nails into his ass. Sparkling stars appeared before her eyes as her stomach muscles shuddered and her internal muscles grasped his cock one final time.

Ears ringing, balls burning, Alex shoved his cock into Belle as far as he could and erupted. He collapsed, falling to her side, sucking in air in huge gasps.

Next to him, Belle shuddered with the final tremors of her orgasm.

He looked down. Cum was still seeping from his cock.

Alex lay back. Christ. When had he ever fucked a woman so hard? He closed his eyes. When had one ever driven him to fuck so hard?

Chapter Nine

ဆ

Belle's breathing slowed and became steady. "Wow."

Alex turned his head toward her and smiled. "I feel pretty much the same way."

Sitting up, she rubbed her arms. "Brrr. The night breeze is getting colder."

Alex looked up at the clouds slowly drifting across the almost full moon. "Storm's coming in. We'll have rain by morning." He rose and held out his hand. "Come on, I'll take you home."

She lifted her hand. "I can find my way myself. You don't have to run all the way to my cabin. It's got to be miles out of your way."

He grabbed her hand and pulled her up into his arms. Looking down into her face, he snorted. "In New York a man might let his date go home unescorted, but we're a little more old-fashioned out here. I brought you out, and I'll take you home."

Smiling, Belle reached up and brushed a stray strand of midnight hair back behind his ear. "Yeah, but in New York, none of my dates turned into wolves and raced me twenty miles or so up a mountain."

Alex leaned down and kissed her soundly. When he raised his head, he grinned. "See what you've been missing."

Wrapping her arms around his waist, Belle chuckled. "Oh, you've showed me very clearly what I've been missing." She licked a bead of sweat off his collarbone.

Cursing under his breath, Alex unwrapped her arms and stepped back. "As much as I'd like to stay here and discuss New York with you, I don't want to get drenched. Those storms rolling in aren't going to be gentle sprinkles."

Raising her arms above her head, Belle rose on tiptoe as she stretched.

Alex's gaze leaped from breast to breast as they jiggled.

Belle settled back onto her feet. "Then we'd better get going. It's got to be well after midnight anyway." Mist swirled, and her wolf form appeared.

Alex shifted and both wolves loped out of the clearing and into the forest.

Belle shifted back into her human form as she ascended the steps to her front porch.

Alex reached the door before she did and pulled it open for her.

She smiled. "Thanks for a wonderful night."

Cupping her chin, Alex tilted her head back. "Tonight was one of the best nights of my life." Bending, he kissed her, his lips moving gently over hers.

He drank in her sigh.

The rumble of distant thunder broke them apart.

His soul struggled against him. *No. Stay. Mate more.*

He forced his Were half into submission.

"I have to go."

Her lips twitching, Belle nodded. "I know. Your pack. You're a good leader, Alex. Your pack can be proud of you."

White teeth flashed as he grinned. "Oh, there are those who would disagree with you."

Her chuckle followed his grin. "You can't please everyone, you know. As long as the majority of them are happy, the hell with the rest."

Shaking his head, Alex turned away. "You can't run a pack like a business, Belle. They're humans—more or less—not numbers."

Belle followed him and leaned against the porch railing as he descended the steps. "I know that. But wouldn't it be nice, if just once, you could just say the hell with all of you?"

You don't know how often I've wanted to do just that. When he reached the base of the steps, Alex turned once more. "I'll be back. Soon." Black mist and a wolf leaped toward the woods.

Arms crossed over her breasts, Belle watched him until he disappeared beneath the trees.

A stronger wind tumbled around the corner of the cabin and wrapped itself around her naked body, raising goose bumps before it gusted away.

Rubbing her arms, Belle turned and entered the cabin.

Callie jumped off of the back of the sofa. *Why did your mate leave? Shouldn't he have stayed here? Isn't that what wolves do, stay with their mates?*

Chuckling, Belle picked up the kitten and cuddled it in her arms as she headed for her bedroom "Yes, we do. Alex just doesn't know I'm his mate yet."

Callie spit. *Doesn't know? Is he stupid? Why would you want a stupid mate? You want your cubs to be smart, don't you? If your mate is stupid, your cubs might be stupid.*

Belle dropped Callie on the bed and pulled an oversized tee shirt over her head. "He's not stupid, Callie, just confused. His pack is very important to him, and he wants to do what's best for it."

Tail straight up in the air, Callie stretched, extending first one paw then the other. Then she settled down, tucking her paws into her snowy chest. *Pack this. Pack that. You canines worry about too many things. Independence is better. Mate with whom and how often you want. I had four siblings in my litter. We had three different fathers. A much better way, I think.*

Hands on hips, Belle shook her head. "Felines and their multiple sex partners. No thank you. I think I'll just stick to a single mate."

Callie closed her eyes. *Suit yourself. I, however, when I'm old enough, intend to enjoy myself to the fullest.* The sound of her purr filled the room.

"Cats," Belle muttered as she crawled into bed. "No wonder they don't like werewolves. We aren't promiscuous enough for them."

Snuggling a pillow in her arms, Belle soon slept, the werewolf in her soul content with the night's events. Her male had left again, but he would be back, she'd seen it in his eyes. The man part of him was still unsure, still worried more about his pack than himself. The werewolf in his soul, however, knew she was his one and only mate. Soon, Alex the man would realize this, and the werewolf would come for her.

Belle stirred in her sleep.

Her werewolf soul closed its eyes. It too needed to rest, to gather strength. When Alex came to claim her, he would discover his mate was just as much an Alpha as he was.

As he ran through the forest, Alex replayed the events of the evening in his head. Belle was far wilder, far more passionate than any woman he'd ever met. She satisfied him far more than any other woman he'd ever been with.

Once again, his werewolf soul had demanded that he mount and mate Belle. The struggle for control had been brief but hard. If he hadn't already had his cock buried to the hilt inside her willing body, the fight for control would have been a lot harder.

Alex shook his head. Best get rid of thoughts like those. Belle was a city girl. She'd be going back to New York. The sooner his Were half understood that, the better.

A deer exploded out of the thicket to his left.

He ignored it, concentrating instead on the enigma that was Belle. She was the first person he'd ever met who'd expected nothing from him. His tongue lolled out and he grinned a wolf grin. Well, except for great sex, but he received as much or more than he gave for that. No, Belle was an enigma. An enigma he would soon see again.

His werewolf soul growled in agreement.

Chapter Ten

৪১

Josh's fist banged against the table. "Damn it, Alex, pay attention!"

Alex blinked and looked at his Beta. "What?"

"I asked if you thought this was a fair price for the bathroom fixtures," Josh said as he stabbed his finger onto a piece of paper. "I don't want to be cheated."

Alex shrugged. "No one's ever been overcharged at Frank's Hardware, not even after his smart-assed son took over."

"Well, what about the finished lumber we need for the extra room we're adding?"

Alex concentrated his stare on Josh. "Christ, we own the lumber mill. Why would we cheat ourselves?"

Crossing his arms over his chest, Josh said, "I just wanted to make sure you're paying attention. Your mind has been wandering a lot lately."

Dave's voice wafted over the back of the couch. "Chasing a hot piece of tail in his mind, I'd imagine."

Alex's voice was a deep growl. "Shut up, Dave."

Pushing himself up, Dave rested his arms against the back of the sofa. "Touchy today, aren't we? Let's see, how long has it been? Last time you managed to wait four days. It's been three since you saw your New York accountant. How long you gonna last?"

Fists clenched, Alex closed his eyes and sucked in a deep breath. As soon as his temper was under control, he opened them and fixed his gaze on his Omega. "You, I believe, are supposed to be checking on the landscaping for the bed and breakfast. So go pick flowers."

Turning to Josh, he continued. "We've been over the plans and work orders three times. The prices for everything are reasonable. Lumber will be delivered tomorrow, so we need to get that back wall knocked out. Bathroom fixtures are supposed to come next week. I want those bathrooms ready for them when they get here."

"Who should we have work on what?"

Alex raked his fingers through his hair. He still hadn't gotten a haircut. He liked the way Belle buried her hands in it.

"Shit, Josh. You've been making decisions like that since you became my Beta. What the hell are you asking me for? I trust your judgment."

Josh planted both palms on the top of the desk and leaned forward. "Yeah, but do you trust your own?"

Thunder rumbled in the distance.

Nostrils flaring, Alex stared at his brown-haired Beta. "What the hell does that mean?"

Josh's gaze never wavered. "You spend too much time thinking about that New York bitch. Just because Serena left you, you don't have to pick up with the first piece of fresh tail that comes around."

Every muscle on Alex's body tensed. "Serena? What the hell does she have to do with anything? She's gone and married. I wish her well. I was over her months ago. You're the one who kept bringing up her name."

"Yeah, right," Dave muttered from the sofa.

"As for the New York *bitch*, I enjoy Belle's company and will continue to do so for as long as I want. And I don't give a damn what you or anyone else thinks."

"Then find out about her. Who is she? What was her last pack affiliation? Shit, Alex, you're the Alpha. You can't go around fucking every willing bitch."

More thunder rumbled — closer this time.

Heat rushed to Alex's face as Dave leaped across the back of the sofa and hurried to Josh's side. "Come on. We need to get this stuff done if we want to open this fall."

Josh shook off Dave's hand. He opened his mouth, looked into Alex's eyes, and thought better of what he was going to say. Eyes never leaving his Alpha, he rounded the desk and followed Dave across the room and out the door.

Thunder boomed against the mountains.

When his teeth began to ache, Alex unclenched his jaw. Never had he had such trouble controlling himself, the werewolf half of him had wanted to tear out Josh's throat. Belle was his! He would see her when, where, and as often as he wanted to.

"I'm surprised Josh left here with all of his skin."

Alex closed his eyes and sighed. Just what he needed, a visit by Alesandra Morning, Council member, the previous female Alpha of the pack — a position she continued to fill until he mated.

Straightening, he turned to face her. "What can I do for you, Alesandra?"

The short, white-haired woman smiled at him. "I don't need anything, Alex. I've come to help you."

Alex made no attempt to muffle his groan. Whenever Alesandra tried to help, his heart ended up taking a beating. He looked into her bright, blue eyes. "Help me like you did before?"

Lips pursed, she nodded. "I admit I made a mistake trying to bring you and Serena together. I won't make the same mistake again."

Rain started to spatter against the porch.

Stepping across the room, Alex cupped her elbow, spun her around, and guided her toward the door. "Good to hear that, Alesandra. I'm tired of people trying to dictate how I should live my life. You better get home before the rain gets too bad. Don't let the door hit you in the ass on your way out."

Fixing a sharp glare on his face, she rapped her cane on the floor—once. "I'm not leaving until I've said my piece, Alex. So shut up, sit down, and listen."

He dropped his hand from her elbow. "Oh fuck."

"And stop the profanity. I don't appreciate it."

The rafters rattled and dust shifted as thunder exploded above the house.

Mumbling under his breath, Alex spun around and flopped onto the sofa. "So talk. I'm a busy man."

"Stupid, arrogant Alpha," she grumbled as she followed him across the room. Stopping in front of him, Alesandra lifted her cane, poked him in the chest and said, "Do you want her?"

His nostrils flared. She smelled of anger, frustration, and— hope. "What are you talking about?"

"This Belle you've been courting."

He snorted. "Courting!"

"What would you call it?"

He bared his teeth in a toothy grin. "You told me not to use profanity."

She smacked her cane against his shin.

He yelped and grabbed his leg.

Alesandra rapped her cane against the floor once more. "Stop being such an asshole and think—not of the pack—but of yourself. What do *you* want? Haven't you realized yet what's best for you is best for the pack?"

Rubbing his shin, Alex stared at the old woman. Was she right?

He pictured Belle as she had lain beneath him, flushed with passion, and the werewolf in his soul surged into his mind. *My mate. Now!*

Alex's entire body shook.

Alesandra smiled a satisfied smile. "I thought so. Go claim her, Alex, before she gets tired of waiting for you and goes back to New York."

The thought of Belle returning to New York galvanized Alex into action. Belle leave? No! She was *his*!

More thunder rattled the windows as he snarled and sprang to his feet. Tearing his clothing off as he leaped toward the door, he tumbled through it in a cloud of black mist.

Alesandra straightened and smiled. About time Alex found the right woman.

Chapter Eleven

೩೧

Belle flinched when another clap of thunder rolled over the dark cabin.

All her fur puffed out, Callie hissed and dove under the sofa. *I am not coming out until the loud noises stop.*

Lightning flashed around the room. Thunder boomed.

The fine hairs on Belle's arms stood up, and she tossed the mystery novel she was staring at on the sofa. She couldn't concentrate on the story anyway.

Alex was coming to claim her.

He was coming. She was as sure of that as she was of her own existence.

The werewolf in her soul soon had her pacing from the window next to the door to the one over the sink in the small kitchen — back and forth, back and forth.

Shadows dipped and swayed with another lightning flash.

He was coming.

Her heat thudded in time to the thunder.

Tonight.

Rain pounded on the roof.

Now.

As the door slammed open, Belle spun around.

Naked, Alex stood, feet braced apart, hand splayed against the door, raindrops rolling down his broad, bronze chest and firm abdomen into the black curls at the juncture of his muscular thighs. His thick cock thrust out — hard, erect.

His dark, gold-flecked eyes blazed with sexual arousal.

His voice shook with Alpha possessiveness. "Come to me now."

Belle's breath caught in her throat. He was everything she wanted in a mate — strong, powerful, domineering. He was more than worthy of her love.

That didn't mean she'd bow meekly to his demands. He had to earn the submission she'd give him.

Shivering, she straightened her shoulders and raised her chin. "No."

Shock and surprise radiated like heat from his body.

A growl rumbled from deep in his chest. "No games!" He held out his free hand. "Come to me."

Crossing her arms over her breasts, she shook her head. Her voice was firm. "No."

His voice became a snarl. "You are mine."

As a gust of cold, rain-soaked wind blasted past him, her nipples puckered under her crossed arms.

Her chin rose higher. "Prove it."

In the blink of an eye, he was across the room.

Anticipating his leap, Belle sidestepped and started toward the door only to be brought up short. Alex had managed to snag the back hem of her tee shirt. Without a second thought, she grabbed the shirt's neck and ripped the front in two. Sliding her arms free, she sprinted through the door and leaped from the porch out into the rain.

In seconds, she was drenched.

Ripped tee shirt crumpled in his fist, Alex stood on the porch and glared at Belle. She wasn't running. Instead, she stood in the pouring rain, long, black hair plastered to her head, neck, and shoulders, fists planted on her hips, feet spread slightly apart, head thrown back. Her nipples pebbled into hard nubs as the pouring rain sluiced off her pert breasts. The soaked shorts she wore clung to her hips.

Lightning flashed and a diamond glittered in her navel.

A gust of wind swirled, embraced her then raced past him.

She smelled of wet woman and arousal.

He would have her. Now!

Leaping from the porch, Alex changed direction in midair, anticipating her dodge.

He anticipated the wrong direction.

She sprinted left as he landed to her right.

Water slapped him in the face as he landed on his hands and knees in a deep puddle in the wet grass.

Pushing himself to his feet, Alex glared at her. "You aren't fast enough to escape me!"

"Prove it."

As lightning lit up the darkening sky, excitement surged through Alex's body. His balls contacted and his cock hardened even more. The werewolf in his soul howled with joy with the thrill of the chase and promise of sexual dominance at its conclusion. He erupted to his feet and surged after her.

Thunder rolled.

Anticipation rippled through Belle's body when she heard Alex's footsteps closing the distance between them. The thought of being sexually dominated by him had her stomach clenching and moisture pooling between her thighs. He was faster but she was quicker. As long as she dodged, he'd have trouble catching her.

Again Belle shivered, but not from the cold rain pelting her body. The longer Alex had to chase her, the more sexually frustrated the werewolf in him would become. When he finally caught her...

She gulped with anticipation.

Bending over, she grabbed a gob of mud and threw it directly at his chest.

He didn't dodge fast enough.

Wet mud splattered against his breastbone and rolled down over his stomach. In seconds, the rain washed his chest clean again.

Alex snarled again as Belle dodged away from him. Bitch. Didn't she know how dangerous it was to tease him like this? When he finally caught her, he wouldn't be able to control himself.

The rain slowed.

Her laughter slid past him.

Howling, he launched himself to her right…and wrapped his arms around her waist when she dodged into his arms.

Twisting in midair, he landed with a splat in the soft, wet grass with Belle on top of him. He hooked his fingers into the back of her shorts and ripped them in half. Then he rolled her over, grasped both wrists with one hand, pinned her arms over her head, and pulled what was left of her clothing from her body.

She moaned and arched into his mouth as he nipped first one nipple then the other.

Raising his head, Alex looked into her flushed face.

She bucked underneath him.

He nudged his cock between her thighs..

Dipping his head, he captured her mouth in a long, dominating kiss. He slid his tongue between her teeth and raked the inside of her mouth with it. His teeth clicked against hers.

When he finally pulled his tongue out of her mouth, she caught his lower lip between her teeth and bit down until she drew blood.

Sheet lightning flashed in the distance. The thunder rolled away.

As he licked the blood from his lip, Alex's werewolf soul howled in triumph. Belle was meant to be mate to an Alpha. His cock jerked against her thigh. He had to bury himself inside of her, claim her, brand her as his. But not like this. Not like a human. He had to mount her, hold her immobile beneath him as he pumped his seed into her body and merged his soul with hers.

A late peal of thunder cracked around them.

Belle sank her teeth into his shoulder.

Alex smelled more blood.

With a snarl, he released her wrists and flipped her onto her stomach. When his fingers brushed against the diamond piercing her navel, she moaned and bucked. He rubbed his cock against the cleft in her ass. "Submit to me."

Beads of water hit him in the face as she shook her head. "No."

Grabbing her waist with both hands, he lifted her to her knees. "You can't escape me, Belle. Submit!" He kneed her thighs apart and settled between them. Reaching between her legs, he slid his finger into her. She was wet and more than ready for him.

Alex eased his cock between her thighs, sliding it back and forth against her slick lips. He leaned over her back and nipped her shoulder.

She shuddered, moaned again — and bucked against his hold.

Alex's breathing became harsher. "Submit. Now!"

He pinched a nipple.

Wind swirled and the dark clouds raced across the sky.

She shivered, tried to jerk free, then threw back her head. Her "No" echoed off the mountaintops.

His howl of frustration followed. He couldn't claim her until she submitted of her own free will.

Alex rested more of his weight on her back and nipped her other shoulder. His voice was a dangerous rumble in her ear. "Damn it, Belle, without you, I only have half a soul."

The moon burst from behind the clouds, and its soft light enveloped them.

Immediately, the tenseness left Belle's muscles. As she relaxed beneath him, she pushed her ass back against his hips.

Alex thrust his cock home, groaning as her hot, slick, internal muscles tightened around it, grasped it, pulled it deeper. Clamping his teeth on her shoulder, he began to pump his hips.

His balls were on fire. He ached with need and the werewolf in his soul fought to release his seed. But his human half was determined to prolong his—and Belle's—pleasure as long as he could.

Shuddering, Belle dropped to her forearms so Alex could thrust more deeply, not caring that her upper torso and arms lay in a puddle of cold water.

He unclamped his teeth and lapped the back of her neck. Straightening, he grasped her waist and ground his hips against her ass.

"Yes, oh yes, oh yes, Alex. Harder." She arched her back.

Growling, he pulled her hips back against his as he twisted and thrust into her. "So wet. So hot."

Belle spread her legs further apart. "Oh, gods, you're so hard." Her stomach muscles clenched and knotted. Her breasts tightened. Tingling sharply, surrounded by soft, wet grass, her nipples hardened even more. She sobbed. Alex's cock was rock-hard and his thrusts penetrated her more deeply than any man—or werewolf—ever had. Never had she experienced such pleasure!

Alex rammed his cock even deeper. "My mate. My mate."

Belle moaned her agreement. "Your mate. Yes! Oh yes, yes."

The pressure inside of Belle built, and she was unable to control it. Her orgasm erupted outward from her groin and fiery heat spread to every inch of her body.

Alex threw back his head, and his howl of possession and completion echoed from the mountains.

Breathing harshly, he rolled off Belle and onto his back. Wrapping his arms around her, he pulled her down onto him.

She nuzzled his chest, licked a nipple, raised her head, and stared into his eyes. Hers were silver mirrors. She smiled and leaned forward to kiss his mouth tenderly.

Alex cupped the back of her head but didn't fight her when she pushed away from him.

Her voice was low but triumphant. "Mine."

Chapter Twelve

A cool morning breeze stirred the curtains of the open window and caressed Belle's body. Shivering, she snuggled back against the solid, warm form spooned against her back. The heavy arm draped over her rib cage tightened, and fingers brushed against the diamond stud piercing her navel. She sighed. After she and Alex finally made it to the bed last night, tugs on that particular piece of jewelry had sent stabs of heat directly to her groin.

Alex shifted and his hand brushed the diamond again.

Belle grimaced. This pressure didn't travel to her clit. It traveled to her bladder. She rolled from beneath Alex's arm, got out of bed, and headed for the bathroom.

Alex woke as soon as Belle left the bed. Blinking, he focused on her disappearing figure and shifted to get more comfortable. He needed to make the same journey himself.

As he sat up, a multicolored ball of fur exploded onto the bed. *Feed me!*

Alex raked his long hair out of his face. "How did I manage to mate a woman who has a talking cat?"

Callie batted his arm.

He glared at her. "You scratch me, and you'd better learn how to fly—fast."

Chuckling, Belle crossed the room and lifted the kitten from the bed. "Come on, Callie. I'll get your breakfast."

Kitten cuddled in her arms, she sauntered out of the room.

Head cocked to the side, Alex watched her leave. She had the nicest ass he'd ever seen—or fondled.

His cock stirred when he remembered gripping those ass cheeks as he pounded into her. Sighing, he shook his head. He had other needs to take care of first.

When Belle returned, Alex was just leaving the bathroom. "I hope you don't mind, but I used that extra toothbrush I found."

She walked into his arms and wrapped hers around his waist. "I bought it for you." She kissed his chin.

Alex hugged her tight. "You can't go back to New York."

She leaned back in his arms. "I'll have to go sometimes. I'm the accountant for the family business. I can do a lot of work via the internet, but I will have to meet with my dad sometimes.

Alex snorted. "I guess that makes sense." He stared down into her face then grinned. "You know. I don't even know your last name."

She grinned back. "You never asked and the subject never came up. It's—"

The loud blaring of a horn and squealing brakes interrupted her answer.

Alex broke their embrace and headed for the bedroom door.

Belle leaped toward her dresser and grabbed a bag sitting next to it. "Alex, here. Put these on first. You don't know who's out there."

Half-turning, he caught the pair of jeans she tossed to him and slipped them on. He pulled up the zipper but didn't bother with the button. He had a pretty good idea who was out there, and he would make sure their uninvited guest left a lot faster than he arrived.

Alex strode through the living room, wrenched the front door open, and glared at the red pickup. Yep. Josh with Dave in tow. Damn, but his Beta was getting to be a real pain in the ass.

"What the hell do you want?" he yelled as they got out of the truck.

Josh slammed the door closed and stomped toward the cabin. "Damn it, Alex, the least you could do is let me know when you won't be around so I know where to contact you."

Feet braced apart, Alex folded his arms over his chest and looked down from the top of the porch steps. "You found me easily enough. Christ, Josh, you're Beta. You can make decisions without me being there."

Josh stopped and glared at Alex. "Not when I have a couple of women asking for Sanctuary. Only the Alpha can grant that."

Alex frowned. "What's going on?"

"They showed up last night around nine," Dave interjected as he sauntered to Josh's side, "and went straight to Alesandra."

Still belligerent, Josh added, "She had to call me when she couldn't find you."

Rubbing the back of his neck, Alex answered absently, "She knew I was here." Two women wanting Sanctuary. He couldn't remember the last time that happened. "What are they running from?"

Dave answered, "One of them is married to a wife-beater. The other is his sister. She helped her get away."

Alex frowned. "They're all Were?"

Josh's answer was a growl. "Yes."

"Alex, you have to grant them Sanctuary. If her mate truly beats her, she doesn't have anywhere else to turn."

Both Josh and Dave stared as Belle snaked her arm beneath Alex's and leaned against his side.

She was glad she'd taken the time to comb her hair and slip into jeans and a tee shirt before she came out. The Beta, Josh, didn't look very welcoming.

"Well, hello," Dave said with a grin. "We finally meet the mystery lady. I'm Dave."

Belle smiled. "Hello to you too. I'm Belle."

Josh growled, "Enough already. You going to get your ass back to the pack, Alex, and take care of this mess, or you gonna stay in bed and fuck all day?"

Belle gasped.

Keeping Belle at his side, Alex growled low in his throat and started down the step. "I mated Belle last night, Josh, and if you can't accept it, I'll be looking for a new Beta."

A gusty breeze swirled and rolled up the muddy road that led to the house. It carried a new scent.

Dave's head snapped up. "Wolf coming. He's Were."

All three men tensed.

Alex tried to push Belle behind him.

She stepped right back to his side.

All four of them looked down the road.

A large gray wolf loped toward them.

Flaring his nostrils, Alex inhaled the breeze. Something about this particular wolf seemed familiar.

The wolf reached the truck, gray mist swirled, and a tall gray-eyed man strode toward them.

Recognition slammed its fist into Alex's stomach. No way! Not again! This particular werewolf was not going to take another woman from him.

A deep, full-throated howl exploded from his lungs. "Kearnan Gray, you bastard. You won't take *this* woman from me!" Shaking himself free from Belle's arm, he began to strip off his jeans.

Both Dave and Josh tensed and snarled.

Belle grabbed his arm and shook it. "That's not Kearnan. That's Brendan."

He ignored her.

She punched him in the arm. "Damn it, Alex, listen to me."

His snarl didn't faze her in the least. "What?"

"That's not Kearnan."

He froze. "How do you know that?"

Fisting her hands on her hips, Belle snorted. "I *can* tell my own brothers apart."

Alex froze and stared at Belle.

Both Dave and Josh wrenched their attention to her.

"Abomination," Josh snarled.

Belle felt as if she'd been slapped. Frozen in place, she concentrated on the man she'd mated. "Alex?"

He simply stared down at her, the momentary astonishment that had been on his face rapidly shuttered away. Now his face was completely blank.

She lifted her hand. "Alex?"

"Get away from her," Josh snarled.

Without a word, Alex stepped back, slipped out of his jeans, and shifted. Once in wolf form, he sprinted for the forest.

Belle blinked as tears formed.

Brendan reached the bottom of the steps. "Belle? What's going on?"

"You and your sister stay away from our pack, Abomination. Let's get out of here, Dave."

Snarling, Brendan stepped toward Josh.

"Brendan," Belle choked, "don't. Let them go."

Josh stomped away.

Dave hesitated and looked back at Belle. After tossing her a quick grin and a wink, he followed Josh to the truck and climbed in.

Gears grinding, Josh backed the truck and roared down the road, mud flying in all directions.

Brendan looked at his sister. "Who were they and what the hell was that all about?"

Shoulders slumping, Belle didn't bother fighting the tears. "The wolf is my mate and the other two are his Beta and Omega. He just found out about our mother."

Brendan gaped at her. "Mate! What the hell are you talking about? You don't even know him." He turned and stared into the forest. "Mother-fucking cocksucker. When I get my teeth on his throat…"

Belle grabbed his arm. "No. Let him go."

"Damn it, Belle. He took advantage of you! He was probably only after a quick fuck. What do you know about him anyway?"

The force of her slap snapped his head to the side. "Don't you dare talk about him like that! I am *not* a quick fuck, Brendan. I am his *mate*."

The angry imprint of her hand obvious on his face, he focused his attention back on Belle. "Are you?"

Her head dropped and her chin rested against her chest. She stared at her feet as tears dropped to the ground.

Brendan cocked his head to the side. "Do you want to repudiate him?"

She shook her head.

Placing his knuckles under her chin, Brendan lifted her head. His voice was gentle. "You can, you know. Pack law allows it."

She closed her eyes. Her voice was barely a whisper. "I can't."

"Why?"

"I love him."

* * * * *

Eyes tearing from the wind caused by the speed of his passage through the forest, Alex ran until his muscles ached — no specific destination in mind. Belle Gray's mother was a wolf, a full-blooded wolf. To many Weres, an Abomination. Werewolves who ran feral and mated a wolf were supposed to stay wolves. Their cubs were supposed to stay wolves. But Belle's mother had died, and her father had taught his children

83

how to change from their wolf forms to human forms. Abomination. Or was it?

Alex shook his head as he ran. The First Law of the WerePack — Above all else, honor and respect the brothers and sisters of the forest, for it was they who guided us through the dark days.

If he'd have ever met Belle's mother, he'd have treated her with all the respect she deserved. Why then, shouldn't Belle and her siblings be treated with respect?

A howl exploded from Alex's throat. Even to his own ears, it sounded anguished.

As he burst into a stand of pines, the small group of deer that was bedded down there leaped to their feet and scattered in half a dozen directions, fear lending them speed.

Alex scented their fear on the wind, tasted it in his open mouth. The satisfying taste of hot blood flooded his memory. The thrill of the hunt soothed his warring emotions.

He allowed the wolf in his soul to take charge of his body. Food. Kill. Eat.

The plump, yearling buck before him dodged left then right in vain. After a short chase, Alex lay panting on his kill, licking fresh blood from his jowls.

A shift of the wind brought a faint scent, a fainter sound.

Brush rustled. An old wolf followed by his mate slunk from beneath the low hanging pines.

Above all else, honor and respect the brothers and sisters of the forest.

Rising to his feet, Alex faced the two wolves.

Both bowed their heads.

Our pardon, Alpha.

Alex nodded, not surprised that the male knew he was Alpha. All wolves recognized an Alpha when he or she met one.

The same way Alex recognized that this old wolf and his mate had been pack Alphas themselves.

We have traveled far and eaten little. We ask only the remains of your kill.

Alex licked his jaw again and continued to stare. They were both thin—and tired. He closed his eyes. *Honor and respect the brothers and sisters of the forest.*

He opened his eyes and stepped away from the dead deer. *My kill is yours. Eat as much as you like.*

Our thanks, Alpha. Both wolves attacked the carcass ravenously. Obviously, they hadn't eaten well in days.

Stretching out on his side, Alex watched the two wolves eat. He was curious and wanted to hear their story. Anything anything to keep his mind off Belle.

The old female finished before the male. After licking her jaws clean, she turned to Alex. *My thanks. I am Willow. My mate is Silver. You are Were.*

Alex nodded his head once. *Yes. I am Alex.*

You are mated?

Alex felt his heart wrench. *Yes, yes, yes*, his soul howled in his mind.

The old female lay down and stared at him. *What troubles you?*

Sitting up, Alex shifted back to human form and stared at the white-headed wolf. "I think my problems might be too complicated for you."

A wolf grin appeared on her face. *Why do you Weres always believe your brains work better than a wolf's?* Slowly, a white mist gathered. It thinned, strengthened, thinned, then thickened, and an old woman sat before Alex.

With a low whine, the old male hurried to her side and lay down against her.

The old woman groaned. "This is the last time, Silver. I promise."

Alex's voice was gentle. "You old fool. You almost couldn't control it. You could have died."

She smoothed the fur on top of the old wolf's head. "Then I would have run the shadow path just a bit sooner."

Alex nodded to her mate. "And what of him, if you had?"

I would have followed her.

"Why did you change?"

She smiled. "You look like a man who needs to talk. Talking to a friendly stranger is sometimes easier than talking to a friend."

Alex leaned forward. "How long have you been his mate?"

Willow smiled, glanced down, and caressed his head.

The old wolf sighed and closed his eyes.

"When we were younger," she answered with a faraway look in her eyes, "I'd change sometimes, just to pet him like this."

"Why did you…"

Her gaze shifted back to Alex. "…run feral? I met Silver in the woods one night and knew I wanted no other."

"But your family, your pack…"

She shrugged. "My soul sang with joy the night I met Silver. Being with him was the one thing I was absolutely sure of."

Alex leaned back against a tree. "Your cubs?"

"Chose to remain wolves…all but one. And I taught him to shift."

Alex's sharp inhalation brought a smile to her face. "What? You think he's an Abomination because he chose to live Were? Why?"

Alex sputtered then shrugged his shoulders. "I don't understand, Willow. Why do Weres look upon a child such as yours as unnatural?"

"Fear, Alex. The fear of someone different. You get it from your human blood. How do humans treat those who are different?"

Alex stared at the old woman. Was it nothing more than prejudice? That's what Serena had said when he tried to take her away from Kearnan Gray. *How can you be so narrow-minded? For years, our Cheyenne people were discriminated against because they were different. Now you want to do the same thing? How can you be such a hypocrite?*

Pushing himself to his feet, Alex began to pace. Was he a hypocrite? What was wrong with Belle, anyway? Before her brother showed up, he'd had no idea that her mother had been a wolf. She was no different than any other Were he'd ever met.

The old wolf whined.

"Have I helped, Alex? Silver wants to continue our journey."

Shaking himself from his thoughts, Alex turned his attention back to her. "Where are you going?"

She shrugged. "South, to warmer weather. We don't have many seasons left, either of us."

"Stay here, for the spring and summer, at least. There's a cabin not so far, with a warm cellar beneath it. My pack will make sure you're comfortable for as long as you want to stay."

Willow glanced at Silver. "It would be nice to stay in one place and rest a while."

"Good." Stepping to what was left of the deer's carcass, he hoisted it over his shoulder. "Follow me." He stared into Willow's eyes. "Will you be able to shift back?"

She smiled. "Yes. It was mostly lack of practice that had me wavering before." After a deep breath, she closed her eyes. This time the mist formed and didn't waver. She shifted to her wolf shape with no problem.

Alex smiled and headed south, his heart lighter.

Chapter Thirteen

✿

Teeth clenched, Belle fisted the tears from her eyes—again.

Now wearing some of the clothing Belle had bought for Alex, Brendan set a mug of steaming tea in front of her then squeezed her shoulder. "All cried out?"

She cupped the mug in her hands and let the warmth soak into her fingers and palms. "Shut up."

"Fucking, prejudiced, asshole purists." He jerked out the chair across the table and sat down. "Are you *sure* you want to keep him?"

Belle closed her eyes and nodded. "I don't have a choice. He's my mate, the one meant for me."

Brendan snorted and threw up his hands. "What a load of crap."

Shaking her head, Belle wiped more tears away. "Remember when Dad met Moira? Well, that's how it felt for me, too."

Leaning back, Brendan crossed his arms over his chest. "What was his reaction when you stated 'Mine' and demanded he come to you?"

A ghost of a smile appeared on hers as Belle remembered Moira's reaction. "I'm a little more diplomatic than Dad."

Reaching across the table, Brendan pried her left hand off the mug and laced his fingers through hers. "How in the world did you two mate without him knowing who you were?"

Pulling her hand free, Belle grabbed another tissue and blew her nose. "He never asked. It didn't matter, not to him, not to me. You'll understand when you find your own mate."

Brendan snorted even more loudly. *When hell freezes over.* "What are you going to do now?"

She shrugged. "I don't know."

He smiled hopefully. "I can go beat the shit out of him until he sees how much of an asshole he's being."

Another ghostly smile on her lips, Belle shook her head.

He grabbed her free hand and squeezed. "Come on, Sis. You're tougher than this. I've seen you face down some of the most powerful executives in New York. Hell, I've seen you face down Dad. What kind of chance does this Alex guy have against you? If you want to keep him, you have to fight for him."

Callie looked up from where she lay purring in Belle's lap. *Your sibling is right. If you want a male, you must make him understand he has no choice.*

Brendan sat back and shook his head. "A werewolf with a cat — that talks. No one will ever believe me."

Sighing, Belle stroked Callie and stared at her brother. "How? How do I fight for a man who thinks I'm an abomination?"

"Alex doesn't truly believe you are an abomination, child."

The chair clattered to the floor as Brendan leaped to his feet to face the woman who stood just outside the screen door.

"May I come in?"

Gathering Callie into her arms, Belle rose.

Kicking the chair out of his way, Brendan grabbed her arm to stop her and stepped in front of her. "Who the hell are you?"

"Another stiff-necked Alpha," the white-haired woman muttered with a sigh and a shake of her head. Then she smiled. "I'm your sister-in-law's grandmother."

He frowned. "You're Alesandra Morning?"

She nodded once. "Yes."

Blinking the remaining tears from her eyes, Belle planted her hand in the middle of her brother's back and shoved. "Damn it, Brendan, what's wrong with you? You have better manners than this."

He glanced over his shoulder. "And you're really in the mood to entertain?"

"Shut up." She stepped from behind him and turned her attention to Alesandra. "Please, come in. Don't mind Brendan. Sometimes he forgets his manners."

Alesandra smiled as she opened the door. "A quirk of all Alphas. Your brother Kearnan is much like him."

Alesandra entered, followed by a large man.

Yowling, Callie scrambled out of Belle's arms, all of her fur standing straight out. *Bear! Danger! Run and hide.* She scrambled from the room, leaving claw marks in the wooden floor.

Nostrils flaring, Brendan grabbed his sister and pushed her behind him.

As the tall man held his hands out palm forward, Alesandra stepped in front of him. "George TwoBears is my friend. He won't hurt you."

Still tense, Brendan stared at both of them. "Are you the same werebear who helped Kearnan?"

George nodded.

Brendan relaxed—a little.

Alesandra looked at the door where Callie had disappeared. "You have a cat? How did you make friends with her?"

Belle grabbed her brother's arm and jerked him out of the way. "Damn it, Brendan, will you please stop shoving me behind you! I'm big enough to take care of myself."

He crossed his arms over his chest. "Really? Didn't seem that way fifteen minutes ago."

Taking a deep breath, Belle closed her eyes and counted to ten. Okay, he was right. Fifteen minutes ago she was a basket case, well, almost a basket case. She'd fix things with Alex, somehow. And maybe this Alesandra Morning could help her.

Belle opened her eyes and bared her teeth at her brother. "That was fifteen minutes ago. Now move, asshole, before I move you. I have guests." She motioned to Alesandra and George. "Please sit down. Would you like some tea?"

Turning his head away from his sister as he stepped out of the way, Brendan smiled. Get Belle angry enough and she'd conquer the world. This Alex Whitehorse didn't stand a chance. Of course, if he was too stupid to realize what a treasure he had in Belle... Well, there'd be one less werewolf roaming this forest.

Chapter Fourteen

ॐ

Alesandra shook her head. "No thank you. We're here to take you back with us."

The teakettle clanged onto the top of the stove.

"Like hell you are!" Brendan interjected as he stepped toward them. "My sister isn't going to crawl on her belly to any man."

Alesandra shook her head. "No, you misunderstand. No one in our pack would respect her if she did that. I want her to come back with me as my guest—and possible business partner. At least that's what I'll tell everyone."

Brendan curled his lip. "Business partner? With you? Us? In what?"

"This." She set a small, pink block on the table.

Belle picked it up. "It's soap." She sniffed. "Rose-scented."

Brendan snorted.

Alesandra ignored him. "We make soap for a local store frequented by tourists. I've told the other women I heard from the owner of the store you were vacationing here, and I was going to approach you about investing." She smiled. "I know a large company such as yours isn't interested in the little bit of soap we make, but it is a way to get you close to Alex."

Before Belle could answer, Brendan interrupted. "And I just bet the members of your pack will be thrilled to have an 'abomination' visiting with them."

Belle snapped. "Enough, Brendan. What I decide to do is none of your business."

Arms crossed over his chest, he stepped in front of his sister and glared down at her. "Like hell. You're my sister, and I'm not going to allow you to be harassed and vilified by a pack of backwoods werewolves who don't like your ancestry."

"That won't happen," Alesandra interjected.

Fists clenched, Brendan spun to face her. "Bullshit. Your own Beta called her an abomination. I was there."

Stamping her cane against the floor, Alesandra shook her head. "No! It will *not* happen again. Not all our members think like he does."

Arms now crossed over his chest, Brendan straightened to his full height and looked down his nose at her. "I'll just bet they don't."

Frowning, George straightened from where he was leaning against the wall.

"That's enough," Belle said in a calm voice. "I'm not a little girl who needs her big brother watching out for her. I can take care of myself."

He turned to face her. "Like you took care of yourself this morning?"

Temper flaring, Belle fisted her hands on her hips. "Just what did happen to me this morning, Brendan, that I couldn't have handled myself if you hadn't been here? As a matter of fact, you're the one who caused all the problems. If you hadn't shown up, I wouldn't have had to defend you, and Alex wouldn't have found out about my ancestry in front of other pack members." She stabbed her finger into his chest. "You, my dear brother, are the one who screwed everything up."

He glared down at her. "Like hell I did."

Belle inched closer, stood on her tiptoes, and glared up into his face. "Yes, you did, moron."

"No. I didn't, you naïve, little idiot."

Shaking her head, Alesandra sighed. This girl Belle was more Alpha than any female she'd ever met, including herself. She was the perfect mate for Alex, if the two of them could get back together without Josh's interference.

As Belle and Brendan's argument became more heated, George placed his hand on her shoulder. *Are you sure she is the one for Alex? Will he be able to control her?*

Patting his hand, Alesandra nodded. *Yes. She's perfect for him. According to her, they're mated, so she accepted his dominance. What you see here is sibling rivalry. These two are Alpha and won't accept the other's superiority. I'm not surprised that Artemis Gray would father such children, especially since their mother was a true wolf.*

Alesandra smiled. *Look at them. Even as they argue, both are wrapped in dignity and self-confidence. Some of that comes from their mother. Wolves have an innate feeling of self-esteem found in few other living beings, something many werewolves have lost. I've come to believe that these infusions of wolf blood will make werewolves stronger.*

George smiled down at her. *Something we werebears have never forgotten.*

She chuckled. *Your people just forget to come back out of the woods.*

A wide grin appeared on his face. *Best place to hibernate.*

Alesandra's short laugh caught Belle's attention. Baring her teeth and shooting an angry glare at Brendan, she pushed him out of her way and sat down. "Please forgive us. My brother always seems to bring out the worst in me."

The older woman chuckled. "There's nothing to forgive. My sister and I were very much the same way."

After snarling once more in her brother's direction, Belle motioned Alesandra to a chair. "What exactly do you have in mind? Brendan may have the manners of a pig, but he's right about your pack not exactly welcoming me with open arms."

Snorting, Brendan leaned back against the sink, arms crossed over his chest.

Belle could feel his stare on the back of her head, but then, she really didn't give a damn about what he thought. She loved Alex. He was the one destined for her, and she wasn't about to give him up just because some members of his pack were prejudiced. And the sooner Alex realized he loved her too much to live without her, the happier they'd both be.

Focusing her attention on the older woman, Belle steepled her fingers. "What's your plan?"

Alesandra shook her head. "I don't have a plan, and we don't need one. Once you're underfoot, so to speak, Alex won't be able to resist you."

Muttering something about women and idiocy under his breath, Brendan stomped out of the house.

Belle grabbed the bar of soap still lying on the table, squeezed it, and dropped it again. "I can't wait until the day some woman wraps him around her little finger."

Alesandra chuckled and picked up the disfigured bar of soap. "Don't fault him for caring about you."

Shaking her head, Belle sighed. "I don't. It's just sometimes he doesn't know when to back off. Now, why don't we need a plan? I'm an accountant. I'm always happier with a plan."

Leaning back in her chair, the older woman smiled. "I've known Alex since he was in diapers. He was a serious child, an even more serious teen, interested in pack lore and tradition much more than any of his friends. Ever since he's become Alpha, he's put all his energy into caring for and maintaining the Pack. Even when he thought he was in love with Serena, the Pack came first. However, since you've come into his life, there are times he isn't sure what day it is. You're the only woman who's been able to completely break through that wall of responsibility he's built around himself." Dropping the soap, she leaned back across the table and clasped Belle's hands. "You've made him remember what it's like to truly live...and love."

Gently pulling her hands free, Belle rose and wiped the soap residue still on them on the seat of her jeans. "I'd better pack my things. I also have groceries that will have to be packed up, and the stuff in the fridge will have to go in coolers." She glanced at Alesandra. "You do realize I plan to move in until Alex comes to his senses, right? Once I'm there, I'm not leaving until that stubborn fool of an Alpha remembers he was the one who demanded that we mate in the first place."

Pushing herself to her feet, Alesandra chuckled. "You're welcome in my home as long as it takes." She glanced at George, who leaned nonchalantly against the wall next to the door. "As long as you don't mind having a bear shuffling around."

He grinned.

Belle chuckled. "Callie is just going to love living with a bear."

Chapter Fifteen

ဆ

"Where are the women asking for Sanctuary?"

Both Josh and Dave started. They'd driven home expecting to find Alex. Instead, his house had been empty. So they sat down to wait.

"Alesandra put them in that empty cottage next to her house so she could keep an eye on them."

Moving quickly, Alex disappeared into his bedroom only to return almost immediately in a fresh shirt and jeans. "What kind of shape are they in?"

Dave shrugged. "Alesandra said she treated them for their injuries and then gave them both one of those sleeping potions of hers. As far as I know, they haven't come out since they got here."

Alex didn't hear most of Dave's explanation. His mind was locked on one word — injuries. "What kinds of injuries?"

Both men shrugged. "We didn't see them, and Alesandra didn't give us any details."

Raking his fingers through his tangled hair, Alex cursed under his breath. Just what he needed. A couple of women running away from trouble. He had enough trouble of his own right now. Gritting his teeth, he headed for the door. May as well get this over with now. Then he could figure out how he'd talk the pack into accepting Belle.

A sharp stab in the general vicinity of his heart drew a quick gasp.

Dave was instantly at his side. "You okay, Alex?"

Alex shook him off. "I'm fine. Just hungry. The sooner I find out what's going on with these women, the sooner I can get something to eat. Let's go." He glanced over his shoulder. "You too, Josh."

A sheepish look on his face, Josh ducked his head. "Ah...is it okay if I miss this? You can fill me in later."

"Christ, Josh. You're the one who dragged me home because of these women. What's so important now that you can't be there when I question them?"

Dave grabbed Alex's arm and whispered. "Better brace yourself, old man."

Josh glanced up into Alex's face then dropped his gaze. "Tabitha's home."

Alex could feel his blood pressure rising. "What the fuck does your sister want now?"

Josh shrugged. "You know Tabitha. She comes. She goes."

Chucking, Dave leaned over and whispered, "Hell, Alex. She wants you."

Alex cursed all the way to the cottage where the strangers were staying. Two years ago, when he'd made it very plain that he wanted Serena as his mate, Tabitha had thrown a huge temper tantrum and stormed off, shouting that he'd be sorry he didn't mate her. Even after Serena ran away, he'd never been sorry that Tabitha was gone. No other woman in the pack was more self-centered. She expected the world to revolve around her. She could never be an adequate Alpha female.

But now she was back and knew he hadn't mated Serena. That he had mated Belle wouldn't matter to her. On a personal level, he doubted that she cared who or what anyone's parents were, but she'd whip up discontent within the pack if she could with the false impression that he'd eventually break down and mate her. Hell would freeze over first.

Dave paced along beside him. "Did you say something?"

"Shut the fuck up."

Stopping before the door of the small cottage, Alex knocked loudly.

A muffled voice drifted out from behind the door. "Who is it?"

"Alex Whitehorse. I'm the Alpha of this pack. I'd like to talk to you. Please," he added as an afterthought.

After a few moments, the door opened a crack, and a pale face appeared. There was a dark bruise beneath her left eye. "Is Alesandra with you?"

Alex stiffened when he saw her face. Someone had hit her! *That* was an abomination! Taking a deep breath, he counted to ten, slowly subduing his anger and frustration. Fear was evident in this woman's voice, posture, and expression. The last thing she needed to think was that he was angry with her. He needed to be gentle and delicate. The woman who stared out at him was scared to death.

Gentle and delicate! Me? I need Belle here to help me with these women. Calming his roiling emotions, he fixed what he hoped was a compassionate gaze on her and shook his head. "I'm sorry, but she's been called away. I promise you have nothing to fear from me."

She looked over his shoulder. Her voice trembled with fear. "Who's that?"

"My Omega, Dave Forrest."

"Omega?"

Alex did his best to smile reassuringly. "He wouldn't hurt a fly. As a matter of fact, he won't even kill fleas."

A slight smile appeared on her face and she opened the door wider. "Come in. I'm Jillian, my friends call me Jill."

Alex nodded. "Thank you, Jill."

Both men followed her into the house.

All the drapes were drawn and no lamps were lit. Alex knew there was another woman sitting in a shadowy corner more by smell than by sight.

"That's my sister-in-law, Eileen. Please, sit down," Jill said.

Alex nodded to Dave and they sat on chairs closest to her. Both sensed her pull away.

Frowning, Alex contemplated the shadowy form. An interview in the dark just wasn't going to work. "I'd like you to open the drapes, please."

Both women gasped.

"Please," Jill began, "don't make her..."

Sighing, Alex used his calmest voice. "I'm sorry. Believe me, the last thing I want to do is distress you, but I have to know exactly why you're claiming Sanctuary before I grant it. The trouble between our packs will be bad enough as it is if your brother chooses to challenge the Sanctuary. I have to know what I might be fighting for."

Jill walked over to the other woman. "You have to show them, Eileen. I know they'll help us. I can just feel it."

A strangled sob escaped Eileen, but Alex saw her nod.

Jill walked across the room and opened the drapes.

"Dave, get the ones on the other side of the room."

The Omega obeyed instantly.

When the light illuminated Eileen's face, she cringed.

Alex understood why.

The string of curses that rolled out of his mouth caused a deep flush to flood her face—at least the parts that weren't covered with bruises in almost every color of the rainbow. Her left eye was swollen shut and her upper lip was half again its normal size. Three stitches held a cut on her right cheek together, and a large chunk of skin was scraped off her chin. Her right arm was in a sling, and she breathed slowly and carefully like someone with broken ribs.

Alex's voice was low and, even to his own ears, deadly. "Who did this to you?"

Jill hurried to Eileen's side. "My brother Bill, her husband." Tears began to roll down her cheek. "I had to get her out of there. I thought he was going to kill her after she lost the baby."

Alex didn't think he could become more angry than he already was. He did. His nostrils flared. "She lost a baby? Was it his fault?"

Eileen shook her head. Her voice was a mere whisper. "It was the only time he ever treated me nice—when I was pregnant. But I had a miscarriage, nobody did anything wrong. It was just one of those things, the doctor said, nature aborting a malformed fetus. But Bill didn't believe the doctor. He said I killed his baby, and he was gonna make me pay."

Tears rolling down her cheeks, she sniffed and blinked. "I didn't hurt my baby. I'd never do that. I was so happy when I knew I was pregnant and not just because Bill started treating me nice. I love babies and want to have my own. I would never…"

She hiccupped and broke down.

Jill sat down next to Eileen and pulled her sister-in-law into her arms.

Dave stared at Jill. "What happened to you?"

She blinked. "I tried to stop him from locking her in the closet when he went to work."

Dave gaped. "He locked her in the closet?"

Jill nodded. "He didn't want her getting away." A satisfied smile appeared on her face. "I unscrewed the hinges."

Growling, Alex practically leaped to his feet. "Sanctuary is granted to both of you as long as you want it, and I for one, hope your husband does challenge me. I'd like to break every bone in his body." He nodded to Dave. "Stay a while and see if they need anything."

Dave nodded. "I'll take care of them."

Alex stopped. "I invited a pair of wolves to stay under the deserted cabin up on the saddleback. Make sure they have plenty to eat."

Dave grinned. "I'll take care of them, too."

Josh met Alex back in his office. "Well?"

Alex leaned back in his chair and stared at his best friend. "I used to agree with you about how werewolves are superior to any other living thing. What I saw today makes me question that."

Josh scowled. "Why?"

He tossed a manila folder across the desk. "This is a list of Eileen Fletcher's injuries. Split lip, swollen eye, broken arm, broken ribs, assorted cuts and bruises. A werewolf did this, Josh. He beat his mate to within an inch of her life because she miscarried his child. Werewolves aren't supposed to do this. Our wolf blood is supposed to make us better, more noble."

His face pale, Josh swallowed. "There are always aberrations."

Alex cocked an eyebrow. "Aberrations? Only a bad seed here and there?" Shoving his chair back, he rose and paced to the window where he stared out at the mountains. "What about Sam?"

"What does Sam have to do with this?"

Alex turned and leaned back against the window. "Werewolves don't leave their mates and offspring, Josh. But Sam has—to live with a human woman. And more reports like these are filtering in all the time. You've seen them. Packs from all over the country, the world, are reporting the same problems. More and more pack members are returning to the forest. Even worse, some werewolves are becoming—human."

Chapter Sixteen

✂

After slinging her backpack over her shoulder and gathering Callie into her arms, Belle nudged the car door shut with her hip and followed Alesandra up a stone-lined path, across a wide porch, and into a large kitchen.

The kitten sniffed the air. *Interesting smells. Mice are hiding in the walls. Maybe staying here won't be so bad. Are you sure you can trust the bear?*

A deep chuckle rolled across the room as George carried the rest of Belle's bags into the house. *I swear on the bones of my ancestors, little sister, that I mean you no harm.*

We shall see. Her nose twitching, Callie dropped from Belle's arms and slipped under the table. There she licked her already pristine paws, watching George as he crossed the kitchen and disappeared into another room.

Chuckling at the kitten, Alesandra turned to Belle. "George will put your bags in the guest room. I hope you'll be comfortable. Come along and I'll show you where everything is."

Instead of following her hostess, Belle dropped her backpack on the floor and slowly spun in a circle, her nostrils flared, inhaling the myriad aromas and scents that permeated the spacious kitchen. Following her nose, she stepped through an open door and into a large, well-lit workroom.

Tiny dust motes danced through the broad beams of sunlight shining through wide windows. Sweet-smelling flowers and pungent herbs of all kinds hung drying from the rafters, teasing Belle's sensitive nose. Clay pots and glass jars of all sizes lined shelves on the back wall. Bars of differently scented soaps lay drying on a wide counter while others, packaged in colorful wrappers, were stacked on a small table.

Drawing an even deeper breath, Belle walked over to the unwrapped soap, picked up an egg-colored bar, and held it to her nose. "Mostly lily of the valley and," her eyebrows rose, "thyme?" She picked up a green bar and sniffed. "Pine and," another sniff, "a hint of marjoram." A purple bar. "Violets and" she smiled, "aconite—wolfsbane." She turned and stared at Alesandra. "These combinations are absolutely amazing. How did you get the fragrances to meld so cleanly?"

Alesandra smiled. "Would you like to learn?"

Setting the bar down, Belle smiled at her hostess. "How would you like to be a very rich woman?"

* * * * *

As the screen door slammed, Alex looked up from his paperwork into Dave's face. "Are Eileen and Jill settled in? Do they have everything they need?"

Nodding, Dave flopped down onto the sofa and stared into the fireplace. "I didn't think a werewolf would do that to his own mate."

His anger surging again, Alex shook his head. "I know."

Dave glared into space. "If I could get my teeth on him, I'd tear his throat out."

Leaning back, Alex contemplated his Omega. Dave was one of the gentlest men he knew. "Don't even think about it. I don't want my Omega getting violent. I need someone everyone else can trust."

After a sigh, Dave's usual cocky grin appeared on his face. "Alesandra has another guest."

Alex glanced back down at the list of necessities for the new bed and breakfast. The words on the list disappeared and Belle's face appeared—her face the way it looked this morning when he'd turned away from her.

His heart clenched. The werewolf in his soul snarled angrily.

Dave leaned forward. "Don't you want to know who it is?"

Clearing his mind and focusing on his list, Alex shrugged. "Not really." The pack's matriarch often had women from other packs visiting her.

Rising, Dave sauntered over to the desk and leaned against it. "You sure?"

Snapping the pencil he was holding in half, Alex snarled, "Dave, I have other things on my mind than some old woman visiting Alesandra."

Dave's laughter rolled around the room. "More old women should look like that."

Alex glanced up.

Dave grinned down at him.

Muttering a curse under his breath, Alex threw the pieces of the pencil into the trash and glared at his Omega. "I'm not going to get any work done this way. Who's visiting?"

"A certain accountant from New York."

Alex froze. He hadn't expected this, but he should have. Alesandra had made meddling in his life a priority. Gritting his teeth, he shoved his chair back and lurched to his feet. "Why can't that old woman leave well enough alone? When everyone finds out, the pack will be in an uproar."

As he stepped around the desk, Dave grabbed his arm. "I think you're overreacting."

Rising, Alex jerked his arm free. "Her mother was a wolf, damn it. The pack—"

"—will get over it."

Alex shook his head and walked around the other side of his desk. "Josh won't."

Dave bit out a curse. "Josh needs to get over his mother going feral."

"That's what I keep telling him," said a sultry female voice from the doorway. The tall, voluptuous woman standing there pushed the door open and walked in. "Hello, Alex. I've missed you."

Taking a step back, Dave stared at the woman then barked with laughter. "Christ, Tabitha, what the hell did you do to your hair?"

Alex's lips twitched. Tabitha's hair was cropped short and dyed a vibrant red.

She tossed her head. "Hot, isn't it? It's one of the latest styles."

Dave walked to her side and messed her hair. "Your head looks like that flashing red light on the top of a cop car."

She shoved her elbow toward his diaphragm.

He sidled away and grabbed the door. "I'll stop by the cottage to check on the women, then head on down to the bed and breakfast to see if they need a hand."

Never taking his eyes from Josh's sister, Alex nodded. "The electrician was supposed to finish the wiring today. Check and see if it's done." *Damn it, Tabitha. What the hell did you come back for? I don't need you stirring up trouble.*

Her smile an invitation, Tabitha glided over to Alex, flattened her hands against his chest and began to caress him.

He stepped back.

Undeterred, she followed. "Still running away from me, Alex. Why? From what I hear, Serena left you and mated someone else." Her hand slid down to his waist. "By now, you should be — needy."

Grabbing her wrist before her hand could dip lower, Alex pushed her away. "What do you want?"

Tilting her head to the side, she smiled a toothy smile.

Alex's nostrils flared. She was aroused. If he wasn't careful, she'd attack him right here. She was certainly brazen enough.

Sidestepping, he walked away from her. "I don't have time to play games, Tabitha. Why don't you go back to where ever you came from before you have half the pack wanting to tear every one of those red hairs out of your head?"

Chuckling, she hurried after him and tucked her hand under his arm.

Alex tried to shake free, but she dug her nails into his flesh. So be it then. "I'm going to see Alesandra. Would you like to come along?" He pulled her out onto the porch.

She faltered. "Alesandra? You know, I do have some more unpacking to do. Why don't I come by later, and we'll catch up on old times."

He stopped and looked into her eyes. "Tabitha, I'm going to say this one time and one time only. I am *not* interested in you in any way. I don't want to talk to you, to have sex with you, or to mate you. You're an intelligent woman. Leave and find yourself another man, wolf, werewolf, hell, go mate a werebear for all I care. Have I made myself clear?"

Her sharp nails scoured deep gouges in his arm. "You cocksucking shithead. You think you're too good for me. You always have. Well, I have news for you, high and mighty Alex Whitehorse, pack Alpha. You'll be sorry you tossed me aside like a used blanket. I'll get even with you, just see if I don't." Whirling, she leaped from the porch and disappeared around the side of the house.

Grinding his teeth together, Alex watched her go. When she was out of sight, he descended the four porch steps and headed for the path that led to Alesandra's.

Birds shrieked and warbled with fear as he stomped through the small grove of trees separating his house from Alesandra's. Tabitha was a pain in the ass and a troublemaker. Alesandra was a meddling, old bitch. And Belle, Belle was the woman he wanted and couldn't quite figure out how to have.

Chapter Seventeen

෨

"What do you think of these numbers?" Belle asked.

Alesandra stared silently for a moment then looked up at Belle. "You're sure? We could make this much money?"

Grinning, Belle nodded. "I can't be exactly sure until the company does a complete analysis with a test market, but it's a conservative estimate. The personal fragrance market is very good right now and your soap is *different*. With the right kind of advertising campaign, the sky is the limit."

Alesandra sank onto a kitchen chair. "My goodness. I never thought…"

Belle gathered up the papers spread out over the table. "…that your simple homemade soap would interest me. Well, it does. Of course, my father will have to approve the deal. Too bad Brendan left. I could have sent the details back with him. You don't have a fax machine, do you?"

As the older woman shook her head, the door slammed open and Alex stalked into the room. "What the hell are you doing here?"

Nostrils flaring, Belle turned to face him. "Are you talking to me?"

"You aren't the one who lives here."

Eyes narrowing, Belle asked, "Where did you learn your manners? A barn with the pigs?"

Clenching his fists, Alex glared at Belle. What was she doing here? If the pack found out, half of them would be beating down his door in outrage. "Damn it, Belle, are you so insecure that you had to follow me?"

Her mouth dropped open. She snapped it shut. "Insecure? About what?"

He snapped his gaze to Alesandra.

She smiled and folded her hands on her lap.

Gritting his teeth, he said, "We need to talk about our relationship, but not now, not here. Go back to your cabin, and I'll be down in a couple of days."

Heat rising in her face, Belle stared at Alex. Who was this jerk? He certainly wasn't the same man who'd declared she was the other half of his soul. Well, she wasn't going anywhere. Crossing her arms over her breasts, she glared back. "Go back to my cabin and wait for you to come to me. Just like that?" Closing the distance between them, she stabbed her finger into his chest. "You listen to me, you arrogant, self righteous, asshole Alpha. *You* came after me. *You* chased me down in the mud and the rain and mated me! I didn't tie you down and demand that you choose me as your mate. You made that decision on your own. Now, I *am* your mate whether you like it or not—and not you or anyone else is going to tell me where I can or can't go."

She stabbed his chest again and he backed up a step. "Furthermore, I did *not* follow you here. If I had, I would be in *your* house right now, not this one. And if you keep acting like a jackass, I will move into your house and you won't be able to get me out. I understand the ramifications of our mating to your pack—better than you do. I'm the one who knows what it's like to be ostracized because of my heritage. That's why I'm in this house."

Another finger stab in the chest. "Besides, Alesandra and I are doing business. After I hear from my father, we'll iron out the details of the contract. In the meantime, our pack will have time to get to know me before I assume duties as Alpha female."

Still another stab in Alex's chest. "That is, unless you plan to repudiate me?" She looked up into his face. "Do you? If so, you're going to do it in front of the Pack Council under the next full moon. I will *not* just walk away from you, idiot. I made a commitment, one I intend to honor to my dying day. So stick that in your pipe and smoke it."

When she started to jab her finger into his chest again, Alex grabbed her hand. His voice was tight with controlled anger. "That's enough. What kind of crazy scheme have you and that old woman hatched? If you think I'm going to let you lead my pack on about some business deal just so you can insinuate yourself into their good graces, you're crazy."

The sharp crack of her hand as it connected with his face echoed around the room. Her handprint appeared on his cheek immediately.

Shaking, Belle clenched her hand into a fist so she didn't slap him again. "You insufferable, condescending prig! How dare you question my integrity! I would no sooner try to *buy* my way into your pack than I would fly off this roof. The contract on the table is tentative but binding. The recipes for the soaps Alesandra has created are some of the most unique I have ever seen. They're probably worth more money than I've offered, but I can guarantee my father will be far more interested in her input than some of the other larger fragrance companies."

Wrenching her other hand free, she spun on her heel and stalked across the kitchen. "I'll find my room on my own, Alesandra. I'd like to freshen up. For some reason, I feel dirty."

The door between the kitchen and living room crashed shut.

Slowly, Alex inhaled then just as slowly exhaled. Stupid, stupid, stupid bitch. She was going to ruin any chance they had at a life together. Why couldn't she just obey him?

Lifting a sheet of paper from the table, Alesandra held it out to Alex. "Here. Look at this."

"What the hell for?"

"Just the last paragraph, the one with the numbers."

Snatching it from her hand, Alex glanced down and then glared at the closed door. The numbers registered, and he looked down at the paper again. He blinked, shook his head, and blinked again. "Is she kidding?"

"No."

"But—"

"Shut up, Alex, and listen. You've finally met a woman who has as much pride and self-confidence as you do. Belle won't meekly follow your orders. She's a successful and confident woman who could live quite comfortably without you or any man—human or Were—if she so chose. Don't be foolish enough to drive her away. With her at your side, our pack could become a major power in the Hierarchy."

With a flick of his wrist, Alex tossed the paper back to the table. "Ha! The Hierarchy would be real impressed with the fact that her mother was a real wolf."

Alesandra shook her head. "She's right. You can be a self-righteous asshole. When was the last time you attended a Hierarchy gathering? Looked over the updates we receive? Or do you just pass them on to me without reading them?"

He waved his hand in dismissal. "I read what could pertain to our pack. I don't have time to read about awards or testimonials or other nonsense like that. We have our own problems to solve."

Alesandra snorted. "You should read about those awards, testimonials, and other nonsense. If you did, you'd know that Artemis Gray has received a number of them for his work helping werewolves—individuals and packs—and will be accepting an appointment this winter to a seat on the Hierarchy. All this after first mating a wolf and teaching his offspring with her to shift, and now mating a human. Sounds to me like the Hierarchy is far more interested in the welfare of pack members than they are about their heritages."

Alex combed his hair back off his forehead, spun around, and headed for the door.

Callie sat before it staring at him.

Mother was right. No matter what the species, males can be extremely stupid.

Chapter Eighteen

෨

Alex dropped his jeans on the floor and fell across his bed, the memory of Belle's angry face in the forefront of his mind. Why did she have to be so damned difficult? She was supposed to obey *him*. He was the male Alpha.

Groaning, he rolled over and stared up at the ceiling. Was it true? Had the Hierarchy changed? Some of the older members had resigned, and eight new members had been appointed in the last seven years. Others had been voted out in political power struggles. Alex groaned again. He'd done his best to keep himself and the pack as far away from Hierarchy politics as possible. Maybe he should have paid closer attention. If Belle's father would be receiving an appointment, politics was not the same as usual.

Muttering, Alex covered his eyes with his arm. The Hierarchy wasn't *here*. His pack was, and some of the members wouldn't tolerate the offspring of wolf-werewolf matings — in human form. None of them had a problem with any cubs that remained wolves. But, Belle wasn't a wolf. He couldn't just demand that the pack accept her. They were all individuals entitled to their own opinions.

Sitting up, Alex swung his legs over the side of the bed, propped his elbows on his knees, and rested his chin on his fist. Josh. Josh was the key. If he accepted Belle, the others would keep their thoughts to themselves. But how to convince Josh? He'd never forgiven his mother when she went feral. Then, when her wolf mate was killed and she tried to bring her cubs back to the pack...

The screen from the window across the room clattered to the floor as a large gray wolf barreled through the window.

By the time Alex was on his feet, the wolf had shifted and Brendan Gray stood before him.

Muscles tensed to spring, Alex glared at Belle's brother. "What the fuck do you want?"

Brendan crossed his arms over his chest. His voice was cold and hard. "For some strange reason, Belle's decided to keep you as her mate. Stupid in my opinion, but then she never did listen to my advice."

Alex's grin was a snarl. "Smart girl."

Stepping forward, Brendan bared his teeth. "Just shut up and listen, asshole. If I ever find out you hurt Belle in any way, I will rip your throat out."

Crossing his arms over his chest, Alex growled, "You and what army?"

Brendan's smile was vicious. "Kearnan's never beaten me in a fight. From what I understand, he kicked your ass—when you challenged him for his mate, no less. Now you're messing around with my sister. Like I said, just one hint that she's unhappy..."

Alex stepped to the other man, stabbing his finger in the general direction of his chest, "What happens between your sister and me is none of your fucking business, and if I find out you've been sniffing around her without informing me you're here, I'll rip you to shreds. Belle is mine."

Brendan's lips twitched with a ghost of a smile. "Do that, and Belle will rip *you* to shreds." He stepped back, then cocked his head to the side. "I'm headed back to New York. Dad's been worried about Belle. She's the youngest of the litter, and the closest to Dad." Mist swirled. The gray wolf disappeared back out the window.

"Fucking prick." Grabbing the screen from the floor, Alex jammed it back into the window before the mosquitoes discovered they could get in. Like he'd ever do anything to hurt Belle. Both her brothers were assholes. Still, unease crept into his mind. Artemis Gray. Rumors were he'd torn the throat out of a werewolf who'd accosted his oldest daughter. And Belle was his favorite?

Rolling back into bed, Alex stared at the ceiling. Sleep eluded him that night.

Belle leaned against the porch railing and stared at the cloudless sky. She'd been here for almost a week, and Alex had spoken to her exactly twice—that first day when he ordered her to go home and then two days later when he'd almost fallen over her. He'd apologized and stomped away.

"Pigheaded, idiot Alpha. If he thinks I'm going to disappear, he's wrong. And I'm certainly not going to crawl to him on my hands and knees begging for his attention."

Callie leaped up onto the railing and rubbed her head against Belle's arm. *When you come into heat, he will not be able to resist you. It's the same with all males. They think with their cocks when confronted by a fertile female.*

Eyes widening, Belle stared at the cat. "Where did you learn that word!"

Balancing herself carefully, Callie sat and licked her paw. *From you. I am referring to the male sexual organ. Cock is the correct word, isn't it?*

Chuckling, Belle lifted Callie into her arms. "It's the correct word, but I never expected to hear it from a cat, especially one that's only half grown. You're still a kitten."

Callie blinked. *All felines are mentally mature when they're born. We just have to wait for our bodies to catch up to our minds.*

Shaking her head, Belle dropped the cat onto a cushioned rocking chair.

Callie immediately curled into a ball for her afternoon nap.

Leaning against the railing once more, Belle stared first at the forest, then at the path that led to Alex's house—she could see the chimney—then at the small cottage off to the left of where she stood now.

The door opened, and Dave walked out. The young woman who followed him waved goodbye and quickly closed the door behind him.

Dave stared at the closed door for a full two minutes, shook himself, and turned. When he saw her, he smiled and trotted toward her.

"Afternoon, Belle. Alesandra keeping you busy?"

Belle smiled and nodded. Dave, at least, seemed happy that she was here. "She's meticulous with her formulas. No wonder her soaps are so fabulous."

"How about her partners in crime?"

Belle cocked an eyebrow.

Dave grinned. "The other women who help with the soap making. Any of them declare you an 'Abomination' and try to throw holy water on you?"

Belle couldn't help but laugh. Dave was the perfect Omega. He could take the most awkward or tense situation and make a joke out of it. "Only one. And there was no holy water—that's for vampires, not werewolves."

He continued to smile, but she noticed a glint in his eyes that wasn't there before. "Who?"

Belle shook her head. Why did all men think women couldn't fight their own battles? "I'm not going to tell you. I handled it myself. I didn't even let Alesandra say anything."

Amusement, followed by approval, appeared in Dave's eyes. "And how did you handle it?"

Belle grinned. "I showed her how much money the pack would be making once production began on their soaps. Amazing how a lot of money can change the perceptions of some people."

Reaching up, Dave patted her hand. "And once she gets to know you, she'll realize how foolish she was in the first place."

"What are you doing here, you scamp? Aren't you supposed to be doing final checks on the plumbing for the bed and breakfast?"

As Alesandra's cane smacked against the railing, Dave jerked his hand away. "Gotta go, Belle. See you later."

Chuckling, Belle watched him jog away. "He's very good, you know, a perfect Omega. Do any of the pack members ever give him a hard time?"

Alesandra shook her head as she handed a basket to Belle. "Oh, there are grumbles now and then, and every pack has a couple of members who don't get along with anybody, but for the most part, everybody likes Dave."

Belle lifted the cloth covering the basket. "What's in here?"

"Food for the shut-ins. Come along. It's time you meet our other guests."

Belle stared after Alesandra as the older woman strolled across the yard to the small cottage much more agilely than any woman with a cane should have been able to. Then with a sigh that was half chuckle, she picked up the basket and followed her hostess. She was curious about the women staying in the guest house.

Chapter Nineteen

🙠

Belle caught up to Alesandra just as she knocked on the cottage door.

It opened a crack and a pale-faced woman looked out. "Who is it?"

"It's Alesandra and Belle."

Belle looked askance at the older woman. In the bare week she'd known her, Alesandra had impressed her as a no-nonsense, damn the torpedoes and full speed ahead type of woman. More than once she had snapped sharply at one or more of the women helping make soap or any of the men who happened to irritate her for one reason or another, even George. Now, however, her voice was low and gentle.

"Belle?"

"She's mated to our Alpha."

Belle almost dropped the basket. Alesandra had just declared her Alpha female. Who were these women?

Slowly the door opened.

Alesandra led the way inside.

Once inside, Belle blinked to adjust her eyesight to the near dark. Every curtain was drawn tightly, shutting out all sunlight. No lights were on.

"Jill, this is Belle. How's Eileen?"

"Here, I'll take that," Jill said as she took the basket from Belle's hand. "She's feeling better, but I still have a hard time getting her out of bed."

Alesandra leaned on her cane. "She can walk without pain?"

Jill nodded as she set the basket on a small table. "Mostly. As long as she doesn't turn suddenly or try to lift something."

Alesandra nodded. "Good. Tell her the Alpha female is here and wishes to see her."

Jill glanced from Alesandra to Belle and back again.

Alesandra sighed. "Eileen can't stay in bed forever, Jill. Since she's well enough to move around, it's only good manners that she come out here to greet Belle."

"I don't know…"

Alesandra stamped her cane against the floor. "Unless there's a grave injury or serious illness that prevents her from doing so, a female does not greet her Alpha's mate in the bedroom. You've asked for Sanctuary, and Belle is female Alpha of this pack. Eileen will come to her."

Face white, Jill disappeared through a doorway.

Anger building, Belle turned to face Alesandra. "How can you tell her that—"

"—you're Alpha female?" Alesandra waved her hand. "Bah. You are. Alex mated you. What I don't understand is why you haven't pushed your claim. You're a strong, independent woman. What are you afraid of? Alex repudiating you? I've known that boy since he was in diapers. Repudiation hasn't even entered his mind."

Crossing her arms over her chest, Belle faced the older woman. "That's easy for you to say—you who've been accepted as Pack since the moment you were born. Do you have any idea what it's like to hear people sneering at your ancestry behind your back—or worse to your face—when you're little more than a child? In the seven years I lived with my grandmother's pack, with the exception of my sister Melody, I only had one real friend who didn't *pretend* to be my friend because of who my grandmother was. She loved me for me and didn't care that my mother was a wolf. When her parents moved their family to another pack and my grandmother died, my life and that of my sister and brothers became intolerable. Why do you think my father moved us to New York? There we were accepted — as humans, true, but accepted nonetheless. Do you have any idea how that felt?"

Alesandra would have spoken, but Belle didn't give her the chance. "You say I'm a strong and independent woman and that I should demand my rights as Alex's mate. What would happen then, do you think? How many pack members would stand against me in Council? What would that do to Alex's authority?"

Slowly, the older woman settled into the chair at her side.

Belle stared down at her. "Don't think that I'll give Alex up. He is *mine*! But I won't undermine his authority by barging in like an angry bull and demanding that the pack acknowledge me Alpha female because I told them they had to. That would be stupid for me and suicidal for pack unity. When all is said and done, we'll probably still lose members because of my heritage. I choose to keep that loss as small as possible. Do you understand, Alesandra? If you don't like the way I'm assimilating myself, just keep quiet and stay out of my way."

Feet planted firmly on the floor, Belle glared down at Alesandra.

The old woman leaned back in her chair and stared back. A smile appeared on her face. "Winning people over slowly with waiting and negotiation is a good, sensible plan — one that probably works very well in the boardrooms of New York. This, however, is not New York, and there are unmated females in this pack who saw themselves mated to Alex. As long as you wait to claim both him and Alpha female status, they'll believe they still have a chance with him. I cannot allow that to happen. As of this moment, I transfer all rights and responsibilities as Alpha female to you."

Belle's mouth dropped open then snapped shut.

Alesandra held up her hand. "However, I will wait to formally make that declaration until Pack Council at full moon. You have two days. I wouldn't go about taking my rightful position in the pack of the man I mated the way you are, but I do acknowledge there is more than one way to a desired end."

Nostrils flaring, Belle spun and stomped across the room. Alesandra could be just as aggravating as Brendan—or worse, her father Artemis. Well, if she could handle those two ultra-Alpha males, she could certainly handle one old woman.

Turning, she glared across the room at Alesandra.

She was wrapped in shadows.

"Oh for heaven's sake, where's the light switch? I can barely see my hand in front of my face, it's so dark in here. Why do they keep it so dark in here?" Belle snapped.

"The light switch is right behind you. It's dark because Jill's sister-in-law was abused by her mate. He beat her badly."

As the lights flared on, Belle froze. "She was mated to a werewolf?"

Alesandra nodded.

"And he beat her?"

Alesandra nodded again. "Both eyes were black with one swollen shut, a couple of ribs were cracked, and an arm was broken."

Belle felt the blood drain from her face, and she gripped the back of the chair before her. "Werewolves don't beat their mates. Humans beat their wives or children. We don't."

The older woman shook her head. "Obviously that isn't true anymore."

"But why? Why would he beat her so badly?"

A quiet voice entered the conversation. "Because I lost the baby I was carrying."

Chapter Twenty

છ

Blinking, Belle wiped the sudden tears from her eyes. How could a male werewolf treat his mate so appallingly? "Did his beatings cause you to lose the baby?"

The woman shook her head. "No. When we learned I was pregnant, he was happier than I've ever seen him. I miscarried spontaneously early in my third month. The doctor told us I didn't do anything wrong. Nature was just asserting herself because there was probably something wrong with the fetus. Bill seemed to accept what the doctor said, but when we got home he started screaming at me, blaming me for losing the baby, saying I must have done something wrong. Then he started to hit me."

Belle stared at her. Something about her was—familiar. "Why did you stay with him if he beat you?"

"Bill never really hit me before. He'd rant and rave, and sometimes he'd push me. But he never hit me."

Belle frowned. The other pack members should have protected her. "Why didn't you go to your Alpha? It's his responsibility to protect Pack members, even from their own mates."

"The Pack Alpha is Bill's brother."

Belle shook her head. If werewolves kept acting more and more like humans, they'd become human. Sighing, she looked back to the battered woman. Her arm was in a sling, and her face was covered with cuts and bruises.

The woman sighed, shuffled to a chair, and sat down carefully.

Belle frowned again. Why did this woman seem familiar? She looked closer.

Alesandra interrupted. "Forgive my poor manners. Belle Gray, this is Eileen Fletcher."

"Eileen Rivers," Belle said at the same time. "Eileen, is that really you?"

Alesandra looked from one young woman to the other. Jill looked confused. A stunned expression was obvious on Belle's face. Tears trickled down Eileen's cheeks as she ducked her head and said, "I hoped you wouldn't recognize me."

Alesandra frowned. "You know each other?"

"Hoped I wouldn't recognize you! I've missed you for years!" Never taking her eyes from Eileen's face, Belle sank into the chair she'd been standing behind. "Eileen's the friend I was telling you about. She's my brother's mate."

Alesandra was on her feet far more quickly than any of the women in the room imagined she could move. "Your brother did this to her?"

"No! Oh, no!" Eileen blurted out in a frightened voice. "Garth would never hurt me."

Alesandra's voice was sharp. "How many mates do you have, girl?"

"Sit down, Alesandra, and listen," Belle interjected in a firm voice.

After the older woman settled back into her chair, Belle leaned forward and continued, "Remember I told you my friend's parents moved away to another pack? They left because my brother Garth started paying too much attention to their daughter. Her friendship with Melody and me they could tolerate because of the respect they had for my grandmother. But when a male 'Abomination' began to show interest in their daughter, they immediately took steps to kill any interest she had in him. They moved."

"How did you know Garth and I mated?" Eileen asked in a trembling voice as she wiped tears from her cheeks with the fingers of her uninjured hand.

Rising, Belle walked across the room, sat on the ottoman at Eileen's feet, and clasped the injured woman's good hand in hers. "After he discovered you were gone, he told me. We did our best to find out where your family was, but no one would tell us. The Alpha wouldn't even tell Grandmother."

Alesandra thumped her cane on the floor. "Not even an Alpha can set aside a legal mating. One party or the other must repudiate it."

Eileen shook her head. "I was sixteen, Garth seventeen. No one would have supported us."

Belle squeezed Eileen's hand. "Dad would have if he'd known in time. Your ages wouldn't have mattered."

Fresh tears rolling down her cheeks, Eileen shook her head. "It wouldn't have mattered. My parents didn't tell me we were leaving. Mother put something in my morning tea that knocked me out. When I woke up, we were miles away. My brothers held me down when I screamed and threatened to jump out of the car. Then, after I finally settled down, they handed me a letter. Looking back now, I know it was a forgery.

"Surely you didn't believe Garth would—"

"It wasn't from Garth. Supposedly, it was from your father."

Belle's mouth dropped open.

"It said that Garth could do better than me for a mate. I was stunned. Your father had always been so kind to me."

"He liked you a lot and believed you were good for Garth."

"I know. I was a fool to believe them, but I was only sixteen," Eileen said. "My family watched me every minute. We'd been in Louisiana for three weeks before I was able to contact a friend back home. She told me your family had left, moved to New York City. When I learned that, I believed the letter was real. When the youngest brother of the Pack Alpha took an interest in me, I let my parents talk me into dating him. He was nice then. Oh, he'd yell, but so did my father and brothers. So, one thing led to another, and I agreed to mate Bill. That was two years ago."

"Why didn't you go to your family after Bill beat you? Surely they don't expect you to stay with him."

Sighing, Eileen shifted and leaned her head back. "My father died in a fishing boat accident right after I mated Bill. My younger brother and mother returned to her natal pack. Unfortunately, my older brother is a lot like Bill. Everything must be my fault because Bill is such a great guy."

"Assholes," Belle muttered. "Well, you're safe here. I'll rip his throat out if he tries to touch you again."

Jill spoke for the first time. "You don't know my brother. It doesn't bother him to hit females. And he's big."

Belle snorted and waved her hand in the air. There wasn't a man on the planet—werewolf or human—she was afraid of. "Doesn't matter. He'll never find you here, will he?"

For the first time, a small smile appeared on Eileen's lips. "I don't know how he possibly could. I'm three states away from my old pack and half a country away from Mom's natal pack. Neither of us knows a soul here, except you now. Bill has absolutely no reason to look for us here."

"Good." After patting Eileen's knee, Belle rose. "You're safe here and may stay as long as you like."

"Eileen and Jill have asked for Sanctuary," Alesandra interjected as she too rose. "It will be granted at the next Pack Council."

Belle smiled. "Good. You'll be safe, and I'll have an old friend here with me."

Tenseness left Eileen's shoulders as she smiled back. "It is good to see you again, Belle. I missed you. How's Melody? Has she mated yet?"

Shaking her head, Belle grinned. "You know Melody— always had to be different. She's a private investigator in

Nevada. Said since she's perfectly capable of taking care of herself, she didn't need a male for anything—except to scratch an itch every now and then."

For the first time since she arrived, Eileen chuckled. "She hasn't changed then." She dropped her eyes. "How are your brothers?"

Over the top of Eileen's head, Belle winked at Jill. "Kearnan is mated to Alesandra's granddaughter. They run a wolf preserve a few hundred miles west of here. Brendan? Well, Brendan is Brendan. He still believes every female on Earth was put here to worship him."

Eileen glanced up into Belle's face. "What about—Garth? Has he—mated?"

Leaning over, Belle stared into Eileen's face. "Yes, Garth is mated. To you. After you and your family disappeared, he told us how he mated you and there would never be another for him. Once he turned twenty-one, he headed out on his own. He's a loner, Eileen. We hear from him now and then, but we're never quite sure where he is. I think Dad knows more, but he won't tell us anything."

Eileen's shoulders slumped again.

Gently, Belle patted her shoulder. "One thing I'm sure of, Eileen. When he finds out you're here, he'll come. Nothing will keep him away."

Eileen turned her face away. "It would be better if he didn't. I don't want him to see what I've become."

"What you've become?" Straightening, Belle fisted her hands on her hips. "Bullshit! Eileen…"

Alesandra grasped her arm. "I think we've visited long enough, Belle. Eileen is tired and should rest more."

Snapping her mouth shut, Belle swallowed the lecture she wanted to deliver. If there was anything she hated, it was weak-willed women who were too timid or insecure to go after what they wanted. Eileen hadn't been like that when they were girls together. But then, she hadn't been beaten to within an inch of her life either. Alesandra was right. Her old friend needed time to heal.

Swallowing her irritation, Belle forced a smile onto her lips. "I'm sorry, Eileen. As you can see, I haven't changed much either. I'm still bossy."

The weak smile on Eileen lips was genuine. "I'm glad, and I'm glad I found you again. But I am tired."

"I'll come back tomorrow to see you, then. Go back to bed and rest. We'll talk more later."

Turning, she nodded to Alesandra and led the way to the door.

Jill accompanied them. "That's the most she's talked since we left Louisiana," she said in a low voice. "I'm glad you're here for her."

Belle smiled. "So am I. Take care of her."

"I'll be back for the basket later," Alesandra added. "There's plenty of soup. And I added some bread and a salad for you, Jill. If Eileen wants some, let her have it. She's healing well."

"I'll make sure she eats some bread with the soup," Jill said as she opened the door. "It was nice to meet you, Belle. Please come back soon."

Belle shook the hand Jill offered. "I will."

As Belle and Alesandra stepped out on to the small porch, Jill shut the door firmly behind them.

Sighing, Alesandra shook her head. "I think Jill may also have suffered from her brother's anger," she said as they stepped off the porch and walked back toward her house.

A shapely shadow blocked their path.

Belle looked up into the face of a pretty woman with hair dyed an atrocious red.

"Who the hell do you think you are, bitch, to come here and think you can take Alex from me?"

Chapter Twenty-One

ଚ୬

Alesandra stepped forward. "Enough, Tabitha. Alex didn't want you two years ago, and he doesn't want you now."

"He'll mate me before he'd touch an Abomination like this bitch."

"Tabitha, I'm warning you—"

"I can fight my own battles, thank you, Alesandra," Belle stated as she pulled the older woman back to her side then stepped forward. "Look, Tabitha, is it? I'm not having a good day. Hell, most of the week hasn't been very good, so I suggest you back off and just leave me alone. You'll be a lot happier."

Squaring her shoulders, the taller, heavier woman stepped closer to Belle and sneered down into her face. "You gonna make me, bitch?"

Belle sighed, remembered her promise to her father not to fight unless it was absolutely necessary. "I don't want to hurt you."

"*You* hurt me! Fat chance, bitch. You're the one who better leave before I hurt you." To punctuate her statement, Tabitha pulled her shirt over her head. Large, round breasts bounced in the afternoon sunlight.

Her patience at an end, Belle snapped, "Oh, look. Big boobs. I'm so scared." Spinning, she kicked Tabitha's legs out from under her.

The larger woman flopped onto her ass.

Arms crossed over her chest, Belle said, "I suggest you stay down there."

"You fucking bitch!" With a howl of rage, Tabitha leaped at Belle.

Just before she reached her, Belle stepped aside, turned, and planted her foot in Tabitha's ass as she went by.

The redhead skidded across the dry grass on her stomach.

Screaming with rage, Tabitha pushed herself up and launched herself at Belle again.

Again, Belle sidestepped, this time tripping Tabitha. When she landed on the hard ground, her breath whuffed out of her lungs.

Alesandra pursed her lips and thumped her cane at Belle. "You're toying with her."

Belle smiled and nodded. "And teaching her a lesson. I don't think she's the kind who learns from a quick knockout."

Tabitha came up throwing dirt.

Turning her head to keep it out of her eyes, Belle shifted away from the dirt.

Anticipating Belle's dodge, Tabitha wrapped her arms around her adversary's waist and tackled her to the ground where she grabbed a handful of Belle's hair and yanked hard.

Gritting her teeth against the pain, Belle snarled. "Christ, Tabitha. Pulling hair? Didn't your mother teach you how to fight?"

Tabitha slapped her face. "Shut up, bitch. When I'm finished with you, you'll regret ever coming here."

Before Belle could reply, Tabitha was jerked off of her.

"What the hell do you think you're doing?" Alex roared.

Shrieking and screaming, her breasts bouncing and heaving, Tabitha twisted in his arms. "Let me go, you bastard. She kicked me."

Rising to her feet, Belle snarled, "Not before she challenged me."

"Tabitha challenged," Alesandra added in a no-nonsense voice. "Belle has the right to answer."

Alex struggled to hold the screeching woman. "They don't even know each other!"

Tabitha snapped her head back into Alex's nose.

Belle heard the cartilage crack from where she was standing and smiled. *Good. He deserved that for interrupting my fight.* "Let her go, Alex. I have the right to answer her challenge."

As blood dripped from his nose, Alex looked around at the small crowd that had gathered. Where had they all come from? Alesandra's house was set away from most of the others. What the hell did Belle think she was doing, answering a challenge from his Beta's sister?

Tabitha twisted in his arms and sank her teeth into his shoulder. "Fuck!" This time he turned away in time. Loosening his hold, he let her fall to the ground.

The redhead scrambled to her feet and leaped toward her antagonist.

Belle met her with a fist to the abdomen.

As Tabitha bent over gagging, Belle simultaneously kicked her legs out from under her and delivered a solid judo chop to her shoulder blades.

Tabitha went down and didn't get up.

Shaking her hair back over her shoulders, Belle said, "There. I was quick. Satisfied?"

Wiping blood from beneath his nose, Alex stared. "How did you do that?"

A satisfied smile twitching at the corners of her mouth, Belle sauntered to him. "A couple of black belts in martial arts. Dad didn't want me running in Central Park without knowing how to take care of myself, and he certainly didn't want me shifting on any muggers unless it was a last resort. So I learned how to defend myself human-style. Be glad I agreed to mate you or you still wouldn't be able to walk." When she reached his side, she patted his cheek. "Better get that bite on your shoulder checked, love. Tabitha may not have had her rabies shots. And you better straighten out your nose or it will heal crooked."

After another pat on the cheek, Belle turned to her hostess. "Don't you have another formula you want to show me before it gets too late?"

Chuckling, old woman locked her arm with Belle's. She couldn't remember the last time she'd seen Alex speechless. "Yes. I finally have enough blackberries. Come along. I think you'll really like this one. The berries add such a lovely purple color to the dye."

Teeth grinding, Alex glared at the back of Belle's head as she walked away. He could hear the snickers and whispers of the small crowd who'd witnessed Tabitha's defeat. Not that he cared. She'd needed her ass kicked for years. There just hadn't been a female in the pack with the strength or courage to do so before Belle.

Tabitha moaned, and Alex glanced down. Looking around, he saw Dave grinning like a fool next to Carl, one of the pack's oldest members.

He too had a grin a mile wide on his face. "Got yourself a good one there, Alex. When you gonna put your foot down and make her sleep in your bed where she belongs? Or you afraid she'll knock you out, too?"

A funny little lurch in the vicinity of his heart stopped Alex's caustic reply. Then his brain registered what Carl had said.

He tilted his head to the side. "You know who her father is?"

Still grinning, Carl nodded. "Always did like Artemis. Daughter is a chip off the old block. He'd never back down from a fight either."

"You don't care that her mother was a wolf?"

The old man laughed outright. "Hell's bells, son. We all have wolf in our family trees somewhere. Just have to look back far enough to find it. Makes us who we are."

Frowning, Alex stared at Carl. How many Pack members felt the way he did?

Tabitha chose that moment to groan again.

Alex snapped his glare to Dave. "Where the hell is Josh? He should be here to take care of his sister."

Dave never quit grinning. "Finally went wolf for a while. Said he couldn't stand staying in the same house with her 'cause she was driving him crazy. He'll be back in time for the Council."

Alex snuffed the blood dripping from his nose, then winced. Christ, but it hurt. "What the hell am I supposed to do with this bitch until then?"

Chuckling, Carl sauntered over to the prostrate woman and nudged her with the toe of his boot. "I'll take her home." Squatting, he grabbed her around the waist, tossed her over his shoulder, and rose — with a small grunt. "Heavier than she looks. Your mate did a hell of a job knocking her out. Wouldn't get her mad at me, if I were you. She moved well enough to kick your ass, too." With those words, he slapped Tabitha's ample ass, turned, and strode away in the direction of Josh's house, adjusting her groaning body whenever she shifted.

"Always did like Carl," Dave said.

"Shut the fuck up," Alex growled as he spun on his heel and headed toward Alesandra's house.

"Wouldn't do that if I were you," Dave called after him. "She's already pissed at you. Try to tell her what is and isn't right, according to you, and she's apt to knock you out."

Blood still dripping from his nose and crusting on his shoulder, Alex kept walking.

Chapter Twenty-Two

ॐ

Alesandra dug a recipe card out of a small box. "Tabitha is Josh's sister, you know."

Groaning, Belle closed her eyes and buried her face in her hands. "Why did I ever leave New York? My life was so much simpler there," she mumbled from between her fingers.

Alesandra chuckled. "But then you would never have met your soul mate."

"Soul mate!" Slapping her hand against the table, Belle bit out a curse. "Damn it, why does Alex have to be so pigheaded!"

Alesandra looked out the open door to where Alex was talking to a group of men. "He's an Alpha. They're all stubborn."

Belle muttered something under her breath then gasped as a sharp jab of desire stabbed her groin. As perspiration slid down her forehead, she groaned and bent over the table.

Alesandra was at her side immediately. "What is it?"

"Oh gods. My wolf heat."

"Now?"

Belle shook her head. "Not full blown yet. Not for a few days—full moon."

As Alesandra rubbed the small of her back, Belle inhaled and exhaled then straightened. "I'm all right."

"You're still pale, and unless you want Alex asking what's wrong, you better get to your room. He's coming this way."

"Oh shit. The last thing I need is an arrogant Alpha telling me about my own body."

Alesandra chuckled. "He'll take one sniff and want to do more than talk."

Belle stared into the other woman's eyes, then smiled. "Yes, he will, won't he?"

Alesandra pursed her lips. "What are you plotting?"

Smiling, Belle shook her head. "I'll let you know when I have it all thought out. Just make sure you have a lot of aconite handy. I'm not ready for babies yet. I'll be in my room."

As Alex placed his foot on the first step to the porch, Callie jumped from her chair, stretched, and placed herself squarely in his path.

Are you finally coming to claim Belle as your mate?

Stupid cat. "Get out of my way."

The kitten licked an immaculate paw. *Why do you hesitate? You claimed her when she was alone. Why do you not claim her now? Why do you worry about what others think? Her happiness and yours is all that should matter.*

Reaching down, Alex picked up the kitten and dropped her onto a chair. "Go back to sleep."

Yawning, Callie curled her paws into her chest and mentally thanked all the venerable ancestors that cats are not so stupid.

Muttering, Alex pushed the door open and stomped into the kitchen. "Where's Belle?"

Alesandra was shuffling cards in her recipe box. "I know your mother taught you better manners than that."

A drop of blood splattered on the immaculate floor. "I'm not in the mood, old woman. Where is she?"

Straightening, Alesandra stepped in front of him.

Her head barely reached his chin.

Crossing her arms over her chest, she said, "Belle's in her room, and you are leaving now. She doesn't want to see you."

He slid his hand under his nose and wiped the blood on his jeans. "Well, I want to see her."

George stepped into the kitchen from the living room. "Too bad."

Fuming, Alex glared at the big man. No way could he get past that bear of a man without the help of at least two other pack members. "Damn it, Alesandra! Belle got into a fight with a pack member. You know how a lot of them feel about her mother. The pack won't tolerate her behavior."

"Really? Why not? Because she fought with Tabitha—over you? She was challenged by another female for her rightful place as Alpha female. What was she supposed to do? Turn around and walk away? What would the pack think of that?"

Alex clenched his teeth. He hated when Alesandra was right.

"They'd have called her a coward. She had to fight. And, in her place, I wouldn't have reacted any differently." Alesandra paused then continued, "No, I *would* have reacted differently. I would have shifted and ripped my challenger's throat out if I'd had the chance. Think about it. Belle didn't shift and didn't give Tabitha the opportunity to do so either. No blood was shed." She grinned and stared pointedly at the bloodstains on Alex's shirt. "Except yours."

He crossed his arms over his chest. "Your point?"

Muttering something under her breath about the stupidity of men, she continued, "If they had shifted, blood would have been shed, most of it Tabitha's. Because Belle kept her head and kept the fight short, no one died."

Alex stared down at Alesandra. Again, she was right. Tabitha had challenged Belle and had lost the fight. He felt his lips twitching. Belle had certainly kicked Tabitha's ass. Tabitha had too much pride to stay after she'd lost a fight. With a little luck, she'd be gone in a day or two.

Raking his fingers through his hair, Alex played the fight back through his mind. Belle had been magnificent. Once she got serious, Tabitha never had a chance. And he thought he'd been helping Belle when he lifted the bigger woman off of her. She hadn't needed his help at all. Hell, she could probably kick the shit out of half the males in the Pack.

Alesandra prodded him with her cane. "You just going to stand in the middle of my kitchen, stare at the wall, and drip blood on the floor?"

Alex looked down at her. "One of these days I'm going to burn the damn stick."

Placing her left hand over her heart, Alesandra leaned heavily on her cane with her right. "You take away my cane? I might fall! What then? Would you care for me?"

"I know when I'm not wanted, old woman. Tell Belle I want to talk to her. I'll be in my office for the rest of the day." Spinning on his heel, he stalked across the kitchen and out the door.

Straightening, Alesandra smiled. Belle was definitely the best thing that had happened to this pack in years.

Back against her closed door, Belle stood in her bedroom listening to the muffled voices drifting up the staircase. As usual, Alex sounded angry. Jeez, but what had happened to the passionate man who mated her in that thunderstorm? She knew he worried about how his pack felt about her. She pushed herself away from the door and ambled across the room to the window.

Callie was just disappearing into a small stand of trees bordering the yard, stalking something undoubtedly.

Belle smiled. Never in her wildest dreams did she ever imagine a cat would like her—and talk to her.

Standing behind the curtains, Belle watched as Alex walked across the yard in the general direction of his house. Damn, but he had a great ass. If only he didn't have such a thick head.

She frowned. Did the fact that her mother was a wolf bother him? She replayed the morning Brendan appeared in her mind. Josh had been very vocal about his feelings, but Alex hadn't said anything.

Turning, Belle flopped across the bed. No, he hadn't said anything, but the blood had drained from his face and he'd shifted and run away.

She rolled over and stared at the ceiling. Full moon was two days away and her wolf heat was coming on. In a few days, she'd know one way or the other how he felt about her ancestry.

Chapter Twenty-Three

Alex finger-combed his hair back behind his ears. Late afternoon had come and gone, the Pack Council was in a few hours, and Josh still wasn't back. Having his Beta showing his support by standing at his side would silence any grumblings when he informed the Pack that he'd granted membership to Eileen and Jill. Not that he expected anyone to complain. There were more male members anyway. Admitting two more females was a logical move.

Gingerly, he touched his nose. There was a bump that hadn't been there before, and he had two black eyes. Stupid bitch, Tabitha. She was still here, and until she did something really heinous, he couldn't demand that she leave. This was her natal pack.

He glanced down at the plans for the bed and breakfast. After a slow start, renovations to the big, old hunting lodge were ahead of schedule. Once they decided on a name and chose a couple to be host and hostess, they'd be able to open for business—just in time to take reservations for the winter ski season.

Then there was Belle's business proposition. If the majority of the pack agreed, he and Alesandra would sign the contract tomorrow. If profits were even half as good as Belle said they'd be, the pack would never have to worry about supporting its members again. They'd be able to update the equipment at the sawmill and buy the hardware store that was for sale in town.

Shaking his head, Alex stared out the window at the forest. He should be a happy man. After tonight, his pack would be far more financially secure than he'd ever dreamed possible. He should be the happiest Alpha on Earth.

But he wasn't, and it was all Belle's fault.

He hadn't seen her since her fight with Tabitha, even though he'd told Alesandra he wanted to see her. Her ancestry was rapidly becoming a moot point since rumors of the contract she'd offered Alesandra had been circulated. Money talked. The prospects of good jobs and full bellies for their children had all but the most virulent purists willing to accept a female Alpha whose mother had been a wolf.

Problem was, Belle had been away from pack life so long, she either didn't understand the dynamics of pack government or, worse, she didn't think it mattered. The other females would look to her for leadership, come to her for guidance. Her independence was going to cause problems.

Clenching his fists before he ripped the top of his desk from its base, Alex snarled at the empty room. She'd ignored his command! Damn it! Didn't she see that his word was law, that if he expected the rest of the pack to follow his orders, she had to follow them, too? She just couldn't throw his authority back in his face. If he said come, she'd better jump.

His roiling thoughts were broken by the slamming of the door. Josh sauntered into the room, looking calmer and more relaxed than he had in months.

Josh's contentment aggravated Alex even more. "Where the hell have you been?"

Halfway across the room, Josh stopped, crossed his arms over his chest, and said, "How do *you* like how it feels to have someone you expect to be there just disappear and not tell you where he's going?"

Alex's knuckles put dents in his desk. "Fuck."

The screen door slammed again, and Dave sauntered into the room. "New girlfriend, Josh?"

The red flush rolling up Josh's neck to his face stopped Alex's sharp retort.

It didn't stop Josh's. "Shut up, Dave."

Alex raised an eyebrow. "What girlfriend?"

Dave nodded toward the door. "Nice-looking wolf bitch sitting just outside the forest. I saw her follow Josh out from beneath the trees."

Josh shoved the Omega. "Stop being such an ass, Dave. She's curious and followed me home. That's all. She'll be gone in another hour." He turned back to Alex. "What happened to you? Run into a door?"

Ignoring him, Alex walked to the door. "Where is she?"

Pushing the door open and stepping onto the porch, Dave nodded. "There. Can't miss her since she's practically white. Hey! Isn't that Belle?"

Alex shoved Dave out of the way. What was that crazy bitch up to now?

"Looks like they're talking," Dave said as Josh joined them.

Alex leaned against one of the columns supporting the porch roof and contemplated the woman who was twisting his insides in knots.

She was sitting cross-legged on the ground before a whitish-blonde wolf bitch. Both had their heads low and were staring into each other's eyes.

"What do you think that conversation is about?" Dave asked. "Looks serious."

Josh snorted but his voice held no rancor, just curiosity. "They probably discovered they're long-lost relatives or something like that."

Are you sure about this? You know your life will change drastically, and you don't even know if Josh will accept you.

The female wolf, Mia, grinned a wolf grin. *He will accept me. I am his destined mate. He may fight the attraction for a time, but in the end, he will be mine. You say he is Beta here?*

Chuckling, Belle nodded. She really liked this wolf. Mia reminded her of herself.

Yes. The dark-haired man standing next to him is the Alpha and my mate, though he has yet to understand the responsibilities that go along with the privilege.

Mia's tongue lolled out as she stared at the three men. *Males of all species are somewhat dense.*

Belle grinned back. Callie was going to love Mia.

Who is the other male?

The Pack Omega.

Mia turned her attention back to Belle. *A worthy position for a Were. Is he mated?*

Belle shook her head. *Not yet, but I suspect it may not be much longer until he chooses a mate.*

Until she chooses him.

Belle laughed outright. If humans really understood the dynamics of wolf packs, they'd have to rewrite at least fifty years of scientific study.

Mia huffed. *Show me how now. I can change. My father was as you are, half wolf, half Were. Of all my siblings, only I have the desire to change. Until now, I had no one to show me.*

Your father?

He believed I would be safer and happier as a wolf.

Belle nodded. *Okay, this is what you must do.* Closing her eyes, Belle opened her mind to Mia, frowning at the slight discomfort when as the wolf searched out, found, and assimilated the knowledge of shifting. She left Belle's mind as quickly as she came.

Not hard at all.

Belle massaged her forehead. The transfer had been a bit more uncomfortable than she anticipated. Opening her eyes, she stared at Mia. *The shifting will be the easy part. Holding your human form will require a great deal of concentration. Your legs won't work the same way and you'll have hands and arms. You'll have to learn to walk upright. Are you sure you want to do this?*

Josh will not remain a wolf to stay with me. Therefore, I must change. Neither of us will be whole without the other.

Rising, Belle said, "Okay, go ahead. I'll catch you if you start to fall."

"They've been talking a long time," Dave commented with a grin.

As the three men watched, a pearl-colored mist formed, rolled and billowed.

"What the fuck is she doing?" Alex snarled.

All three men leaped from the porch and sprinted toward the trees.

As they reached Belle's side, the mist dissipated and a short, pale-haired woman stumbled forward.

Josh caught her as she fell.

Alex grabbed Belle's arm. "What do you think you're doing?"

Dave reached to help Josh support the woman.

Josh's snarl was low and dangerous. "Do *not* touch her."

Throwing his hands in the air, Dave stepped back. "She's all yours."

Alex shook Belle's arm. "Explain yourself."

Belle jerked her arm free. "This is Mia. She asked me to teach her how to shift, so I did. She's part Were. She had the right to know." Turning her head, she smiled at Mia. "I'll see you later." Spinning on her heel, she stomped back to Alesandra's house.

Alex didn't miss the smile the two women shared before Belle turned away.

Chapter Twenty-Four

ɞ

As she hurried away from Alex, Belle glanced back over her shoulder. Confusion and frustration danced across his face and he took a step to follow her. Before he could take a second step, Mia stumbled and fell against him.

He staggered.

Belle looked away and smiled. Yep. She already liked Mia — a lot.

"I'm sorry. I can't seem to catch my balance."

Mia's voice was low and husky.

"What do you expect," Josh growled as he hauled her back out of Alex's arms, "you never walked on two legs before."

Mia wrapped her arms around Alex's chest as her legs wobbled beneath her.

Alex tried to push her into Josh's arms.

She threw her arms around Alex's neck.

Both men cursed.

After one last glance in their direction, Belle bit her bottom lip to keep from laughing out loud and followed the path into the grove of trees. Mia was doing a wonderful job of keeping Alex's attention.

Belle hurried into Alesandra's house. Whatever herbs the old woman had given her to mute and disguise the symptoms of her wolf heat were wearing off. A dull ache had begun to grow in her groin. That ache combined with Alex's compelling body would wreak havoc on her plans. She had to stay away from him until tonight.

Once Alex had disentangled himself from Mia and Josh had carried her off, he looked for Belle.

She was nowhere to be seen.

Growling in disgust, he headed back to his house. Damn woman. A week ago she couldn't keep her hands off of him. Now, whenever he appeared, she disappeared.

"And whose fault is that, nitwit?" he mumbled to himself. "You're the one who ran away from her as soon as you found out her mother was a wolf. And when she showed up here, all you did was issue commands. Not once have you told her you loved her."

Hearing himself admit his love for Belle out loud brought Alex to a stumbling halt. Bracing his hand against a slender birch tree, he stared unseeing into the forest. Loved Belle? He loved Belle? True, the Were half of him would never be content without her, but his human half? Love?

He blinked and shook his head. What if the pack demanded that she leave, that she wasn't a fit mate for their Alpha?

Instantly, the wolf in his soul howled with rage. What's more, his human half agreed. He needed Belle. She was the other half of his soul. If the pack demanded she leave, he was going with her.

Again, his wolf half snarled in anger. He was going nowhere. He was Alpha. The pack was his. No one would drive him or his mate away. Anyone who wouldn't accept Belle as his mate could leave — or fight.

Taking a deep breath, Alex straightened. He loved Belle. She was his, and she was staying. Tonight, everyone in the pack would learn of his decision, as would Belle. Then she was going to submit to him like a good mate should.

* * * * *

"Does anyone disagree with allowing these two women Sanctuary?"

Alex looked out at the faces of the pack members assembled before his front porch. Eileen's story had more than one woman in tears.

A short man stood and stepped to the bottom of the steps. "What if her mate comes looking for her? He has the right to demand she return to him. He could go to the Hierarchy and demand that we give her back. That's trouble for us, I say. We don't need no more troubles than we already have."

Crossing his arms over his chest, Alex glared down at Sam. Fucking asshole. He caused more trouble than any other three pack members put together. "Every pack has autonomy, Sam, which you would know if you had paid attention to your schooling in Pack Law. Besides, any pack member can leave his or her pack and request Sanctuary in another if he or she believes his or her life is in danger."

A sneer on his face, the short man continued. "How do we know if this woman's life is in danger? Ain't none of us but you and your pussy Omega seen her."

Alesandra's cane thudded against the wooden floor of Alex's porch once, twice, three times, as she stepped forward. When she stabbed it at Sam's chest, he was forced to jump back. "I'm the one who treated her wounds, Sam Irons. Do you think *I'd* lie about them? What about the other women who've been to see her, including your wife? As a matter of fact, I don't see Sally here tonight. Why is that? Maybe she decided she needed to find Sanctuary in another pack, too."

Sputtering, Sam surged forward. "Why you old bitch…"

The steel-tipped point of her cane in the middle of his chest brought him up short. "Yes, I am, and don't you forget it."

"Would you like to see the bruises I still have?"

Alex felt the entire pack surge forward as Eileen, supported by Jill, stepped to his side.

After taking a deep breath, she stepped forward and leaned against the porch railing. "My mate cracked four of my ribs, broke my arm, blackened both my eyes, and split my lip, among other lesser bruises. Why? Because I miscarried the child I was carrying. Then he blackened his sister's eye because she tried to stop him."

Though he kept his face blank, satisfaction surged through Alex at his pack's reaction. Collective gasps rose from the crowd, more women were in tears, and a number of the men were muttering threats. There was no question that Eileen and Jill would be accepted now.

"What if he comes here looking for her? She don't belong to nobody here. Who's gonna fight for her? Anybody who'd do that to his mate is meaner than a rabid wolverine."

"Christ, Sam, if you don't want to grant them Sanctuary, just vote no," Alex snapped. "The Third Law of the Pack states that all males will defend any unmated female. Eileen is not mated to anyone in our pack. But if you're worried about your own skin and if her mate shows up, I'll fight him. Besides, any male who would do that to his mate strikes me more as a bully who picks on those weaker than himself. Facing a pack Alpha is another story altogether." Alex lifted his gaze to the crowd. "Are we ready to vote? Is there anyone here who votes to deny Sanctuary?" He looked back down at Sam.

Sam looked around.

No hands were raised.

Muttering under his breath, he slunk back into the crowd.

After another quick look around, Alex turned to Eileen and smiled. "Sanctuary is granted. We offer you the protection of our pack. By Pack Law, you can now choose to declare yourself unmated. Every male here—" he glanced in Sam's direction, "—will do his utmost to protect you, whether you mate any of them or not. Do you accept Sanctuary?"

Smiling weakly, Eileen nodded. "Yes."

Alex turned to Jill. "Do you wish Sanctuary? Your brother is a pack Alpha. Severing ties to his pack could be considered an insult."

Somebody in the crowd tripped Sam as he hustled forward.

Jill glanced at Dave then back to Alex. Smiling, she nodded. Her voice was strong and clear. "Believe me, my brothers will be glad to see me go. As far as they're concerned, I'm worthless, especially since I refused the last mating they proposed."

More mutters drifted up from the crowd.

Alex nodded. "Very well. Both of you are granted Sanctuary."

With Alex's pronouncement, Eileen sagged against Jill.

Dave beat Alex to her side. With a smile for Jill, he lifted Eileen into his arms. With Jill leading the way, he carried Eileen back to her cottage.

After a quick wink to Josh, Alex turned back to the crowd. He still had an announcement to make, but first he had to ask if anyone else had business to settle. "Is there any other business to discuss?"

People standing closest to the forest began to stir. Whispers drifted to Alex on the breeze—whispers and something else.

The crowd rolled, shifted and parted as a lithe female Were loped toward the porch. The slight wind that preceded her announced her condition. She was in full heat.

Every unmated male snapped to attention.

The wolf in Alex's soul awoke howling.

At the foot of the steps leading to the porch, black mist swirled.

Head thrown back, defiance in her eyes, Belle stared up at Alex. "I have business with the pack."

Turning, she faced the crowd. "I'm in need of a mate tonight. Are there any unmated males interested?"

Chapter Twenty-Five

&

As Belle watched, four males yanked their shirts over their heads.

With a snarl that echoed back from the mountains, Alex leaped from the porch, stripping out of his tee shirt in midair. He landed in front of her, fists clenched, teeth bared. "She is mine!"

Three of the men stepped back. The fourth, a tall, heavily muscled male, snarled back. "She asked for any unmated male."

Shredding his shirt, Alex dropped it and took one menacing step forward. The muscles on his chest and abdomen rippled. "Belle is *my* mate."

The other male didn't back down. "Then why does she ask for others? Does she repudiate you?"

Belle kept her eyes fixed on the big male.

He didn't look like he was going to back down.

A sharp stab of heat lanced her groin, and her nipples tightened to painful peaks. Sweat broke out on her forehead as she gritted her teeth. A sharp, breathy hiss slipped from between her lips. She needed to mate—soon. Alex had declared she was his mate to the entire pack far more quickly than she'd expected. It was enough. Now what did she do with this other male?

In front of her, Alex tensed at her hiss but didn't turn. He didn't take his eyes off of the other male either.

Belle took a deep breath, swallowed her urge to jump Alex right there, and cleared her throat. Before she could say anything, a shrill voice floated over the assembly.

"Abomination. She's an abomination," Tabitha called as she sauntered out from the thickest part of the crowd, a satisfied smirk on her face. "Your Alpha has mated the daughter of a wolf. Will you accept this from him? Is he still worthy to be your leader if he stoops to mate one such as her?"

Alesandra started down the steps. "Enough, Tabitha..."

Alex held up his hand. "No, this is my fight—and I will fight, for I will give up neither my mate nor my pack."

Tabitha turned to face the crowd. "Are you going to accept a leader who mates with an Abomination?"

Mutters and grumbles circulated among the crowd. Many concentrated their stares on her.

Belle did her best to concentrate but was forced to use most of her energy to control her sexual urges. Alesandra's herbs had worn off completely, and her body was on fire. The males closest to her kept shifting, their nostrils flaring, their gazes leaping from her to Alex and back again.

Sweat trickled down Alex's back. Belle was close enough to know the scent of her heat was wreaking havoc with his concentration, too. But he had to cement his position as Alpha and hers as his mate before they could give in to their desires.

"You're just pissed 'cause Alex didn't want you," Carl said from the front of the crowd. "You always were one to stir up trouble. Came back to see if you could snag Alex and when he turned you down, you had to make trouble. But Belle beat you when you challenged her, kicked your ass good. Woulda thought you were smart enough to learn your lesson then."

"Shut up, old man," Tabitha snapped quickly, her eyes darting around the crowd. "People don't care what you think. That woman—" she turned, and pointed at Belle, "—is an Abomination. Do you want an Abomination for your female Alpha?"

Carl spit. "For sure certain I don't want it to be you."

As members of the crowd tittered, Belle closed her eyes and sucked in her breath. The wolf in her didn't give a damn about any of this. All she wanted was a hard, fast mating, but she had to control her urges so she could defend herself to the pack. Alex couldn't make them accept her on his own.

After one last deep breath, she stepped to Alex's side. "My father," she began slowly, her voice strengthening as she continued, "is Artemis Gray. Yes, he mated a wolf, and I am one of the offspring of that mating. I can't change the way you think if you believe all wolf-werewolf offspring are Abominations. If you do, I pity you."

Another deep breath. Another surge of her human will over the wolf in her soul, the wolf that she soon wouldn't be able to control. "Am I more of an Abomination than the male who beat his mate, the woman you just granted Sanctuary? Am I more of an Abomination than the male or female werewolf who ignores his or her children? Do they have more honor, better blood than I do?" Belle shook her head. "If you think so, then you are the Abominations."

"Why you—" Sam lunged forward only to be halted by Alex's fist planted squarely in his stomach. He fell gasping and writhing to the ground.

Alex glanced contemptuously at Sam. "Belle is my mate. I chose her, and she accepted me. Like wolves, we mate for life. There will be no other mate for me."

He didn't wait for the grumbling and whispering to subside. "What's more, I'm Alpha of this pack, and I'm going to stay Alpha. None of you have been able to defeat me in a fight for dominance, and you certainly won't be able to defeat me today," he added glaring directly into the faces of the four males who'd stepped forward earlier. "Anyone who doesn't like this arrangement is free to leave—now." He glanced at Tabitha. "That includes you."

Face flushed, the redhead rounded on her brother. "Are you just going to stand there and let him get away with this, Josh? He's mated an *Abomination*! You're Beta. The pack will follow you."

Scowling, Josh glanced over to where Mia sat leaning against a tree with a grin on her face. Then he glared at his sister. "Yeah. I'm Beta. And I follow my Alpha."

Tabitha's jaw dropped. Then she began to sputter. "But...you...he..."

"Shut up, Tabitha. You don't give a damn about anybody's ancestry, and everybody here knows it. You've been pissed at Alex ever since he chose Serena over you. The only reason you came back was because you heard Serena had mated somebody else and you thought you could weasel your way into Alex's bed. That didn't work, and now you're trying to cause trouble. Well, it isn't going to work. I stand by Alex and his mate."

"So do I," Dave said from behind Alesandra where he'd stationed himself after returning from taking Eileen and Jill home.

Carl stepped forward. "Me too. What about you, Richard?" he added nudging the muscular male who'd seemed on the brink of challenging Alex. "You gonna challenge or support?"

Richard glanced at Belle once more.

She shook her head and inched closer to Alex.

More and more pack members stepped forward or called out their support for Alex.

"What's the matter with you people!" Tabitha shrieked. "You can't do this."

"Shut up, bitch," Carl said, "or I'll toss you over my knee and paddle that behind of yours. 'Course, you might like it too much. But I think I can handle that too. I'm not that old yet."

Her face twisted with rage, Tabitha glared out at the crowd, most of whom were laughing. "You'll be sorry. All of you will be sorry for not listening to me." Spinning, she shoved past anyone who didn't get out of her way.

"I'll keep an eye on her," Josh said in a low voice. "She'll leave in a day or two. I give you my word on that."

"If she doesn't," Belle murmured through clenched teeth, "Mia will take care of her."

More sweat beaded on Belle's forehead. Her knuckles whitened, she stiffened every muscle in her body, and didn't move. If she did, her wolf soul would gain control.

At her side, Alex struggled against his own wild soul. The tantalizing aroma of Belle's heat surrounded him. She was his, and she needed to mate. Now!

Sweat rolled down his back as he stared at Richard. Practically every member to the pack had declared his or her support.

Richard looked at Belle again, speculation in his eyes. Then he grinned. Extending his hand, he said, "I think she'd be too much for me to handle. It takes a lot of sass to do what she did tonight, throwing that challenge in your face in front of all of us. You're going to have your hands full with her. You are Alpha."

Easing his control a bit, Alex clasped Richard's hand. "Thanks. Now that everything is settled, meeting adjourned. Everybody go home. I have other business to attend to."

Dropping Richard's hand, he grabbed Belle, threw her over his shoulder, leaped up the steps, and disappeared through his front door.

Josh glanced over at Mia, who was leaning somewhat unsteadily against a tree. Grinning, he clapped Richard on the shoulder. "I have other business to take care of, too. You've just been promoted to my assistant. Anybody still has any questions, you handle it."

Leaping from the porch, he loped over to Mia, lifted her into his arms, and continued on into the woods.

"But…"

Dave clapped Richard on the other shoulder. "Welcome to management."

Chapter Twenty-Six

฿

As Alex headed for his bedroom, he slapped Belle's bare ass. "Don't you ever put me into a position like that again!"

Twisting, she sank her teeth into the fleshy part of his other shoulder.

He smacked her ass again.

Snarling, she let go. "I wouldn't have put you in that position if you had acknowledged me as your mate right away—like you should have."

Kicking the bedroom door shut, Alex tossed her onto the bed, following her down, covering her body with his in an attempt to hold her immobile. He grabbed her wrists and lifted her arms over her head.

He felt her gather herself to try and throw him off.

She stiffened and shuddered. "Ahhhhhhhhhhhhh!" Her hips jerked. "Oh gods."

The tantalizing aroma of her heat surrounded them.

Alex inhaled deeply.

His cock strained against his jeans.

Holding her wrists with one hand and keeping a leg over her thighs, he slid off her body, dropped his free hand to her crotch, cupped her swollen lips, and pushed.

She lifted her hips and thrust into his hand. "Please, Alex."

His nostrils flared as moisture coated his palm. He shifted his hips, trying to ease the ache in his cock. But he kept his jeans on. Belle's condition would have her insatiable for a good part of the night. He intended to satisfy her completely. "Please what?"

Baring her teeth, she snapped at him. "Damn it, I'm on fire!"

"Where? Here?" He slipped his fingers inside of her.

Arching her back, she thrust against his fingers. "Yes, oh yes." Her breasts jiggled as she shivered.

Alex smiled. She had such lovely breasts. Lowering his head, he sucked on her nipple.

She shuddered, arched even more, and groaned.

He twirled his fingers around her swollen lips again, then caressed her smooth mound. "You shaved again," he murmured against her breast. "I like it. You're so soft and smooth." As he petted her mound, he tongued her nipple.

Slipping his fingers between her thighs, he kissed her between her breasts. "You're wet and swollen—and aching for my cock—*my* cock. Nobody else's."

"Your cock," she panted. "Just yours. Now. Please."

Alex kissed her breast then suckled her nipple. He separated her lips and, as he nipped her nipple, he pinched her swollen clit.

Her body arched as she keened her orgasm.

Panting, Belle stared into Alex's eyes. Her breasts still tingled and a slow fire burned between her legs. That first orgasm relieved the ache in her groin—a little. She needed more.

He smiled down at her. "That help?"

She licked her lips. "More. I need more."

"So do I." Bending, he lapped her pebbled nipple. "You're beautiful, Belle. I love you."

She froze and stared into his face. He loved her? She blinked back the tears welling in her eyes and sniffed. "Took you long enough to figure that out."

He grinned. "Don't you have something to say to me?"

Belle shivered as another twinge of heat stabbed her groin. "Yes, I do. Get those damn pants off, now!"

Laughing, Alex pushed himself up off the bed and shucked his jeans.

Belle followed, settling on her knees on the edge of the bed. She grabbed his thighs, pulled him closer, and sucked the head of his magnificent cock into her mouth. Sliding her hands up the back of his thighs, she caressed his ass cheeks.

Alex buried his hands in her hair and thrust his cock deeper into her mouth. "Christ, Belle."

She slid her hand back down his firm ass and cupped his balls, rolling them while she sucked more of his cock into her mouth. Then she pulled back and circled the head with her tongue.

Another bubble of heat burst in her loins.

She moaned against his cock. As good as he tasted and as much as she enjoyed this, it wasn't enough. "I need you inside of me, Alex, please. I'm burning up."

Without a word, he grabbed her waist and spun her around. Sliding his thigh between hers, he forced her legs further apart.

As the crisp hairs on his leg caressed her inner thighs, Belle spread her knees even further and rested her forearms on the bed. "Deep, Alex. I need you deep."

He fingered her swollen lips and clit.

His cock brushed the inside of her thigh.

Belle shivered as she anticipated his rock-hard cock ramming into her. She pushed back against him. "Please, Alex."

Resting a hand in the small of her back, Alex pressed down. Her ass rose further into the air. Beads of moisture seeped from between her swollen, red lips. He slid his fingers down her lips and pressed against her clit.

She thrust back against his hands and moaned.

Grabbing the base of his cock, he pushed the head against her slippery opening.

Her moan became a sob.

He slapped her ass lightly. "I am your mate, your Alpha. Will you obey me?"

Again, she pushed back against his hips, trying to get his cock inside of her.

He rubbed it against her lips, coating it with her moisture. Bending over her back, he nipped her shoulder. "Will you obey me?" He pinched her nipple then nipped the back of her neck.

Belle buried her face in the blankets. She was so hot, so achy. She needed his hard length deep inside of her.

Another nip, this time on the other shoulder.

Her nipples tightened even more.

He slid his cock back and forth between her legs but he held her immobile, and she was unable to shift so it slid into her.

A sharper nip on the back of the neck. "I am your mate. You are mine. Will you obey me?"

The werewolf in her soul was howling with need. Her entire body was on fire. This man could satisfy her and make her happier than any other man on Earth. She lifted her head. "I'm yours. Your mate. I will obey. I love you, Alex."

Lifting himself off her back, he straightened, slid his thumbs down her slit, and parted her lips.

As Belle trembled and arched her back, he thrust his cock in as deeply as he could, pushing her across the bed with the force of his entry.

Belle shivered with ecstasy and keened her pleasure as he withdrew and thrust home again.

"Harder, Alex. Deeper."

He pulled out and rammed into her again and again and again.

"Oh yes, oh yes, oh yes!" Belle raised her ass and pushed back against his thrusts.

He grabbed her hips and settled into his rhythm.

"Ahhhhhh." The friction of his cock against her aching internal muscles was pure heaven. Pleasure built. "Harder. Harder."

Alex twisted his hips.

She shivered with delight. "Deeper, deeper."

Her internal muscles clenched his cock, squeezing, grasping.

Bending over her back once more, Alex nipped her shoulder. "Mine. Only mine."

He curled his arm around her waist, slid his fingers between her spread thighs, and rubbed her swollen clit.

As her orgasm exploded outward, she howled with pleasure.

Alex twisted his hips, buried his cock as far as he could, and joined his howl to hers.

Gasping for breath, Belle collapsed on her stomach.

Alex fell to her side and pulled her into his arms, content to lie quietly until they both caught their breath.

After a last shiver, Belle sighed and nuzzled Alex's chest.

He pulled her closer. "You'll obey me?"

She chuckled and lapped his nipple. Her hand drifted down to his cock. A few caresses and it was rock-hard again. "If you'll obey me."

Her head followed her hand.

When she wrapped her hot, wet tongue around the head of his cock, Alex shuddered, laced his fingers behind his head, and didn't give a damn about who obeyed whom.

Solstice Heat

ฅ

Chapter One

✂

"Challenge!"

As the door slammed against the wall, the three men looked up from the blueprints they were studying.

Alex's voice was low, deadly. "Who?"

Dave shook his head. "Never saw him before. Big black bastard. He just loped out of the woods as if he already owned the place."

"Not *my* place," Alex growled as he rose to his feet. "Josh, Richard."

Richard glanced at his fellow Beta. "Why would he need his seconds-in-command?"

"Witnesses," Josh said. "Dave will come too as Omega."

Richard cocked an eyebrow. "Why the Omega? He's supposed to calm the Alpha down, not rile him up."

Shrugging, Josh stepped forward. "Dave has a better chance of stopping Alex from killing the bastard. I don't give a damn. Dave's more in tune with pack politics. It's not a good idea to kill a strange Were without knowing who he is or what pack he's from. If he has high status, the other pack could get pretty angry."

As Alex walked by him, Dave grabbed his arm. "He's not from any of the packs we've had dealings with. And, he's the biggest Were I've ever seen."

Alex shook his arm free. "Doesn't matter how big he is. This is my pack and it's going to stay that way."

His three subordinates followed him out the door.

Alex inhaled deeply as he stepped out onto the wide porch

that enclosed three sides of his large cabin. Numerous paths that led to other houses and cabins where members of his pack lived disappeared into the rich undergrowth surrounding the large clearing. This was his land, his pack. He'd devoted his life to caring and nurturing both.

A snarl curled his lips.

No other Were was going to take it from him.

A fresh breeze swirled across the clearing and he inhaled again.

The late spring wind carried the fresh scents of rain-washed pine, verdant forest loam, and late alpine flowers. Off to his right, a jewel-toned hummingbird flitted among the red petunias growing in one of the baskets hanging from the porch eaves. In a huge oak tree next to the porch, an irate blue jay scolded a squirrel.

Then a second light gust brought another scent, a musky, half lupine, half human scent.

A growl rumbled in Alex's chest as he concentrated his gaze on a huge, black wolf sitting calmly in the clearing's center.

As the four men stepped off the porch, the wolf tilted his head back and yawned.

The sun glinted off long, white fangs.

Josh and Richard's reactions didn't instill confidence.

"Christ, Alex, I've seen ponies smaller than that."

"Fuck. Do you have to fight him alone? Can't one of us help you?"

Alex glanced over at the man who he'd recently promoted to be a second Beta and shook his head. "My pack, my fight."

Richard raked his fingers through his hair.

Alex's Omega clasped his shoulder and squeezed. "If I were you, I'd go straight for his balls."

The black wolf continued to stare at them.

Alex never took his eyes from him. "Where's Belle?" The

last thing he wanted was for her to see him ripped apart in this fight. It was going to take everything he had to win.

His three subordinates glanced at each other.

His voice became more demanding. "Where's Belle!"

"Alesandra's cabin. They're concocting a new scent for the soaps."

Alex nodded. "Make sure she stays there, Dave. I don't want her to know about this until it's over. And... If I lose, make sure she doesn't try to avenge me. She wouldn't stand a chance against a wolf like that."

"The Alpha female is permitted to join in a fight if her mate becomes severely wounded."

Fist clenched, Alex rounded on his number one Beta. He would remember that particular clause of Pack Law. "No, damn it! I will *not* have her injured in any way. Do you understand?"

Stepping back, Josh stared at his Alpha then nodded his head — once. "If you end up dead, she's apt to kill me."

Ignoring Josh's comment, Alex turned back towards the huge werewolf sitting so calmly in the middle of his yard. Dave was right. Never in his life had he seen a Were so large. It would take all his skill and every trick he'd ever learned to defeat him and retain control of his pack.

Alex cursed under his breath. Fuck! Who the hell was this — monster? And why did he have to show up now — now, when he'd finally found his mate.

Wiping the sweat from his forehead with his sleeve, he closed his eyes. Pictures of Belle's face flashed through his mind, Belle laughing with him, arguing with him, loving him. He clenched his fists more tightly. He would *not* lose this battle. He would *not* lose her, not now, not so soon after he'd finally found her.

Ripping off his flannel shirt, he stepped forward.

As he walked towards his opponent, a white wolf stepped out of the forest, stared at them, then sprinted in the direction of

Alesandra's cabin.

"Fuck!" Snarling back over his shoulder, Alex snapped, "Damn it, Josh. Can't you control that bitch!"

"As much as you can control yours," his Beta mumbled under his breath.

*****

"This combination of scents is really interesting, Alesandra. I wouldn't have thought of mixing them together."

The older woman chuckled, but before she could answer, the white wolf burst through the screen door.

Silvery mist swirled, and a naked blonde woman stood before them, a hand braced on the back of a chair as she gasped for breath. "Alex…challenge…huge Were… now."

Belle didn't wait to hear any more. Not even bothering to shift, she bolted out the door and sprinted down the path towards the cabin she shared with her mate of barely three weeks. No one was going to put any teeth marks in his skin except her!

Minutes later, she exploded out of the forest to the right of the path and into the clearing, easily avoiding the men who'd stationed themselves there to intercept her, and raced to Alex's side.

He caught her as she reached him.

"Get the hell out of here, Belle. This is no place for you."

"Bullshit!" she gasped as she struggled to catch her breath. "I love you, and I'm not going to let you do anything stupid."

Anger replaced the determination on his face. "Damn it. This is my pack. I'm Alpha. I have to accept this challenge."

Belle stopped struggling. Turning to face him, she cupped his face in her hands. "I'd never expect you do anything else." She blinked back a tear. "But you can't expect me just to stand by and watch you die. I can help you. Pack Law allows it."

Closing his eyes, he wrapped his arms around her and

rested his forehead against hers. "I know, but the thought of bites and slashes on your body. Belle, I couldn't stand it if you were badly hurt. And look at him. You don't stand a chance against something like that."

After kissing her forehead, he turned her to face his opponent.

For a moment, Belle remained frozen in his arms.

Then she gasped.

Then she cursed.

Then she cursed again—loudly.

Bringing her boot heel down on the instep of Alex's now bare foot, she slipped free of his embrace and stomped towards the black wolf who stared at her, tongue lolling out of his mouth.

"You inconsiderate, insensitive, aggravating, unappreciative, idiotic moron! How could you be such a jerk? Do you know what you just did to me? Do you?" Stopping a few inches in front of him, she poked her finger at his nose. "You jackass! Just wait. I'm going to skin you alive for this."

After the initial sharp pain in his foot and shock at Belle's behavior, Alex leaped to her side. "Damn it, Belle! He could kill you."

Baring her teeth, she snarled first at Alex then at the black wolf. "He will *not!* He hasn't beaten me in a fight for the last eight years, have you, ingrate?"

At first, Alex gaped. Then, "You know him?"

Belle ignored Alex and, before the wolf could react, she slapped him across the jowls.

Pulling back his lips to show deadly fangs, the wolf snarled viciously.

Alex grabbed her arm.

She jerked it free. "Of course I know him. This is Garth." Glaring at the wolf, she added, "Go ahead. Try to bite me and see what happens."

Alex shook his head. "Garth? Garth who?"

Throwing her hands into the air, Belle spun on her heel to face her mate. "Garth. My brother. Who did you think it was? The Dalai Lama?"

Alex stared first at Belle, then the wolf.

The wolf grinned at him.

Throwing his hands in the air, Alex cursed—long and loud. Then, "Brother? Another brother? How many fucking brothers do you have?"

Chapter Two

ဢ

Growl rumbling in his chest, Garth eyed his sister. Belle hadn't changed at all—still wanted to boss everybody around. How Dad and Brendan were able to put up with her all these years he'd never been able to figure out. But then, he couldn't understand why they'd all want to spend most of their time trapped in New York City when wild forest and open tundra beckoned. Even Melody lived in a town now, though it was a lot smaller than New York. Only Kearnan had freed himself from the ties of civilization—most of them anyway.

Yawning, Garth closed his eyes and stretched out, his head on his paws. When Belle got really got wound up, she could lecture for what seemed like hours.

"Damn it, Garth. Don't you dare go to sleep. I'll kick you if you do."

Garth opened an eye. *And I'll bite your foot off if you try.*

That brought a snarl from the man at her side, and Garth smiled to himself. According to Kearnan, this Alex Whitehorse had mated their little sister—*after* he knew the truth about her parentage. That was one point in his favor. Then, he'd stepped forward to fight when he thought there was a challenge to his position as any good Alpha should—a second point. Finally, his snarl has just made it clear that he would defend his mate against her own brother. Three points to him. Now that Garth knew Whitehorse was worthy, he was welcome to Belle, a sister with the temper of a wet cat, a sister who was still haranguing him.

She stomped her foot. "Bullshit. You wouldn't hurt a fly."

Garth opened his other eye to see her mate staring at her as if she had two heads. He chuckled to himself. Whitehorse may have mated her, but he obviously didn't hang on her every word or believe everything she said. He went up another point in Garth's estimation.

"Garth!"

I detest flies.

Belle stomped her foot again. "Would you please stop being so damned obstinate and shift to human?"

Two foot stomps. She was really getting pissed. Pushing himself up to his haunches, Garth grinned a toothy grin. *No clothes.*

She threw her hands into the air. "Oh for heaven's sake! Where do you expect me to find clothes to fit you?"

"George?" one of the men now standing beside her mate said.

Becoming still, she stared at Garth and nodded. "That should work. Mia," she continued turning to the white female wolf sitting not far off, "would you go tell Alesandra what we need?"

With a small yip, she sprinted off.

Garth watched her go.

"Get your eyes off my bitch's ass."

Garth transferred his gaze to one of the other men with his sister's mate. Anger and possession radiated from his tense figure. Interesting, that bitch was far more wolf than she was human. Maybe there *was* hope for werewolves, at least this particular pack.

Belle started tapping her foot. "Damn it, Garth. Why didn't you tell me you were coming? Why didn't you tell anyone where you were?"

Before he could answer, Belle's arms were around his neck, and she was hugging him for all she was worth. "I missed you, you big monster."

Belle, you're choking me.

She sniffed into his neck ruff. "Good. You deserve it. I

should have let Alex kick your ass."

Why don't you introduce me?

Straightening, she planted her hands on her hips. "After you shift, idiot. How long have you been feral? Don't you remember any manners?"

I have not been feral. I've been traveling.

She snorted. "Traveling, my ass."

The man on her other side chuckled. "Since you have everything under control, Alex, I'll head on down and help Jill with the final orders and reservations. The phone's been ringing off the hook. See you later, Belle."

"That was Dave, our Omega," she snapped at Garth, "and if you'd have shifted, I could have introduced you to him. Honestly, why do you have to be so modest!"

Garth stretched. *So I don't like standing around naked. I told you I don't have any clothes with me.*

A noise behind Belle and her companions drew his attention. Stepping to his sister's right, he watched an older woman escorted by a huge man approach them. The woman reeked of authority and power—an Alpha female if ever he met one, and the man...

Garth twitched his nose, jerked his head up, and stepped back. Bear? Werebear—here? He glanced at Belle's mate.

Whitehorse hadn't taken his eyes off him. Now he stood there with his arms crossed over his chest, smiling a nasty smile.

Garth nodded once. An Alpha with a werebear ally. Whitehorse and his entire pack were becoming more interesting by the minute.

"You asked for these," the woman said.

"Thanks, Alesandra." His sister dropped a pair of jeans and a shirt in front of him. "These should fit. Now, will you shift? Please?"

Garth grinned another toothy grin. *Since you asked so nicely.*

Black mist swirled. In a few moments he appeared,

standing a head taller than everyone but the werebear. Bending, he shook out the jeans and stepped into them.

As he pulled up the fly, Belle buried her fist in his stomach.

Sucking in a sharp breath and blinking back tears, she jerked it back, shaking and stretching her fingers.

Garth grinned as he shrugged into the soft flannel shirt and buttoned it up. "You should've known better than to try that."

"It always worked for Melody," she snapped as she blinked back more tears.

"Melody lifts weights. You lift pencils." Gathering her into his arms, he hugged her until she squeaked then set her back on her feet. "It's good to see you too. Now, introduce me to everyone."

Grabbing his shirt, she stretched up on her tiptoes and kissed his cheek. Then she turned to the others. "The tall one in the middle is Alex Whitehorse, my mate. Next to him are Josh and Richard, his Betas."

Two Betas? How large was this pack? After a brief nod, Garth held out his hand, pleased when all three men shook it without hesitating.

"This is Alesandra," she continued, "and George."

Again, Garth shook hands. "And the white wolf? Isn't she going to shift to be introduced?"

The Beta named Josh growled.

"That's Mia," Belle answered with a chuckle. "Josh doesn't like her wandering around naked. She only learned to shift a month or so ago and still hasn't come to grips with the necessity of clothing."

"Once summer's over, she will," Alesandra said as she stepped forward. "So, you're the third son of Artemis Gray. I see little of him in you except your height, and you certainly don't favor your mother."

Garth nodded once. Nosy old woman, one who obviously knew his father, but—she deserved his respect. Good thing Belle was as stubborn and opinionated as she was, or this woman would run right over her. This Alesandra would be an Alpha to her dying day. Still, he didn't have to talk about his family if he didn't want to. And he didn't.

"You want to know about my family, talk to Belle. I don't have the time. Nice to meet you though." Ignoring her cocked eyebrow, he glanced back at Whitehorse. "Two Betas, one with a mate even more wolf than Belle, and a werebear ally. Interesting pack you have here."

His sister's mate never stopped smiling. "We are what we are."

Garth chuckled. "I've met werebears before."

"Where?" George asked as he extended his hand. "Few of the lupine race are friendly to us anymore."

Garth gripped the other man's hand. "Canada, Northwest Territory. There's a small clan there that guested me for a few months."

"Probably because they'd never seen a wolf as large as you are. How many matches did you win?" George squeezed his hand tighter.

Garth squeezed back. "Three."

"How many did you lose?"

"Ten."

George's laughter boomed around the clearing as he released Garth's hand. "Winning any is noteworthy. They'll tell the story for generations."

It was Garth's turn to shake the blood back into his hand and stretch out his fingers.

Belle grabbed his arm. "Okay. Enough standing around and chatting out here. Come inside and explain to me why it's taken so long for you to contact anyone in the family. Did you know Dad has mated again—to a human? They have twin girls, Myste and Raven. And Kearnan has a mate now too, Serena, Alesandra's granddaughter. They have a daughter, Morgan."

"I'll get back to the mill since you don't need me here," Richard said.

"I'll finish rechecking the blueprints," Josh added.

Both men turned and walked away, the wolf Mia at Josh's side.

Alesandra laid her hand on George's arm and nodded to Belle. "I'll get back to that formula we were working on."

"Perhaps later you will tell me of your stay in Canada," George said to Garth. After a nod, he escorted Alesandra back the way they'd come.

Looking from Belle to Alex, Garth sighed. "I can't stay long."

Belle's frown was thunderous. "Why not? You just got here!"

"I'm being hunted."

Chapter Three

ഐ

"How long did you stay with Kearnan?" Belle asked as she set a glass of lemonade before her brother.

"Two days and nights. I didn't think it would be safe to stay longer, but I am having some of my possessions sent to him though, disguised as a medical shipment."

"So then you know about everything happening in the family?"

Smiling, Garth nodded. "Serena and the baby are good for Kearnan. I've never seen him happier. He told me all about Dad and Moira and their daughters too. He even had some pictures. Beautiful girls. Then, when he told me about you being here, I decided that northern Wyoming was far enough out in the wilds for me to chance a visit."

Leaning against the back of his chair, Garth stretched his legs out under the table and sighed contentedly. It was nice to just sit and relax. As he sipped his lemonade, he looked around the large combination living room/dining room/office of the cabin that smelled of fresh air and sunshine. Belle's touch was everywhere from the bright yellow curtains and throw pillows on the sofa before the huge stone fireplace to the aromatic, multicolored wildflowers in colorful clay vases on the mantel and in the center of the table where they sat.

Garth grinned to himself. Who'd have believed a city girl like Belle could be so happy in such a rustic setting. But then, they had been born in a forest. He glanced at her. She looked happy. Obviously, Whitehorse was good for her.

Sliding into the chair next to her mate, his sister smiled at him. "It's so good to see you. I've missed you, you know. We all have."

"Enough, Belle." Alex laced his fingers together and fixed a stony gaze on Garth. "Who's hunting you?"

When Belle would have retorted, he held up his hand. "No. He's not talking about some human, great-white-hunter wannabe who thought he saw a big wolf. There's more to it than that, isn't there?"

Nodding, Garth leaned forward in his chair and crossed his arms on the table. "Five years ago I was at loose ends looking for something exciting to do with my life. Dad hooked me up with a CIA agent he knows, Ken Cover, a Were like us, to help ferret out terrorists and extremists — both foreign and domestic — in the Western states and along the Canadian border. It was a totally secret program. Only a few people in the CIA knew about it, but it was very successful. Unfortunately, Cover was wounded in a gun battle two years ago so they transferred in a new supervisor." Lifting his glass, Garth gulped. "The guy's an asshole, has his nose in everything."

Alex nodded. "Saw it as his ticket to a big promotion."

"Exactly. My job was to sneak up on any camps I found and record conversations. I was really good at it."

"As a wolf, right?"

Gulping more lemonade, Garth nodded. "I rigged a miniature camera to a collar I could wear around my neck. Simple. Slip on the collar, shift, and trot off to camp. If any of the suspects ever saw me, and that rarely happened, they saw a wolf."

"You could have been shot!" Belle snapped.

Garth shrugged. "It goes with the territory."

"How was your cover blown?"

"Asshole commander wanted to know what kind of dog I was using and where it was."

Alex cocked an eyebrow. "Dog?"

"He found the collar and pulled some hairs off it. I sneaked into his office and stole them back. I thought I'd gotten them all, but he'd already sent a couple to a lab." Garth shook his head. "I did manage to get a look at the report that came back. It stated the DNA results were inconclusive because of contamination. The hairs were wolf, but human DNA was mixed in with it." Garth grinned. "He got a reprimand about the proper way to gather and ship evidence."

As Belle sat with her hands clasped together, Alex sipped his own lemonade. "So why wasn't that the end of it?"

"With anybody else it would have been." Rising, Garth raked his hair back off his forehead. "I should have had a dog with me, then he never would have stolen those hairs. Emil Sorescu is the son of Rumanian immigrants from the Carpathian Mountains." He turned to face his sister and her mate. "He was eight when his family came to the US. He grew up with the old stories. Unlike most people in this country, he *believes* werewolves, vampires, and such exist, and now he's out to prove it. If he can catch me, he'll lock me up and keep drawing blood samples until everyone believes it."

His sister shook her head. "But Garth, that's so farfetched. Americans don't believe in werewolves, at least most of them don't. What's more, Dad's a member of the Hierarchy now. There's no way the news would ever get out."

Garth smiled at his sister. "No, I'm sure it wouldn't. We're talking about the CIA here, Belle. They wouldn't want this information to get out either. But they would set out to locate and capture every Were they could—with their families. Then they'd coerce them into working for the government."

Leaning back in his chair, Alex stared at his brother-in-law. "How many men are after you?"

"At this point, just one. Sorescu couldn't exactly tell his superiors the real reason he wanted to arrest me. And Cover's recovered from his injury and has been promoted. He's working from the inside to rein in Sorescu."

"If Cover is back, why doesn't he just order Sorescu to back off?"

"Sorescu accused me of being a double agent. He had some trumped-up evidence to back his claim. So, until Cover can prove Sorescu's lying and I'm innocent, I'm on the run."

"Only one guy hunting you?" The tenseness left Alex's body. "There's not a Were in the world who can't disappear if he wants to. Better yet, wait for him and kill him. Lure him here if you want. I'll help you get rid of him, and his body will never be found."

Garth shook his head. "If he doesn't report in, Sorescu will assume he's dead. Then there will be an inquiry as to where and how he died. They might not find the body, but they'll have a general idea about where he disappeared. More agents will be sent. I'd rather just deal with one."

"So lose him."

Sighing, Garth gulped more lemonade. "I've spent the last two years traveling between Canada and the US. But every time I shift, he eventually shows up. Might take a few months, but he finds where I've been. He's that good."

Alex's fist rattled the glasses on the table when his fist connected with it. "Why the fuck are you here then? Belle's your sister. This is one of the first places I'd look."

Garth shook his head again. "The one thing he doesn't know is my real name. I have a false identity, one not even the CIA spooks could determine wasn't real. But then, Cover created it himself in the agency database.. As far as this guy is concerned, Garth Gray doesn't even exist. He's hunting somebody else, so the family is safe."

"Who's he looking for?"

"Best you don't know. Then, if he does show up here, you can honestly say you never heard of me." Gulping the last of his lemonade, Garth enjoyed the tart taste of the cool liquid as it flowed across his tongue and down his throat. Once he left, he'd be back on raw meat and water. "So now you know why I can't stay. Until I get word from Cover that Sorescu's goon's been called off, it's best I shift and head back into Canada. I'll stop back here every six months or so to let you know how I'm doing. Cover's in touch with Dad. Once everything is straightened out, Dad will contact you. Any questions?"

Whitehorse was shaking his head. He seemed relaxed but there was a slight tenseness around his shoulders.

Garth could understand why. If his mate's brother had just shown up and told him a government spy might come poking around his pack looking for werewolves, he'd be tense too. Still, Whitehorse looked like he was in control of himself and wouldn't have any trouble handling anything. Besides, Garth had spent a few days in the area. There were quite a few humans here, some even employed in the pack lumbermill. And from the snippets of conversation he'd picked up, none of them knew they were surrounded by Weres.

He shifted his concentration to his sister.

She was staring at him, a thoughtful expression on her face.

Smiling, Garth shook his head. He knew that look. She was plotting something. "No, I am not going to lose myself in New York City. I am *not* interested in getting into the family business. I told you that six years ago and haven't changed my mind."

She shook her head. "No. It's not that."

Garth chuckled. Belle always had some kind of angle. "What is it then?"

She wet her lips, opened her mouth, then closed it again.

He grinned at her. "This idea really must be out in left field if it's taking this long for you to spit it out."

Sucking in a huge breath, she laced her fingers together and stared at him. "Garth, Eileen's here."

The werewolf in his soul roared to life. *My mate!*

The glass in his hand shattered. Sparkling shards bounced on the table.

Garth stared at his sister. Eileen was here? Now? After all these years? "Where?"

A smile twitched at the corner of her lips. "A small cabin,

five miles north, on the ridge."

Black mist swirled and the clothing Garth had been wearing fell to the floor. As dust motes danced, the mist shifted into a black wolf that leaped for the door.

Belle's chair slammed to the floor as she jumped to her feet. "Garth!"

He was gone before she finished his name.

Shaking her head she stared at the discarded clothing. "I didn't think anybody in the family but Dad could shift while wearing clothing."

Stepping to her side, Alex clasped her arm. "What's going on? Who's Eileen to him?"

Belle smiled a small smile. "His mate."

Chapter Four

ဢ

As he leaped through the dense forest, silky ferns and whiplike saplings slapped Garth's face and body. The enticing scents of deer and elk teased his sensitive nostrils. When he leaped over a downed tree, a ruffed grouse exploded from beneath his feet.

He ignored all of it.

The werewolf in his soul urged him on—faster, faster.

Eileen, Eileen, Eileen.

Her name pounded through his veins as he raced through stands of aspen, oak, pine, and beech.

Eileen, Eileen, Eileen.

Joy exploded in his heart. His first love. His only love. She was here!

Eileen, Eileen, Eileen.

Old anger surged. Her family, parents, two brothers—all four had been appalled that their daughter had stooped to show interest in an Abomination, a Were whose mother had been a wolf. They had stolen her away in the middle of the night and disappeared.

His anger dissipated almost as quickly as it rose. The past wasn't important. *Now* was important.

Eileen, Eileen, Eileen.

Happiness enveloped him. The woman with whom he'd first shared the joys of sexual love, the woman he'd mated on a sultry summer night under the full Solstice moon. Finally, he'd found her.

Eileen, sweet, sweet Eileen.

As he ran, Garth gave over the control of his body to the wolf half of his soul. His mind, his human mind, returned to the memories of that hot, Solstice night almost ten years ago.

* * * * *

She teased him unmercifully throughout the day, appearing seemingly out of nowhere to touch, caress, kiss. Then she'd slip away, her coquettish laughter promising and denying at the same time so that he hadn't been able to concentrate on the small figurines he was carving for his grandmother. Once, when she'd kissed the back of his neck as she passed by, his knife had slipped, and he'd cut himself.

As he cursed, she'd laughed and disappeared.

Unable to focus, Garth set his carving aside. Most of the male members of the pack were in much the same condition he was. On Solstice nights, the desires of females held sway, and they teased their men unmercifully.

As he sucked the blood from his thumb, Garth contemplated the night to come. Eileen and he had both been virgins the first time they'd made love, but that had been two months earlier. Tonight, as the moon rose high into the sky, instinct would drive them, sex would be hotter, harder, more intense. In the middle of the afternoon, he was barely able to keep his cock from hardening.

Many of the men didn't even bother trying to hide the long, thick bulges straining against the fronts of their pants, especially those with mates in heat. They stalked, paced, shifted from human to wolf and back again — snarling and snapping at each other.

The women reveled in their power — teasing, tempting. By the time the moon rose, the men would be stretched to their limits. Once the women shifted and ran, the men would no longer be able to control themselves.

But their anticipation was no stronger than Garth's.

Eileen had agreed to mate him. Tonight, under the full

moon, she truly would become his forever.

Somehow, he made it through the day. That night, as the moon rose and the wolves howled, Eileen had slipped away from her parents' house and met him. Together they'd raced for miles through the forest until they reached a secluded glade. There, Eileen had shifted and stood before him in all her naked beauty.

Even then, with the moon's light enveloping and urging him to take her, to dominate her, he tried to be gentle, but Eileen would have none of it. Launching herself onto him, she knocked him to the ground.

Before he could so much as wrap his arms around her, she rose to her knees and sucked his aching cock into her mouth, sliding her warm, wet tongue up and down and around, nipping the head, nibbling its length. Burying his hands in her hair, he'd spread his legs, and she sucked his balls into her mouth, one after the other, until they burned with a fiery hardness he could barely tolerate.

As his thigh muscles tensed and he arched his hips towards her, she sat back on her haunches and laughed a low, delicious laugh that sent shivers dancing up and down his spine.

Reaching out, she'd wrapped her hand around his cock and pumped him — twice.

As he dug his hands into the soft dirt at his sides, cum seeped from the head, and she laughed again.

"You are so very hard," she whispered. "You'll feel so good buried deep inside of me."

Releasing him, she cupped her breasts, pinched her already pebbled nipples. Throwing back her head, she shivered and moaned. After a deep breath, she looked at him again. "I love when you suck on these, when you nibble my nipples." Her hungry gaze pierced his. "But not tonight, not yet. There's time for that later." She shivered again and slid her hands down her rib cage, over her abdomen, down through the soft, honey-colored curls between her thighs. "I'm wet, Garth. I'm ready for you. Mate me. Now! Grind your cock into me. Bury it so deep I don't know where I end and you begin."

Then Eileen turned around and bent over, resting her forearms on the ground. Her ass was in the air, her legs spread. Between them, she was wet, slightly swollen, her lips a deep, rich red color.

As he rolled to her side and rose to his knees, her scent surrounded him — hot, eager woman, musky with need.

"Now, Garth! I need you!"

The werewolf in his soul howled, and his own voice became nothing more than a full-chested growl as he positioned himself behind her and rubbed his cock along the crack in her ass. This bitch was his!

Her moan mated with his growl.

His balls were drawn tight against his body and his cock ached with a hardness he'd never before experienced.

He slipped his hand between her thighs, slid first one finger then a second between her slippery lips and buried them deep, pushing, twisting, pulling them back.

She ground her hips against his hand. "Yes, Garth, more, harder, deeper."

As her body writhed and twisted beneath his hands, his werewolf soul stripped away the last of his control. Playing with her wasn't enough. He had to bury his cock into her, plunge in and out until she acknowledged that she belonged to him.

Spreading the swollen, red lips of her cunt, he kneed her thighs farther apart and rubbed the head of his cock against her, coating it with her musky moisture.

"Mine!" he growled. "You are mine."

She bucked back against him. "Pleeeease…"

Bending over her back, he nipped her shoulder. "Submit. You are mine!" He nipped the back of her neck.

She bucked once more.

Sweat broke out on his forehead as he held himself back.

He would not, could not satisfy her until she acknowledged him. He slid his cock between her legs, sliding it back and forth against her clit.

She shuddered under him. "Yours," she finally moaned. "Yours."

Letting go of his control, Garth plunged into her, driving her forward in the process. After a final nip on her shoulder, he straightened. When he placed his palm on the small of her back, she arched back against him. He grunted with satisfaction when he slid even more deeply into her. "That's it, tighten your muscles around me. Squeeze my cock."

"Damn it, Garth, move!" She swiveled her hips.

He twisted his the other way, pulled his cock out, and rammed it back in again.

She pushed her ass back against his hips to meet his thrust. "Yes! Harder! Deeper!"

"You want it harder?" Grabbing her hips to steady her, Garth complied, sliding in and out, twisting left and right, groaning as her hot, wet muscles tightened around his cock, squeezing, sucking, causing his balls to burn and tighten even more. He ground his hips against her ass. "Gods, you're so hot, so tight!"

In and out, in and out, twist left, twist right. Garth thrust and plunged, faster, harder.

Finally, when he thought he couldn't hold back any longer, Eileen shuddered and cried out—half howl of joy, half scream of ecstasy.

At the same time, fire exploded from his balls and erupted through his cock. Hips jerking, he tilted his head back and howled his triumph.

*****

Lost in his memories, Garth ran on. Somewhere up ahead of him was the woman he'd never stopped loving.

Chapter Five

෨

A soft breeze danced amongst the trees, teasing the fresh green leaves into dips and shimmies. Shadows lengthened as the sun slowly dropped behind the mountains. Deep in the forest, an owl hooted. Leaves rustled as two young squirrels chased each other.

In the clearing before the small cabin, Eileen leaned against a beech tree, a wolf on either side of her.

She inhaled, smiled, and inhaled again. Myriad scents floated on the breeze, fresh, clean, wholesome. No gasoline fumes, no smoke, no—humans. Nothing but nature. Other than leaving Louisiana, coming to this cabin was the smartest thing she'd done in a long time.

She looked up at the sky. Only a few more days and Solstice would be here. She sighed, her memories straying to a Solstice night long ago.

The owl hooted again and Eileen wrenched her mind to the present. Traveling down memory lane wouldn't do her any good. Best to live in the present and plan for the future with her new pack. The past was the past, and it was best that it stayed buried.

A soft snore slipped from the wolf's head cradled in her lap.

Eileen giggled as the old white wolf on other side snorted. *Humans aren't the only ones who snore.*

Eileen dragged her hand over the top of Silver's head.

He sighed in his sleep.

"What's it like, Willow, to give up being human? To live only as a wolf?"

The gray wolf turned her head and stared into Eileen's face. *It's a choice not to be entered into lightly. Every Were I've met who made that choice did so to stay with a mate. Is there a full wolf you wish to mate? Or do you just wish to run from your human problems?*

Sighing, Eileen shook her head. Maybe she shouldn't have told the old wolf her story when she first came to the cabin, but she'd felt it was the right thing to do. Willow was a Were, one who'd left her human side behind and returned to the forest to live out her life with the full wolf she'd mated. Besides, talking about how Bill had abused her made it easier to bear, helped her to heal.

The old wolf pushed herself up onto her haunches. *Returning to the forest for a few days or a season is a good way to clear the head. Returning to the forest to hide from your problems will not resolve them.*

Leaning her head against the tree at her back Eileen closed her eyes. Willow was right. She didn't really want to spend the rest of her life in the forest as a wolf. Not that she didn't love that part of her. Nothing could compare to the exhilaration of racing through a wild, primordial forest for the sheer joy of running. Very few things could compare to the hot rush of adrenaline that pumped through her veins as she made a kill or the taste of hot blood gushing in her mouth. Eileen snorted mostly to herself. Then again, nothing could compare to the soft silkiness of soaking in a tub of hot, fragrant water, a house with four walls and a solid roof when rain was pouring down or snow was piling up, or the taste of a cinnamony apple pie.

Nothing.

Except…

Again her past intruded on her present, and a man's face appeared in her mind. Not Bill, the arrogant Were her parents had pushed at her until she agreed to mate him, the bastard who had beat her just because she'd miscarried his child. No, not him. The only time she thought of that asshole was when she moved too quickly and her almost healed ribs ached. If she ever saw him again, it would be too soon.

If I ever see him again, I'll be ready for him, she promised herself. *He'll be the one with scrapes and bruises, not me.*

No, the man whose face she saw was Garth's, her first love, the Were she'd thought she'd spend her life with.

Eileen smiled as she remembered him. Tall and gangly with an open, honest face topped by a crop of thick, black hair, he'd been so serious, so sure of himself—and her. She hadn't really paid that much attention to him when his family had first come to live with her pack, but then, most members didn't.

Whispers had followed all of the Grays. After his wolf mate died, their father Artemis had done the unthinkable—returned from the forest with five half-wolf, half-Were children. Many in the pack had been outraged, but Artemis' mother was a powerful woman, female Alpha when she was younger, godmother to the current female Alpha. The pack had reluctantly agreed to allow the Grays to stay—after Artemis explained they'd be staying only long enough for his children to master their humanity. Then they would leave.

Her parents hadn't cared one way or the other, they said. When Eileen had become close friends with Artemis' two daughters, Belle and Melody, they'd encouraged the friendship. Her family didn't have particularly high status, and for Eileen to spend time in the house of the old Alpha was a coup.

Eileen opened her eyes and smiled at Willow. "You would have liked Garth."

Garth? The wolf sat with her ears pricked forward, watching, waiting.

Eileen nodded. "I met him at his grandmother's house. He was sitting on the porch, carving a fox. His hands were so big, yet the carving was so small, so exquisite, so realistic."

Pushing Silver's head off her lap, Eileen drew up her legs, wrapped her arms around her legs and rested her chin on her knees. "He gave me that carving. I still have it."

"Why?"

Staring up at the darkening sky, Eileen sighed. "I fell in

love with him."

The other half of your soul?

She nodded. "I had no doubts. Neither did he. We mated on Summer Solstice two years later. That's when I found out just what my parents thought of 'Abominations' like Garth." She blinked back a tear. "We were gone before the week was over. They never told me we were leaving. All I remembered was going to sleep and waking up in a car halfway to Louisiana. I tried to get away, but they watched me all the time, my parents and my brothers. And Mom gave me a letter that was supposed to be from Garth's father, one that said I wasn't good enough for his son. It was a lie, but I was young and naïve."

Sighing heavily, she blinked back more tears. "I wonder what he thought of me after that, leaving him without a word right after we'd mated. He probably hated me. I made a fool out of him."

At her side, Silver jerked his head up, struggled to his feet. *Someone comes. Were.*

Willow's nose quivered.

Eileen lifted her head and inhaled, but the fickle breeze shifted and swirled away, taking the new scent with it.

A burst of blue exploded from the edge of the clearing as an angry jay flew away.

The playful squirrels scurried up a stout oak.

A velvet-antlered deer burst into the clearing, skidded to a halt when he saw the two wolves before him and bounded off to the left.

The werewolf in Eileen's soul awoke, shifted, raised its head.

The breeze shifted again, dipped and eddied, swirled around them.

As her werewolf soul howled with joy, Eileen froze. The wind carried a scent she'd never forgotten, *his* scent.

As she scrambled to her feet, a huge black wolf leaped into

the clearing. Almost immediately, mist enveloped him. In seconds, the man she'd just been daydreaming about was striding towards her.

As she rose to her feet, elation exploded in Garth's heart. It was her. True, she was older, more mature. She was still short, still slender, but her figure was slightly more voluptuous, curvy in all the right places, flaring hips, slender waist, high breasts. Nor had her features changed much. He'd have recognized her anywhere. Honey-brown hair tumbled around her shoulders. Her mouth was still wide, her lower lip still pouty and full. Upturned, small nose, high cheekbones and forehead.

Garth stopped before her.

Her eyes, her lovely golden eyes were wide with surprise.

Before she could utter a word, he wrapped his arms around her and hugged her to him.

The wolf in his soul howled with triumph. *My mate. I have found my mate.*

Chapter Six

ဆာ

"Need something, Belle? Dave said you wanted to talk to me."

Belle turned away from the window.

Jill was dusting off the seat of her pants. "Sorry about the sawdust, but the carpenters are just finishing up the deck at the back of the B&B."

"It doesn't matter." Belle paused. "Jill, my brother Garth is here."

Jill shrugged. "I'm glad for you, but what does that have to do with me?" Then she frowned. "You don't expect me to be interested in him, do you? I've already agreed to mate Dave on Solstice."

Smiling, Belle shook her head. "No, I don't. Everybody knows you're going to mate Dave, and we're all happy about it. You two are perfect together. No, Garth's being here will affect Eileen."

Belle waited, but her new friend still looked confused.

Then, comprehension leaped onto Jill's face. Her eyes widened. "Garth? *The* Garth Eileen mated before she came to Louisiana? The one her parents took her away from?"

Belle nodded.

"Where is he?"

Belle glanced out the window again. "Considering he can run pretty fast when he wants to, probably at her cabin."

A worried look appeared on the other woman's face. "You told him where she was? Are you sure that was such a good idea?"

Walking across the room, Belle flopped down onto the sofa and clutched a pillow to her chest and shrugged. "I don't know, but I felt like I had to. He was so devastated when he lost her. As far as he's concerned, they're still mated. He would never have forgiven me if he found out she was here and I didn't tell him." She looked up at Jill. "How do you think Eileen will feel? We were pretty close when we were younger, but it's been so many years since I've seen her. How is she going to react to having him get close to her? I'm totally lost on this one, Jill. Human women who've been beaten by their husbands often have a hard time trusting men again, and your brother did beat her pretty severely. How will she react when Garth gets close, tries to touch her? He will, you know. She's his mate. Will she freak out?"

Sliding down into a comfortable leather chair, Jill pulled her legs up, crossed them, and propped her elbows on her knees. She stared into the fireplace. "I'm not a hundred percent sure, but I don't think so. Bill's attack took her completely by surprise, and she was still emotionally drained from losing the baby." She glanced at Belle. "You know what we're like, we female Weres. We're not like human women, some of whom take the abuse for years and years. We fight back. Eileen just never got the chance, he was on her so fast. His first punch practically knocked her unconscious. One of the few things she regrets about leaving Louisiana so fast is not being able to get a few licks in on Bill."

Belle nodded. "That's what I figured. I mean, if it had been me, I'd have shifted and done my best to rip his throat out." She leaned back. "And she did say it was the first time he'd ever hit her."

Nodding, Jill sat up, shifting her feet to the floor. "Bill always yelled a lot, but he never hit her before. I don't know what bug he got up his ass, because he even hit me when I tried to keep him from locking her in the closet. I think it scared him, the way he reacted, because he tore out of the house like all the demons from hell were after him."

"Why didn't you fight back?"

Sighing, Jill grimaced. "When he slapped me, I lost my balance and slipped. My head hit the corner of the table. By the time I wasn't seeing stars anymore, he was gone. So I got a hammer and screwdriver out of the basement and took the closet door off the hinges. Eileen was a real mess, so I threw some clothes in a suitcase, loaded us both into my parents' car, and took off. You pretty much know the rest."

"You think Eileen will be okay?"

Jill rubbed her chin. "I think she will. It's not like she was physically abused for years." Then she grinned. "She left a note on the table telling Bill to go fuck himself. She also wrote that if she ever saw him again, she'd rip off his balls."

Belle grinned. "Sounds like he didn't break her. That's the Eileen I knew."

"Yeah. She's a lot tougher than she looks."

Before Belle could reply, the sound of a small scuffle slipped through the screen door.

"Meeeeeeerrrooooowww!"

Tossing the pillow back onto the couch, Belle pushed herself to her feet. "Why can't you learn to open the door yourself?" she said as she crossed the room and opened the door.

A gangly, almost-grown calico cat sauntered in, a struggling mouse between her jaws.

"And why do you keep bringing them back alive?" she continued as the cat released the mouse and chased it across the room.

They're more fun to play with this way.

Jill giggled. "A cat living with a werewolf. I wouldn't have believed it if I hadn't seen it myself."

You have no idea how lucky you people are that I choose to stay. The cat pounced on the mouse, trapped it between her paws, and looked over her shoulder at Belle. *Where would your mate least like to find it?*

Both women burst out laughing.

Bracing her hand on the back of the sofa, Belle grinned and struggled for breath. "I—*hiccup*—swear, Callie—*hiccup*. One of these—*hiccup*—days, Alex will ban—*hiccup*—you from the house."

The cat smiled a cat smile. *He'll have to catch me first, won't he?*

* * * * *

Eileen wiggled and squirmed until she was able to get her arms in front of her and plant her palms on his chest.

Corded muscle flexed beneath the smooth, bare skin under her hands. Soft, curling hairs teased her fingers. His chest had more hair on it, and he'd grown taller. Her head barely reached his collarbone, and his chest was also broader, much, much broader.

His scent surrounded her, filled her.

She pushed. "Garth! Let me go," she said in a muffled voice. "I can't breathe."

Instantly he loosened his hug, but he didn't let her go. "Is it really you? Are you really here?"

She felt his gaze on the top of her head.

Another deep breath. She could taste him now. Hot, male, Garth.

Shuddering mentally, she stared at his chest. When did he get all these muscles? Her gaze wandered upwards. His shoulders and neck looked like they were strong enough to carry all the troubles of the world. Tilting her head back, Eileen stared up at him. His chin was still firm though now there were real whiskers sprouting, not the peach fuzz she remembered. Fine, white teeth gleamed as he smiled down at her. She stopped her perusal at his nose. There was a bump that hadn't been there before, and it was slightly crooked. Sometime during the long years since she'd seen him, he'd broken it.

She looked higher. His hair was still dark as night but longer than he used to wear it. Wisps of it fell forward over his shoulders. Then, finally, she looked into his eyes. They were the same silvery gray she remembered, gray that turned into hardened steel with anger and soft mountain mist with passion.

His eyes were locked with hers as he stared intensely into her face. Silvery mist swirled in his eyes.

Eileen shivered. No one had ever looked at her like this, like she was the most desirable woman in the world. She shivered again as he slid his big hands up her arms.

"Eileen?"

His deep voice held the promise of passion.

She swallowed. He still wanted her. His hips and rock-hard thighs pressed against her stomach, as did his twitching cock.

Garth. Her Garth, so open, so honest. They'd promised they'd always love each other, that no one would ever come between them.

Closing her eyes, Eileen dropped her chin onto her chest. She'd been so young, so naïve. She should have known her parents would never let them stay together. Now, she'd changed. She wasn't the same girl he'd known.

"Garth," she acknowledged with a whisper as she struggled to escape his gentle clasp.

"Gods, but I've missed you." After a momentary lightening of his hands on her arms, he let her go.

She didn't answer him. Her heart felt like it was going to burst.

"Eileen?" Confusion mixed with the passion in his voice.

She took another step back. "Garth. How are you?"

He stepped forward. "Eileen, what's wrong? It's me, Garth, your mate."

Tears welled. Oh gods. She shook her head. "Garth, I... Oh shit."

His forehead wrinkled as a frown slid onto his face.

"What's wrong?"

Blinking back tears, she spun away. Hugging herself, she rubbed her arms. "You know I didn't leave you, don't you?"

She felt rather than saw him step behind her.

"I know. Your parents took you away. I, we, my father tried to find you. Where did you go?"

"Louisiana, a small town on the Gulf. There's a pack there that runs shrimp boats. They keep mostly to themselves. It was the perfect place for my parents to hide me."

His warm breath caressed the back of her neck. "But now I've found you." His lips followed his breath.

She wrenched herself away. "No. I can't." Spinning, she planted her palm on his chest. "I was miserable without you, but my parents didn't care. I wanted to run away, to come back to you, but they watched me. Then they gave me a letter they said was from your father. It said I wasn't good enough for you."

His nostrils flared. "My father never…"

Eileen nodded. "I know that—now. But I was so young, so naïve. I believed it. My family had such low pack status. And your father… Even though he'd run feral all those years, his status was still so much higher than my family's."

A growl rumbled in his chest. "I told you before that didn't matter."

She shook her head. "Let me finish." Staring up into his eyes, she continued. "My parents pushed me to date the unmated males of the pack in Louisiana. Months had gone by since I'd seen you, then a year, two. I was so lonely, I gave in."

She ignored his louder growl.

"The pack Alpha had an unmated brother. When he showed interest in me, my parents were ecstatic. They pushed me at him. So did my brothers. And he had a sister who had become my friend."

Eileen continued to stare at him. "Please, you have to understand. I was alone, so alone. I needed…"

Anger cracked in his voice. "What?"

She swallowed. "To feel like someone loved me."

His voice echoed off the mountains. "I loved you! I always loved you!"

"You weren't there!"

He stared back at her. "What did you do?"

She dropped her gaze and concentrated on the hand she still had pressed against his chest. "I mated him when I was twenty."

"No! You were already mated—to me."

Tears rolling down her cheeks, she shook her head. "It had been four years since I'd seen you. I believed your father didn't want us together. What was I supposed to do? I believed I'd never see you again."

The pain in his voice wrung her heart. "You could have waited. I did." He stepped back, and mist swirled as he spun away. The black wolf sprinted into the forest without looking back.

Tears streaming down her cheeks, Eileen sank onto the steps that led up to the cabin's porch. She hadn't thought she could ever feel any worse than she did after Bill beat her. She was wrong. He'd hurt her body. She'd just broken her own heart.

Chapter Seven

ഌ

Belle looked up as the door slammed open.

Garth heard wooden splinters trickle to the floor behind it. He didn't give a damn.

Jumping up onto the back of the sofa, Callie stretched. *Why are you half-humans so noisy?*

Stopping in mid-stride, Garth stared at her. "What the hell are you doing with a cat? And did she just talk?"

"It's a long story," his sister said as she rose to her feet. "Did you find Eileen?"

Garth's snarl rattled the windows. "She mated another Were! Mated someone else! She was mated to me! I loved her. What kind of Were is she?"

When his fist hammered down onto the table, it shuddered then collapsed.

The cat hissed, fluffed out all her fur, and catapulted off the sofa to disappear through another doorway.

Garth snarled after her. Good. He didn't like cats anyway.

"Damn it, Garth! That's my table."

"I don't give a damn about your fucking table. Eileen mated somebody else!"

Planting her fists on her hips, Belle snapped. "And this surprises you? You know how manipulative and controlling her parents and older brother were, how young she was. How was she supposed to hold out against them?"

Garth stopped in front of her. "I don't know, but she should have."

She glared up at him. "Why?"

He towered over her, did his best to intimidate her. "Because I still love her!"

Belle wasn't intimidated in the least. "And how was she supposed to know that when she hadn't seen you for years?"

As he clenched and unclenched his fists, Garth's entire body shook. Damn Belle and her common sense. "Fuck you!"

For a moment, her mouth dropped open. Then her soft gray eyes hardened to steel. "How dare you talk to me like that!"

A tiny part of Garth's mind told him he might have gone too far with that last comment, especially when Belle started ripping at her clothing, but he didn't care. Closing his eyes, he struggled to draw a breath. His chest felt as if it were wrapped in bands of steel. His heart had never ached like it did now.

A sharp pain in his calf pulled him out of his misery.

Blood trickled down his leg.

Belle had shifted and bitten him.

"You bitch."

When she leaped through the screen door, he shifted and followed her.

In the middle of the clearing, she spun around and faced him, growling and snarling.

He charged right at her.

She deftly leaped to the side and nipped his haunch as he went by.

Whirling on his hind legs, he leaped at her again.

Rolling underneath him, she bit his tail.

Howling with rage, Garth turned to face his sister again.

Belle stood with her four feet planted firmly, lips drawn back in a vicious snarl.

Simultaneously, they launched themselves at each other.

"What the hell is going on?" Alex snapped when he reached the clearing.

"Belle and her brother are having a disagreement," Dave answered. He grabbed Alex's arm when his Alpha started forward. "Don't worry. She's not hurt. As a matter of fact, she's beating the crap out of him."

"What? How?"

Dave jerked his chin towards the fighting wolves. "See for yourself."

As Alex watched, Belle slipped in and bit her brother's ear.

Unclenching his fists, he willed his body to relax. He wasn't going to have to defend his mate, not today anyway. "Her brother's holding back."

Dave nodded. "Yeah. Still, she's faster than any Were I've ever seen and has moves I didn't think a Were could do."

Alex grunted as he watched the two black wolves feint and dodge around each other. The big one was bleeding. He grunted again. He knew exactly how quick his mate was in a fight.

A roaring cough off to their left had both Alex and Dave both stepping forward at the same time.

The two wolves stopped their fighting and whirled to face the new danger approaching them, a silver-tipped grizzly lumbering out of the forest.

With a howl of triumph, Garth charged towards it.

Shifting immediately, Belle sprinted to her husband. "Stubborn, idiotic moron. He's impossible when he gets like this."

After holding her at arm's length to make sure there wasn't a scratch on her, Alex shrugged out of his shirt and wrapped it around his naked mate. "Gets like this?"

Shoving her arms into the sleeves of his shirt, she buttoned it up. "When Garth gets pissed, he needs to work off his anger. I was just obliging him."

Alex didn't hide the anger in his voice. "You could have been hurt."

She snorted. "If he put one tiny scratch on my skin, he'd

have to deal with Dad. Not even Garth will challenge Dad. Besides, I'm too quick for him." Fisting her hands on her hips, she glared at the two fighters. "Pain in the ass brother. Now I'll have to spend the rest of the evening patching him up. The cuts I gave him were nothing. I have a feeling George won't be so gentle."

Dave snorted. "I have a feeling your brother doesn't want him to be."

In the clearing the wolf charged.

Rising on his hind legs, the bear swung his heavy paw, connecting solidly with the wolf's ribs.

Garth flew four feet and bounced when he hit the ground. He immediately scrambled to his feet and leaped towards the bear. Feinting left, he swerved to the right and opened a long gash on the bear's unprotected flank.

Roaring with rage, the bear turned far more quickly than anyone could have imagined and slashed his claws along the wolf's ribs.

Garth's howl was a mixture of pain, frustration, and anger. He charged again, feinted left then right then left again.

Unimpressed, the bear coughed a rumbling roar and swiveled to face him.

Arms crossed over his chest, Alex watched the battle. He didn't mind in the least if one of Belle's brothers wanted to get the shit kicked out of him. He just wished it was Brendan instead of Garth. "What brought this on?"

"Garth found out Eileen had mated again," Belle answered in a piqued tone. "Honest to Pete, he knew what her parents were like. I don't know why he was so surprised."

"She repudiated that mate."

She nodded "Yeah, but I bet my thick-headed brother didn't stick around long enough for her to tell him."

"Maybe she didn't want to," Dave interjected. "Jill told me Eileen said she didn't want anything to do with any man or

Were again."

"That was before Garth got here. I'll bet she changes her story real quick," Belle muttered. "But she's just as stubborn and hardheaded as he is. Shit, it's not like I don't have enough to do as it is." She turned to Alex. "You're Alpha. Don't you think it's time to stop this before one of them really gets hurt?"

Alex grinned at her. "But it's a good fight. I'd say they're pretty evenly matched, don't you think, Dave?"

The pack Omega looked from Alex to Belle, shook his head, turned without a word, and disappeared into the forest.

Chuckling, Alex looked at his mate. "Smart man, Dave."

She was glaring at him. "Smarter than his Alpha sometimes. You want to sleep on the sofa with Callie tonight?"

"Okay," he said with a snort. "You want me to stop them, I will."

He didn't get the chance. By the time the two of them walked out into the clearing, both the bear and wolf stood still, facing each other, panting heavily. Both shifted at the same time.

"Draw?" George growled.

"Draw." Garth snarled back.

Blood from numerous cuts dripped from both. George had a nasty bite on his thigh. Garth had three parallel slashes on his ribs.

George smiled. "Good fight. Thanks."

Garth didn't. "Don't mention it," he snapped back.

Grunting, George turned and limped away.

"He's a brave man going to face Alesandra looking like that," Alex muttered as he and Belle halted not far from her brother.

"Feeling better now, moron?" his mate taunted.

Her brother snarled at her. "Enough, Belle. I'm not in the mood."

Alex grinned.

Belle didn't stop. "Jeez, Garth, how you can be so stupid!" she snapped as she prodded his cuts. "What do you think Eileen is doing here if she's mated to some Were in Louisiana?"

"Visiting."

"Who? She doesn't know anybody here."

"She knows you."

Throwing her hands into the air, she glared at him. "And how was she supposed to know I was here? We haven't been in contact for ten years. Neither of us knew where the other one was."

Alex grinned. Belle's brother was still pissed as hell. He and Belle were a lot alike.

"What does that have to do with anything?" Garth roared.

Belle's voice was full of disgust. "How you survived all these years I'll never know. Eileen repudiated her mate, idiot. She and her sister-in-law have asked for Sanctuary. The asshole her parents pushed her into mating beat her after she lost their child. She's *here* because she's *hiding*."

Alex chuckled as brother and sister stared at each other. Belle was pissed off, her brother was shocked speechless.

"He beat her?" he finally choked out. His entire body shuddered.

Deadly fury such as Alex had never seen appeared on Garth's face, enough fury to make the Alpha step back.

Black mist swirled once more as Garth shifted again. He leaped towards the forest, towards Eileen's cabin.

As Belle stepped after him, Alex wrapped his arms around her waist. "No. Let him go. They have to sort this out for themselves." He slid a hand under his shirt and cupped her between the legs. "There are better things for us to do, or do you still want me to sleep with that damn cat?"

Chapter Eight

ॐ

"Hoo. Hoo. Hoooooooooo."

"It's me. Who did you think it was?" Frowning into the darkness, Eileen sat on the edge of the porch, feet resting on the top step, elbows propped on her knees, chin resting on her fists.

The sounds and scents of the night surrounded her as she contemplated her life. Her body was almost healed, and she'd gotten her head together. She wasn't afraid of men. She didn't even hate them—not even Bill. Though every now and then she did wish she'd see him again so she could get in a couple of good bites before he knew what hit him. Yep, one good bite on his cock and one on his balls, and she'd be willing to call it even.

Sighing, Eileen looked around the moonlit clearing. She liked it here in this small cabin in the middle of nowhere with no one to bother her. What's more, she had two wolves for company, so she didn't even feel lonely. If she wanted human—well, partial human—companionship, it was only a short, five-mile hike down to Belle's. Life was good, better than it had been for longer than she cared to remember.

Shifting her butt, she sighed again. Trouble was, she wasn't content anymore, and it was all Garth's fault. Damn it, because of him, she was sitting here in the dark feeling miserable. She looked around again. Hell, it wasn't even really that dark. Stupid moon was almost full. It was practically as bright as day in the small clearing before the cabin.

She would have preferred utter darkness. It would fit her mood better.

The owl hooted again.

Stupid owl. Why did it have to hunt here? Why did all those happy insects have to chirp and whirr and hum? Why was the moon shining so brightly? It was supposed to be cloudy and damp and rainy and foggy — miserable weather to go with the way she felt.

Bushes rustled.

Willow and Silver trotted into the clearing. Silver carried a plump rabbit. As they passed Eileen, Willow licked her jowls. *A stupid one. It ran right into Silver's mouth.* Both wolves disappeared around the corner of the cabin.

"Stupid rabbit? Humph!" she muttered to the moon. "Stupid me. Stupid, stupid, stupid. I've gone and chased off the one Were I could really love. Could love? Bullshit. I've always loved him."

Blinking, she stared at nothing. Why did she tell him about Bill? She sighed and shook her head. "Because he deserved to know. Not telling him would have been a lie."

Eileen rubbed her arms — it was getting chilly — and contemplated a stray moonbeam that floated through the leaves of the tree next to the cabin. Even if she never saw Garth again, telling him about Bill had still been the right thing to do.

Rubbing her arms again, she looked up at the stars. Garth. She probably would never see him again.

The night breeze swirled.

The scents of wolf and blood tickled her nostrils.

Nostrils flaring, Eileen tensed and inhaled. What?

The breeze shifted.

After a few minutes, she relaxed. Wolf and blood. Willow and Silver and the rabbit they were sharing.

A single cloud floated across the moon, plunging the clearing into darkness.

Closing her eyes, Eileen inhaled fresh night air again. A late-night run. That's what she needed. Running always relaxed her. She could immerse herself into her wolf's soul and run and run and run until she was too exhausted to feel anything. Yes, that's what she'd do.

Standing, she loosened her ponytail, shook her hair free, and began to unbutton her shirt.

The cloud slid past the moon and soft light illuminated the clearing again.

Garth was striding across the clearing.

One button undone, Eileen froze.

He stopped a few feet away. "How much did he hurt you?"

As Eileen stared into Garth's face, she mentally cursed his sister.

Anger radiated from his tense body. "Tell me where he is and I'll kill him."

Tears welled in her eyes. Why did he have to be so damn noble? Blinking, she shook her head. "No. He's not worth it."

A deep growl rumbled from his chest. "Any Were who treats his—mate—in such a way deserves to die. That—Were—deserves to die for what he did to you."

She lifted her hand. "Oh Garth…"

She'd never seen him so angry.

Then she smelled blood, his blood. Her gaze snapped to his rib cage.

Though they were beginning to crust over, three parallel cuts still seeped blood. More of it was dried on his abdomen and hip.

She looked closer. "What happened to you?"

The nasty gashes on his ribs weren't his only injuries. His left earlobe was crusted with dried blood, and there were bites on his shoulder and calf. His right eye looked puffy. Most of his body was covered with a mixture of dirt and bloody mud.

After another quick perusal of his body, she looked up into his face. "How did this happen?"

His eyes looked as hard as steel. "The bear and I sparred."

"Sparred! Bullshit. This isn't sparring! It looks like George tried to gut you. Why? And those bites aren't from a bear.

They're from another wolf."

Shrugging, he rubbed his wrist. "Belle got mad at me." His stare never left her face.

As she bit her lip, Eileen felt her anger flare higher. Bill had never answered her questions either. Whenever she asked him for explanations, he'd told her it was none of her business or not to worry about it. Well, no man was going to ignore her questions again. She wasn't going to be treated like her thoughts and opinions didn't matter. "Damn it, Garth. You picked a fight, didn't you? Two fights. One with Belle and one with George. You weren't sparring with him, you were fighting. I remember how you and your brothers used to 'spar'!"

He narrowed his eyes. "What do you care?"

Curling her hands into fists, Eileen glared at him. "What do I care? You ass! Why wouldn't I care?"

He cocked an eyebrow. His stare became more intense. "You mated someone else."

Digging her nails into her palms, Eileen stamped her foot. Damn him. How could he not understand being taken away from him was the most traumatic experience of her life? "I was kidnapped — by my own parents — dragged off to a pack where I didn't know anyone in a place I'd never been before with no way to leave! I was lied to, manipulated into believing I was unacceptable to your family! I was pushed into mating another Were."

He wiped some dirt off his arm. "So?"

She gaped. She blinked back the tears that threatened to fall. "So? So! You are such an ass." Balling her fist, she punched him — on the still seeping cuts.

Fresh blood splattered, then more blood began to flow.

Shock and surprise leaped onto his face.

Eileen didn't even try to hide her smug smile.

He grimaced, grunted, sucked in a breath. "Fuck, that hurt."

She wiped her hand on her shirt, stretching her fingers to bring the feeling back. Punching him was like punching a wall. "Good. It was supposed to. Now let me stitch you up before you bleed to death or those cuts get infected."

"Why should I?"

"Because, you stupid ass, I love you."

Chapter Nine

ജ

Garth closed his eyes, all of his uncertainty and most of his anger flowing from his body.

Eileen loved him. For now, that was all he needed. He'd discover the name of the Were who'd hurt her another time. Then, he'd have revenge for both of them.

"Come on."

Opening his eyes, Garth looked at her. She was standing on the top step, the handle of a small, wicker basket over her arm. A couple of towels were thrown over her shoulder.

"Where are we going?"

Irritation flashed in her eyes and she snorted. "You don't honestly think I'll let you in my clean house looking like that, do you? It took me a week to get this place cleaned up, and I'm not going to have you dropping bloody mud and dirt all over. The stream that flows behind the cabin has a nice-sized pool in it about five minutes from here. You're going to take a bath and get that dirt off of you and out of those cuts and bites."

She stomped down the steps and pushed past him.

He inhaled.

She smelled like flowers—and sexy woman.

Her voice cracked. "Come on. I don't have all night."

His chuckle became a groan as he turned and followed her. Fighting with Belle was nothing—but the bear... Garth groaned again. George had slammed him to the ground more than once. Twice, he'd bounced. He ached all over, and those freaking cuts on his ribs were beginning to burn. As he followed Eileen, he gritted his teeth. She obviously didn't feel sorry for him in the least. The pace she set was practically a trot.

Garth pressed his arm against his side. Fuck, but that side of his ribs hurt too. At least they didn't ache enough to be cracked.

A pine branch snapped back and slapped him in the face.

"Don't dawdle."

His anger began to build again. "I'm not fucking 'dawdling'!" he snarled as he wrestled the branch out of his face.

"And don't curse at me or you can fix your own cuts."

He swallowed a sharp retort. Getting her even more angry with him wouldn't help, and he did need these cuts stitched. Even though werewolves healed faster than humans, they could still have cuts become infected if they weren't cared for properly.

He snarled quietly as she disappeared between two pine saplings. "Wouldn't be the first time." He dodged another branch and stepped from beneath the trees to the side of a stream. About thirty yards up the side of the mountain, water poured out of a rift in the face of a small cliff and tumbled into a pool at its base.

Her back to him, Eileen was hiking up the steep trail. "The water is only about two feet deep, and the floor of the pool is smooth rock. It's like sitting in a bathtub."

Painful fire now spreading outward from his cuts, Garth grunted and followed her. When he reached the top of the ridge, he strode past her straight into the water and sat down.

The burning pain was replaced with an icy ache. "Christ, woman! This water is cold!" He began to rise.

She grinned a malicious grin. "What did you expect from a mountain stream? And don't you dare get out of that water. You'll get used to it in a minute or two. Here." She threw a washcloth into his face. "Scrub yourself." A cake of soap plopped between his legs.

Teeth gritted, Garth glared at her as she busied herself with the basket she'd carried. A shiver raced up his spine, and he grabbed the soap. The sooner he got cleaned up, the sooner he'd be out of this freezing water.

Leaning back, he sucked in a breath and stuck the top of his head under the water cascading into the pool. After sitting up straight again, he lathered his hands and began washing his hair.

"I brought shampoo," Eileen interjected in an exasperated tone.

"This is good enough." He leaned back, shuddered when the icy water hit his head, and washed the soap out. Then he grabbed the washcloth floating on his knee, rubbed some soap on it, and scrubbed himself, being very careful when he finally got to his ribs.

His gasp drew her attention.

"Are you finished? I want a closer look at those slashes."

Garth waited until the pain in his side subsided—he shouldn't have rubbed the cuts so hard—then pushed himself to his feet and waded out of the pool.

"Sit here," she ordered.

He sat then stretched out on his back. Throwing his arm over his eyes, he said, "Do your worst."

"Don't tempt me," she snapped.

Garth felt rather than saw her kneel as his side. "Honestly, grown men fighting like children. What's the matter with you?"

Garth sighed. Was she going to be angry all night?

Her touch surprised him. He expected her to poke and prod. She didn't. Her fingers were gentle.

He heard a click. "What's that?"

"Flashlight. The moon is pretty bright, but do you want me to sew by its light?"

He shuddered. The thought of a needle in his flesh... "Do you have to? I mean, do you have the right kind of needle and thread?" He lowered his arm and stared at her.

Her head was bent, and she was using the flashlight to

study his wounds. Her sigh was more exasperated than anything. "Listen. These are deep cuts. You're going to have scars no matter what I do. And just bandaging them isn't going to work, even with as fast as you'll heal. Infection could set in if they reopen, and I can't see you staying still for the week or so it would take them to heal then."

He snorted. "Sew them up, but I sure hope you know what you're doing."

Her touch remained gentle, her voice low and soothing. "I took care of minor injuries while I was in Louisiana. Remember how I studied with the pack healer before my family up and left? The new pack didn't have a healer, and Mom went and told them I was one. She lied, but they didn't care. They didn't have anybody else. I learned as I worked."

Garth grunted then gasped as she pushed the needle through his flesh. She was being careful, but it still hurt.

"I'm sorry, really, but this is the best I can do."

Sweat beaded on his brow. "I know. Just get done as fast as you can." He grimaced and added, "Please."

"Not much longer."

Finally, after what seemed like an eternity, no more needle pricks. He felt her swab and wipe the cuts. "I'm going to pour some peroxide on them now."

"Peroxide!"

Hissing, fizzing, liquid fire attacked him.

Her hand on his chest kept him flat on his back. "I'm sorry, but at least it isn't alcohol. Now, I'm going to dab it dry, put on some ointment and then bandage you up, okay?"

Garth answered her with a grunt.

As she wiped, the fire receded. The ointment she slathered on his wounds was cool and soothing, and the last of the fire died away.

"Sit up so I can wrap this bandage around you to hold the other ones in place."

He complied.

When she finished, she looked into his face. "I have to clean the bites Belle gave you. Peroxide will work best."

Nodding, he closed his eyes and suffered in silence, though after his ribs, the slight pain he endured as she cleaned the bites was nothing.

"There," she finally said, "I think you'll live."

Opening his eyes, Garth stared at the woman kneeling by his side. "Good."

Ignoring the sharp ache that burst in his side, he wrapped his arms around her, pulled her onto his chest as he lay back down, and rolled over, trapping her beneath him.

Eyes wide, she stared up into his face. "What do you think you're doing?"

Garth smiled down at her. "Kissing you."

Chapter Ten

ตา

Garth's lips found hers before Eileen could say anything. Soft and gentle, his kiss was more comforting than passionate.

She sighed against his mouth.

As he lifted his head, his wet hair fell forward and caressed her cheek. "Belle told me what happened to you. Am I hurting you, frightening you?"

With his face only inches away, Eileen could see the hot desire in his misty gray eyes, desire tempered with uncertainty. One word from her, and he'd release her. All she had to do was tell him to let her go.

Her entire body rebelled at the thought, including her werewolf soul. His hard body rested mostly against her side. His heat permeated her entire being. She felt safe—and more desirable than she'd felt in years. The last thing she wanted was for him release her.

Lifting her head, she nibbled his lower lip, licked it, sucked it into her mouth. After she released it, she smiled up into his face.

His body shuddered against hers as he slid his arm beneath her shoulders and pulled her closer.

Thumbing her cheek with his left hand, he smiled. "I want you."

"Not as much as I want you," Eileen whispered back. "Love me, Garth. Love me until I can't think anymore."

His answer was another kiss. But this one wasn't gentle— this one tempted, excited, demanded. Lacing his fingers through her hair, he tilted her head back and slanted his mouth over hers. When he nipped her lip and she gasped, he stabbed his tongue into her mouth, slid it along her teeth, twined it with hers.

Sucking on his tongue, Eileen caressed it with hers. She sucked it deeper.

Their teeth clicked and clashed.

He pulled his hand from her hair, fumbled with a button on her blouse, then simply ripped it open.

Buttons bounced against his chest and ricocheted to the ground.

Cool air caressed Eileen's braless chest and she shivered.

Then his big hand cupped her breast, and she shivered again, this time with anticipation.

When his mouth replaced his hand, Eileen arched her back and pushed her breast closer. "Yes, oh yes."

He twirled his tongue around her taut, aching nipple, lapped it, nibbled it, then sucked it into his warm mouth. When he lifted his head, it puckered even more in the cool air. He began to play with her other nipple.

Eileen shifted and a rock gouged her back. She gasped. "Ouch!"

Instantly, he lifted his head. "Did I hurt you?"

Pushing him away, Eileen sat up. "No, you didn't. This rock did." Half turning, she tried to pull it from the ground. It was buried too deep.

Chuckling, he buried his face in her neck and kissed it. "Shift over then."

With a sigh, she complied and leaned back on her elbows. "Mmmmm."

He trailed kisses over her shoulder and down to her breasts, across her stomach, pushing his body back as he did so.

He jerked up. "Fuck"

Eileen opened her eyes. "What?"

"Branch poked my ass."

Her giggles became outright laughter.

Growling, he rose to his feet, pulled her up, and lifted her into his arms.

"Garth! You'll tear your stitches."

"Then you can sew them up again. That cabin does have a bed, doesn't it?"

"Yes, but…"

"No buts." Holding her close against his chest, he headed back towards the cabin.

"My basket!"

"You can get it tomorrow."

They were down the path far more quickly than they had gone up it, and Garth was pushing the door to the cabin open and carrying her inside before she had time to think.

"Where's the bed?"

Biting her lips to hold back her chuckles, she nodded to the right. "There, on the other side of the stove.

Three steps had him next to the bunk, the small, one-person bunk.

His groan echoed around the small room.

Her giggles mixed with it. "I tried to tell you…"

Setting her on her feet, he reached for the snap of her jeans. "Be quiet and lose these before I tear them off."

Shivers of anticipation dance up her spine. His voice, the look on his face—he wanted her. Now.

And she wanted him.

Her werewolf soul whined with anticipation.

Her fingers trembling with excitement, she pulled off her jeans and panties and shrugged out of her open shirt, then stood before him.

The cabin was dark, but he'd placed her in a shaft of moonlight that streamed in one of the small windows.

His voice rumbled. "You're so beautiful."

Sucking in a quick breath, Eileen blinked back a tear. How had she lived all these years without him? "You make me feel beautiful."

Sitting down on the bunk, he held out his hand. "Come to me."

She didn't hesitate to put her hand in his. "The bunk's too small."

As he pulled her into his arms, his teeth flashed in the darkness. "We'll manage." He remained sitting, wrapped his hands around her waist, and lifted her onto his lap. "Put your legs around me."

His cock brushed her inner thigh. "Oh, yes."

He kissed her, sucked her tongue into his mouth, then lifted his head and stared into her eyes. "Are you ready for me?" He slipped a hand between her legs, slid his fingers along her cleft. His chuckle followed, and he slid his finger into her. "More than ready. You're so wet."

"Ahhhh." Eileen ground her hips against his hand, forcing his finger deeper. "I need you inside of me." She arched her back.

Bending his head, he sucked a nipple into his mouth.

Eileen wrapped her arms around his neck and inhaled. He smelled like cool antiseptic, hot man, and eager, musky wolf. "Oh, yes."

Pulling his hand free, he clasped her waist, lifted her, and slid her down onto his thick cock.

He stretched her, filled her completely, deeply. "Oh, gods!" She wiggled her hips, and he slipped even further into her. "Yes!"

"That's it, love. Take me deeper." He lifted her and dropped her again.

Moaning, Eileen locked her legs around his waist and began to slide back and forth. "You are so hard!" She dropped her head, kissed the side of his neck, nipped his shoulder.

An excited growl answered her. "Faster, love. You're so wet, so tight. Slide faster."

With his hands guiding her, timing her rhythm, Eileen complied. Back and forth, back and forth she slid, grinding her hips against him, riding his cock, sucking it in as far as she could.

His breathing became panting. "That's it, love. Fuck me. Fuck me hard."

He pushed his hips up. His cock plunged even more deeply.

Heat rolled in her groin. Her cunt muscles shuddered. She dug her fingers into his shoulders. "Garth! I can't…"

"Come for me, baby. Come."

The heat exploded in her groin, radiated upward to her belly, rose to her nipples.

"Ahhhhh!" Throwing back her head, she shuddered and keened.

He twisted his hips, pushed his cock further into her.

Her entire body vibrated. Then, shuddering, she collapsed onto his shoulder.

Slowly, Eileen's senses returned. She heard the ropes holding the bunk's mattress squeak, tasted his sweat when she lapped his neck, lifted her head and saw the unfulfilled passion in his eyes, smelled the scent of her passion enveloping them, and felt the strong arms he still had wrapped around her and the long, thick cock still buried deep inside her. She shuddered, shifted, easing the slight strain on the insides of her thighs, thighs that were still spread wide, locked around his waist.

His cock pulsed inside her. He pushed his hips forward.

As she sucked in a deep breath and moaned from the exquisite feeling of pleasure, he said, "We aren't finished yet, love. Hang on. Before this night's over, the past will be gone. I'm going to love you until you don't even remember your own name."

Chapter Eleven

෨

In his arms, Eileen moaned and shuddered again. She tightened the muscles of her pussy around his cock, and Garth forced down the urge to come, to shoot his cum into her. No, not yet. He'd wait, bring her to orgasm again before he let himself go. She was his again, and he intended to keep her.

Again, her internal muscles sucked his cock, clamped and unclamped around it. She bit his shoulder.

The werewolf in his soul howled with glee, urged him on, urged him to drop her to the floor, roll her over and mount her, reclaim her for his own. He fought the urge. Another time, he would reclaim her, revel in the pleasure of pounding his hips against her ass as his cock slid deep—but not tonight. Tonight was Eileen's. Her pleasure came first. Beside, she felt too damn good sitting on top of him like this for him to even want to move her.

He slid his hands around her ass and cupped her cheeks. He wiggled his hips.

She groaned against his shoulder.

He kissed her where her neck and shoulder met, nibbled her skin, inhaled her hot, female scent. The odor of sex, of her feminine cum surrounded them.

Deep inside her, his cock pulsed.

Lust throbbed in his veins. His woman, his mate. He wasn't done with her yet. A sharp nip followed his tender kiss. "You're hot and wet, love. My cock aches, my balls are on fire. Don't stop now."

Shuddering, she lifted her head and stared into his face.

Her shimmering, golden eyes were unfocused, her pupils dilated. Her nostrils flared as she inhaled. Leaning forward, she captured his lips, thrust her tongue into his mouth to mate with his. After a long moan, she tightened then loosened her cunt muscles around his cock. She began to slide back and forth again.

Perspiration coated her body as Garth slid his hands up her sides and cupped her perfect breasts. He sucked her tongue deeper.

The soft cotton of the sheet rubbed against his balls. The gentle abrasion made them tighten even more. Again, his cock pulsed as her wet muscles clasped it. Her moisture dampened the bunk beneath him.

The scent of sex permeated the room.

His werewolf soul was howling for release.

Groaning, he slid his hands back down her sides and around to her back. Sliding them lower, he cupped her ass cheeks and squeezed them, pulled her back towards him. When had he ever been so deeply buried inside a woman? "Fuck me, love. Don't stop now."

Pulling her mouth from his, Eileen grabbed his shoulders and arched her back. "Oh, gods. You're so hard, so deep."

Garth thrust his hips upward.

She tightened her legs around his waist, sobbed, and fell forward shuddering. Her nibbles stabbed his chest. Her cunt muscles pulsed around his cock.

Beads of sweat broke out on his forehead.

Shuddering, she cried out, collapsed against his chest. She'd come again.

How long could he hold out? How often could he drive her over the brink?

Once the tenseness left her body, Garth started moving again, slowly.

Throbbing and vibrating deep within her, his cock was

surrounded by pulsing wet heat. He wasn't going to be able to hold back much longer.

"Once more, love. Ride me. You have me so hard. Take me as deep as you can." He cupped her ass again, guided her, helped her.

She nipped his nipple, and delicate pain flashed to his groin.

Faster and faster, she slid back and forth on his cock. She sobbed and moaned. "Garth! I need…"

Her muscles tightened around him yet again.

He gritted his teeth. "Not yet, love. Don't stop. Fuck me. I'm ready to come. I want to explode deep inside of you."

"Garth, oh Garth, oh Garth." She chanted his name and threw her head back.

He watched her breasts bounce.

The odor of sexual heat and release permeated the room.

"That's it, love. A little more, just a little more.." His cock was completely buried inside her. Her silky pubic hairs tickled his stomach.

A sob escaped her throat, followed by another and another. "Garth! I can't—wait—any longer!"

He surged into her one final time. "Now, love, now!"

As she melted around him, fire exploded from his balls, surged up the length of his cock, and blasted into her.

Tears rolled down over his shoulder and chest as she sobbed against his neck.

As he leaned back against the wall, Garth held her shuddering body close. Bright motes of light danced before his eyes. Never had he experienced anything like this. Eileen had taken him beyond the realm of gratifying sex into the bright fire of undying passion. Gods, how he loved her.

"Garth, I can't stop…" she sobbed against his shoulder. "I can't control…"

He hugged her more tightly. "Shhhh. Let it go. Let it all out. I'll keep you safe. I love you."

"I love you too," she sobbed against his neck. "I'm...so sorry... I didn't...mean to... I hurt you."

Sucking in another deep breath, Garth lifted her off his cock and set her back down sideways across his lap. He combed her silky hair off her forehead with his fingers. "Shh. It's over. You're back with me now, and I'll never let you go again."

She sighed against his chest. "I'm...so...drained. I can't stay awake."

He smiled against the top of her head. "Sleep. I'll be here. I'm not going anywhere."

She rubbed her cheek against his chest, nuzzled him, kissed whatever piece of skin she could reach. "I love you," she sighed.

As Eileen slept in his arms, Garth shifted to make himself more comfortable, leaned his head back against the wall, and smiled. He never thought he'd see Eileen again, but he'd found her, reclaimed her as his mate, and, in the process, had the best sex of his life.

All he had to do now was find the Were who'd hurt her and kill him.

Chapter Twelve

∞

Garth woke with a crick in his neck and his cold feet dangling over the edge of the bunk. Sometime during the night, he'd stretched out on the bunk. They definitely needed a bigger bed.

Eileen was draped over him.

Careful not to disturb her, he eased out of the bunk, biting back a groan when his stiff and aching muscles protested. Once he was up, he grabbed the quilt that had been kicked to the floor and covered her.

She muttered something in her sleep and rolled over.

After staring at her for a moment, Garth turned, padded to the door, and slipped outside.

The sharp nip of cool morning air raised goose bumps on his skin as he stepped to the edge of the porch. After sucking in a deep breath—nothing smelled as good as a mountain forest in the morning—he lifted his arms over his head and stretched, stifling a groan at the stab of pain from yesterday's cuts. Lowering his arms, he glanced down at his bandage. No blood. The stitches had held.

Who are you?

Stiffening, Garth turned.

Two elderly wolves sat on the edge of the porch.

"Eileen's mate."

New or old?

"Her first."

The old female dipped her head once. *It is time you came to her. She's been very sad.*

The male drew back his lips. *You will not make her sad again.*

Smiling slightly, Garth shook his head. "No. I won't."

The female continued to stare at him. *I am Willow. This is my mate Silver. The Alpha of this territory has given us permission to hunt here for as long as we like. He remembers the old ways, the laws the wolves taught the Weres.* She rose and padded to him, nose twitching. *There is much wolf in you — and a scent, somewhat familiar.* She sniffed again. *You are sibling to the Alpha's mate.*

Garth nodded. "Belle's my sister. My mother was Myste of a high mountain pack, my father a Were."

She stared unblinking with yellow eyes. *Your sibling has told us the story.*

The old male stepped to his mate's side. *She will not go with you.*

Frowning, Garth stared at Silver. "What are you talking about?"

The scent of the forest, of the Wilde, is strong on you. Your wolf's soul is strong. Eileen's is not as strong. She will not turn to the Wilde even for you.

Garth shook his head. He'd stayed away from wild wolves while hiding from the CIA. He'd forgotten about *the Wilde*, their term for Weres who became feral. "I never planned to ask her to."

Willow stared into his face, locked her gaze with his. *You flee from danger. A human hunts you so you seek safety in your wild soul. If you stay, he may find you — and Eileen. Which will you choose?*

Cursing silently, Garth tore his gaze from the wolf's. The mind meld all wolves shared allowed them not only to communicate but to read each other's thoughts. To wolves, it was nothing. They didn't hide anything from each other. The part of Garth's soul that was human, however, was disconcerted. Not only did Willow know what he was thinking, she was right. By staying, he was putting Eileen in danger.

He fisted his hand and rubbed his knuckles with the other. He would not leave Eileen! Not now, after just finding her again.

If he tried, his soul would be ripped in two. No. She was his, whether he stayed here or went somewhere else, Eileen would be with him. He wouldn't lose her again.

"I see you've met Willow and Silver."

Turning to face the woman he loved, Garth said, "I'm being hunted."

That brought her up short. "By whom?"

"CIA."

She gaped then snapped her mouth shut. "What in the world do they want with you?"

He sighed. "To make a long story short, my superior believes in werewolves and thinks I'm one. He's got a man after me. He wants to capture me to prove we exist. Then the CIA would take our families hostage to make us work for them."

Nostrils flaring, Eileen fisted her hands on her hips. "If that son of a bitch thinks he's going to take you away from me after I just got you back... Well, I'll rip out his throat myself."

Thrusting all uncertainty to the back of his mind, Garth smiled at his mate. "Have I told you how much I love you?"

Relaxing, she smiled back. "Well, we'll deal with this man if he finds you. How's your side? Are you hungry?"

"Fine and yes, especially for you."

Her smile broadening to a grin, she chuckled. "I'll make you breakfast. As for your other hunger, well, we'll see." She winked, turned, and strolled back into the cabin.

Garth's gaze was glued to her shimmying ass.

The mind snorts of both wolves had him wrench his attention back to them. "Go hunt something."

Wide wolf smiles had their teeth gleaming in the early morning light as they carefully jumped from the porch to the ground.

Silver trotted towards the forest.

Willow looked back over her shoulder. *Remember, a lone wolf is not as strong as the pack.* After a nod of her head, she trotted after her mate.

Absentmindedly rubbing his side, Garth stared after the two wolves. He'd always taken care of himself, and he was good at it. But this man chasing him was very good too. And now he had Eileen to consider. Turning, he walked into the cabin. Maybe pack life wouldn't be so bad.

* * * * *

"Let me get this straight. You want to stay here, join my pack?"

Garth leaned back in his chair and stared at his brother-in-law.

Alex stood behind his desk, his hands flattened against the smooth oak top, and leaned forward. "Why should I let you stay here when you're a potential danger?"

Garth nodded. "You've taken Eileen into the pack. She's my mate. Guess you could say that makes me a member already."

Anger flickered in the Alpha's eyes. "I've met your brothers. Both are Alphas, and you're just as arrogant. How long before you challenge me?"

Shaking his head, Garth leaned forward and rested his elbows on his knees. Alex's question was legitimate, especially since he'd met both Kearnan and Brendan. However, of all Artemis Gray's children, he was the only one without Alpha tendencies. But his sister's mate didn't know that. "Never. Belle will vouch for me in this. I'm a Loner, Alex. I don't much care for a lot of company. Just let Eileen and me stay in that cabin she's been using, and I'll be the happiest Were on Earth. I've some skill at carpentry and carving. I can earn my keep. And I give you my word that I'll never challenge you for the leadership of the pack."

Alex lowered himself into his chair. "Belle says you owe her a new table."

First smiling then chuckling, Garth felt some of the

tenseness leave his body. "She wouldn't have let me leave here until I made her a new one."

"What about the danger you bring to the pack? You're a hunted Were."

Raking a hand through his loose hair, Garth nodded. "I know. I don't doubt that he will show up here sooner or later. Maybe you were right about killing him. Accidents happen in the wilderness."

"And what about the men who would come looking for him?"

His chair skittering back across the floor, Garth surged to his feet. "Fuck. What do you want me to say? I mated Eileen ten years ago, had her stolen away from me, yet managed to find her again. She's here, a member of your pack, and she wants to stay. What would you do? How much does Belle mean to you? What would you be willing to chance for her?"

As the other man stared at him, the wolf in Garth's soul paced nervously, snarling once, then twice. He would take Eileen and leave here if he had to. He could find a place for them so deep in the forest, no one would find them. But—Eileen wouldn't be happy, and her happiness was more important than anything.

Garth stiffened as Alex rose.

The Alpha held out his hand. "Welcome to my pack."

Chapter Thirteen

ഌ

Brilliant sunshine streamed through the sparkling kitchen windows of the pack's new bed-and-breakfast inn as Eileen watched Jill check the new cutlery, dishes, and pots and pans. Bending, she sniffed the daisies that were stuck in a vase sitting on the counter. As the sweet scent tickled her nose, she mentally hugged herself. What a fantastic day it was!

The teakettle whistled merrily.

"I've never seen you this happy, not even when you found out you were pregnant," Jill said as she set two mugs of tea on the table.

Sliding into a chair, Eileen cupped the mug in her hands, propped her elbows on the table, and blew on the steaming tea. "I haven't felt like this since before my family dragged me to Louisiana. I never thought I'd see Garth again, even with Belle here. When we were young, he was obviously a Loner, happiest when he was working wood with his hands." She chuckled. "Except when he was with me."

Jill grinned at her. "Who would have thought when we left Louisiana, we'd both end up this happy?"

"Dave treating you right?"

"Better than anyone else ever has. We're making our mating official on Solstice."

"Two more days. You are going to make him work for it, aren't you?"

Jill's laughter rolled around the room. "Believe me, he's never run as far as he's going to run when he's chasing me."

"Good." Eileen's laughter joined her friend's.

"What's so funny?" Dave asked as he sauntered into the

kitchen.

Both women grinned at him. "Nothing."

He looked from one to the other. "I'm leaving, now, before I get into trouble."

Both laughed again as he hurried through the door.

Once she regained her breath, Eileen smiled at her friend. "I've never met an Omega before. He's not what I expected."

Jill nodded. "I know. The pack in Louisiana hasn't had one for two generations because no one would take the job. Everyone thought it was too demeaning. But Alex and the others here don't treat Dave like he's less than they are. They respect him, and other pack members come to him with the minor squabbles instead of bothering Alex."

"This is how it's supposed to work, I think," Eileen answered as she sipped her tea. "In a wolf pack, the Omega has the lowest status, and the other members pick on him. But taking their frustrations out on him keeps tempers from becoming too volatile. I guess the humanity in Weres gives us the opportunity to give Omegas respect and responsibility. At least Alex has. The others follow his lead. Alex is a good Alpha. I'm glad we came here."

Jill sipped some tea then put down her mug. "Will you be staying?"

Eileen nodded. "Garth's talking to Alex now. He wants us to stay in the cabin on the ridge. We're close enough to be part of the pack, and far enough away for him to still feel like we're alone."

"You don't mind."

Shaking her head, Eileen grinned. "Not at all. I was afraid he'd want to move to New York and get involved in the family business. I mean, could you see me living in a big city? I'd always be getting lost and doing a lot of other things to make a fool out of myself. No, we'll be happy in that little cabin. Besides, what's five miles to a wolf?" she added with a grin. "I'll just keep a couple changes of clothing here and visit whenever you'll have me."

Jill grinned back. "And you'll always be welcome, well, at least most of the time." Her chuckle was deliciously sexy. "So, what are you going to do with yourself all day? You won't be able to make love all the time, you know. Your bodies won't be able to take it."

Tea spurted across the table as Eileen tried to stifle her laughter. After her coughing fit passed, she said, "Garth is going to go back to carving and furniture making again. Eventually, he's going to set up a website and sell pieces via the internet. That will mean a generator or running a power line up the ridge, but he's already planning how to enlarge the cabin. I'm going to keep studying healing. I won't be able to do what a doctor does, but I can treat stomachaches, bumps and bruises, and such."

Grinning, Jill looked at her wrist. "It's two o'clock. You guys made all these decisions today? That's fast work."

"We had these plans years ago," Eileen answered after another sip of tea. "They were just—delayed." She swallowed more tea then looked at the clock on the wall. "If you're going to show me the rest of the B&B, we need to get moving. I told Garth I'd meet him at Belle's house around 2:30."

Before they left the kitchen, Eileen hugged her friend. "Thank you."

"For what?"

"For bringing me here."

Sniffing, Jill pulled away from Eileen. "Now you're making me cry. Let's go see the rest of this place before I'm sobbing." Sliding her arm through Eileen's, Jill steered her towards the front of the B&B.

"It's really great that you and Dave will be running this place. Have all the rooms been reserved?"

As they walked into the small lobby, Jill nodded. "Eight of the ten starting the middle of next month. And we're already getting calls about ski season. We're close enough to the resorts for people who were too late for reservations there for a particular date to be happy to stay with us. Buying this old lodge and converting it to a B&B was a brilliant idea. And Alex bought the hardware store in town too. With the sawmill and contact with Belle's father, the pack isn't going to have to worry about taking care of anyone for a long time. Dave told me Alex is even planning on offering a couple of college scholarships next year if things keep going well. He'd love to have one of our younger members go to medical school too."

"I thought the doctor in town was Were."

Jill nodded. "He is, but he also takes care of all the full humans. And there are a lot of Native Americans who come to him since he's Cheyenne too. What's more, the pack is growing. He needs a partner." She pulled Eileen to a stop. "This is the lobby."

Gazing around, Eileen smiled. Jill's touches were evident everywhere from the muted, earth tone throw pillows on the sofas before the huge fireplace on one side of the room to the Native American pottery sitting on the end of the admissions desk.

"This room runs from one side of the lodge to the other. Instead of breaking it into two smaller rooms, Alex, Dave, and Josh decided to keep it like this. The guests can sit in front of the fire or use one of the smaller tables set around the room to play cards or board games or something. You've already seen the kitchen. The dining room is next to it. Come on, I'll show you the bedrooms now."

Grabbing Eileen's hand, Jill pulled her towards the stairs behind the desk.

They'd gone barely two steps when the front door slammed open and a woman sauntered in.

"I'm sorry," Jill began as she turned to her, "but we aren't open yet." She stopped. "Wait a minute, aren't you..."

The woman chuckled and looked back over her shoulder at the two men who followed her. "Bill, honey," she said, "your runaway mate is here."

Chapter Fourteen

ဢ

Her stomach rolling, Eileen stared at the scruffy mate she'd repudiated. Bill—here? How did he find her?

"I told you she'd be glad to see you. She's just speechless with joy," the woman said with a snicker.

Wrenching her eyes from Bill's face, Eileen glanced at the woman. Did she know her?

"Tabitha!" Jill blurted out. "What have you done?"

Eileen started. Tabitha, Josh's sister, that's who she was. She'd never met the woman who'd tried to turn the pack against Belle. The night she and Jill had been granted Sanctuary, she'd gone back to her house after showing her bruises to the pack. Dave had come later and told Jill and her every detail of what happened after that, including the pack's acceptance of Belle in spite of her wolf heritage. Tabitha had left the next day vowing never to return to a pack that took in "Abominations".

Stepping past Tabitha, Bill grabbed her arm and jerked her forward. "Get your stuff. We're leaving. You too, Jill. You're both going home where you belong."

Eileen tried to yank her arm free. "I'm not going anywhere with you."

An ugly snarl burst from his throat, and he jerked her towards him. "I'm your mate, and you'll do what I tell you." He glanced at his sister. "As soon as we get back, you're mating Frank here. Once he's fucking you every night, you won't have time to meddle in other people's business."

"Like hell I will," Jill stated. "I'm mating into this pack in two days."

"Fuck this pack. You're coming home."

Chuckling, Tabitha sauntered closer, stepping between both Bill and Frank.

Both men stiffened and shifted. Their nostrils flared. Bulges appeared in the front of their jeans.

As the other woman's scent reached her, Eileen started.

Tabitha was coming into her wolf heat. She traced her finger down Bill's arm. "Thanks for the ride home, honey." She smiled at Frank. "You too."

Frank grabbed her wrist. "Fuck me."

Chuckling, Tabitha cupped his groin. "Now or later? You want some too, Bill?"

Jill fisted her hands on her hips. "And you want me to mate him? He'd mount her right here in front of me if she dropped her pants. Get the hell out of here, Bill. Go home."

With his attention fixed on Tabitha, Eileen was able to yank her wrist free and step back. "Go with this bitch. She's more your type."

Jerking his attention back to Eileen, Bill growled, "I'll fuck you both at the same time if I want to. I'm your mate. You have to obey me."

Crossing her arms over her chest, Eileen stared at him. How had she ever let her parents talk her into mating him? He was worse than a pig. And judging by his scent and appearance, he'd been living like one too. "Like hell I do. Jill and I have been granted Sanctuary. I repudiated you before the entire pack. Considering the bruises you gave me, it wasn't hard. Didn't your new—girlfriend—tell you?" she asked as she nodded towards Tabitha.

Chuckling from where she stood between Frank's outstretched legs—he was leaning against one of the sofa's backs—Tabitha rubbed her ass against his erection. He had his arms wrapped around her, one hand squeezing a breast, the other jerking at the button on her jeans.

"He didn't care, honey. Says you belong to him."

"And it's time to teach you another lesson. This time you'll stay where I put you." Raising his fist, Bill started towards her again.

* * * * *

Garth was just rising when the Beta Richard strode into Alex's cabin. "Tabitha's back."

The Alpha frowned. "Fucking bitch is more trouble than she's worth." Then he waved his hand. "She's Josh's sister, so she's his problem." Then Alex grinned. "I have a feeling Mia will put her in her place."

"She's brought two men with her," Richard added. "They were asking around town for two women, Eileen and Jill. The bigger one says Eileen is his runaway wife."

The wolf in his soul howling to life, Garth leaped from his chair. "Eileen's at the B&B with Jill. Where are these men?"

Richard stepped back. "They probably reached there by now."

"I'll kill him." Dark mist swirled, the clothing Garth was wearing fell to the floor, and he shifted to his wolf form. The wire screen was ripped to shreds and wooden slats splintered as he barreled through the door.

Sighing, Alex shook his head. "I don't know why I even bother having a door."

"What was that?" Belle asked as she walked into the room.

"Your brother didn't bother to open the door before he went out."

"Why?"

"Eileen's other mate has shown up."

"Oh, shit. Come on. We better get down there before Garth kills him." She started to unbutton her blouse.

"I brought a jeep," Richard said with a grin.

Grabbing Garth's clothing from the floor, Belle headed for the door. "Don't just stand there, Alex. You're the Alpha. It's your job to deal with this mess." She stepped through the broken door.

Shaking his head, Alex looked at his Beta. "Find yourself a mate without siblings. Life will be a lot less complicated."

Chuckling, Richard followed his Alpha out the door.

* * * * *

As Bill advanced, Eileen stumbled back. When her back rubbed against the desk, she was forced to stop. A shudder ran through her body. She remembered how much Bill's fists hurt. He hadn't held back when he'd beaten her before. If she weren't Were, she probably wouldn't have survived.

She blinked. Why was this happening to her? Why now? After she'd just found Garth again?

"Fucking bitch. I'll teach you to run away from me "

"Bill! No!" Jill leaped at her brother, grabbed his arm.

Since she was off balance, he had no trouble shoving his sister away. "And when I finish with her, I'll teach you not to help a man's mate leave him."

Jill flew back and slammed into one of the small tables. It clattered to the floor.

"Jill!" Eileen leaped towards her.

"Get back here."

He managed to grab her wrist.

Without a second thought, Eileen bent and clamped her teeth into his hand, biting until she drew blood.

"Goddamn!" Bill yanked his hand away. He stared at the blood on his hand then looked at Eileen. Fury radiated from him. "You'll pay for that."

Kneeling at Jill's side, Eileen barred her teeth and snarled. "Touch me again, and I'll rip out your throat."

He stalked towards her. "Go ahead and try, bitch."

Chapter Fifteen

ഇ

As Bill reached her and Eileen rose to meet him, a black whirlwind exploded through the doorway. Howling with rage, the wolf slammed into Bill, knocking him across the room. He shifted, and Garth stood in front of Eileen, hands fisted, muscles bulging. "She—is—mine!" His vicious growl echoed off the walls as he leaped to Bill, grabbed him with both hands, and tossed him back across the room where he slammed into the other wall. Plaster shattered and dribbled to the floor from the hole the back of his head put in the wall. The glass on two framed prints shattered when they bounced off the hardwood. A curtain rod jerked upward then dragged down the colorful cloth hanging from it.

Bill slid slowly downward and crumpled to the floor. He didn't get back up.

Eileen jumped forward and locked her arms around Garth's waist as he stepped towards his foe. "Stop! You'll kill him."

Freezing in place, he never took his eyes off the prone man. "He deserves to die."

On her knees, Eileen buried her face in his hip. "Garth, please."

"Jesus fucking Christ," Frank gasped as he pushed Tabitha away from him. "Who the hell are you?"

Eileen tightened her arms around his waist as Garth snarled and turned towards him. "Her mate."

"But she's mated to Bill."

Eileen tightened her hold as Garth shook with fury. Just how stupid was Frank?

His howl rattled bric-a-brac sitting on shelves. "She was mine first! And she is mine now! If you want to keep your friend alive, get him out of here and never come back."

"Well hello, gorgeous," Tabitha purred as she stepped closer to Garth. She reached out to caress his arm. "We haven't met. I'm Tabitha."

Teeth barred, he snarled, "Touch me, whore, and I'll rip off your arm."

Jerking her hand back as if she'd been bitten, Tabitha stumbled back just as her brother rushed through the door from the kitchen. Spiteful anger on her face, she hurried to his side. "Josh! Did you hear what he called me? Challenge him!"

After a quick perusal of the room, Josh stared into her face. "You want me to challenge *him*? Are you crazy? No way. I want to stay in one piece."

Snarling, she backed away. "Coward! I'm your sister and he called me a whore."

"If the shoe fits," Belle said from the front doorway.

Whirling, Tabitha glared at her. "Why you! I'll..."

"What?" Josh asked from behind her. "Let Belle kick your ass again? She did it once, you know."

"What the fuck is going on here!" Alex demanded as he stepped into the room.

Richard stood behind him, tense, ready to spring if necessary.

Relaxing slightly, Eileen closed her eyes. The pack Alphas were here.

"He's the one who beat Eileen," Garth snarled as he jerked his chin towards Bill. "I'm going to kill him."

On the other side of the room, Bill groaned and tried to push himself up. He collapsed again and lay still.

Belle stomped across the room until she stood a few inches from her brother. Growling, she stared into his face. "Like hell you will, Garth Gray. You aren't killing anybody in our new bed-and-breakfast, and if you try, Eileen will be stitching up a lot more slashes and cuts."

A vein pulsed on Garth's forehead. "Get out of my way, Belle, before I move you."

Snarling, Alex stepped forward.

"Jesus fucking Christ," Frank said again.

Nobody answered him.

Letting go of Garth's waist, Eileen rose to her feet and slid between him and Belle. "Garth. Let it be. He's learned his lesson."

Nostrils flaring, Garth threw back his head and howled. Then he grabbed Eileen's upper arms. "You are *mine*!" Throwing her over his shoulder, he spun around.

"There are ten beds upstairs," Belle called after him as she tossed his clothing over the back of a chair. "Pick whichever one you want."

"Shut up, bitch," Garth snarled. Nevertheless, he leaped across the room and up the staircase.

* * * * *

"What's wrong with you, Alex, to let someone like that in the pack?" Tabitha spat as she rubbed her arms. She'd left her brother's side and now leaned against a sofa. Her lower lip stuck out.

"Shut up." Alex turned to Frank. "Pick up your friend, get out of here, and never come back. If you do, I won't stop Garth next time. Understand?"

Adam's apple bobbing as he gulped, Frank nodded then scurried across the room, grabbed the unconscious man beneath his armpits, and dragged him out the door. The sound of a truck door slamming and an engine gunning announced their departure.

Tabitha stomped her foot. "Alex! You can't let someone like that Garth in the pack."

A muscle in Alex's cheek began to tic. "Like what, Tabitha? A Were who'll fight for his mate? He's a better pack member than you'll ever be."

"How dare you!"

Stomping across the room, Alex halted before her. "You have done nothing but cause dissension within this pack since you reached puberty by setting one male against another. You leave for months at a time then come back expecting us to bail you out of whatever problems you've caused. Now you return, bringing the repudiated mate of a Were who's gained Sanctuary here because of the abuse she suffered at his hands. Who the hell do you think *you* are?"

Hands curled into fists, she dropped her arms to her sides. "Who am I? I'm your Beta's sister. I should be your mate. I should be Alpha female, not that puling New York bitch!" After sucking in a deep breath, she gasped and shuddered. Then, in a calmer voice "Come on Alex. You know me. You know how good I am." She leaned closer. "Can you smell me, Alex? My heat's coming on. Remember two years ago when we..."

"As far as I'm concerned, you smell like garbage. And as Alpha, it falls to me to determine your punishment."

She started and stepped back. "Punishment? For what?"

"Placing a pack member in danger of her life." Alex glanced at Josh. "You're her family. Is there anything you want to say in her defense?"

After staring at his sister for a moment, Josh shook his head. "No. She only causes trouble whenever she's here. Punish her how you see fit." Spinning on his heel, he left the way he came in.

"Josh, you fucking asshole, get back here."

She would have followed him, but Richard grabbed her. His nostrils flared at her scent, and sweat broke out on his forehead, but he held her immobile.

Alex stared at her a moment then crossed his arms over his chest. "Three days in the cage."

Color drained from her face. "No! Alex, you can't do that, not now, now when I'm in heat! Please! You can't lock me away all by myself."

"I can and I will."

Her face white, Belle laid her hand on his arm. "Alex…"

He shook his head. "I know she'll suffer, but Eileen could have been seriously injured or killed. It's no less than Tabitha deserves."

Tears were streaming down Tabitha's cheeks. "Alex, you can't lock me up alone while I'm in this condition."

"You should have thought of that before you brought these men here."

"A trouble-making bitch in heat. Want me to take care of her for you?" came from the doorway.

Everyone turned.

Grinning, his arms crossed over his chest, Brendan Gray leaned against the doorjamb.

Chapter Sixteen

ɜୠ

When he reached the top of the stairway, Garth shouldered open the first door he came to. Once inside he kicked the door closed, tossed Eileen onto the bed, and leaped down beside her, trapping her with his body.

"You're mine!"

Beneath him, Eileen shuddered. The wolf in Garth's soul was fighting for control of his body.

"You are mine," he snarled again. He leaned more weight on her when she tried to wiggle out from under him.

"Get off me. I can't breathe."

The growl that rumbled in his chest would have any male backing away from him.

Eileen wasn't male. She was Garth's mate, and he was ready to forget he was part human.

She shuddered again. Almost. He was almost at the point where his wolf half would control him completely. Anticipation rolled in her stomach causing the muscles to tighten, her nipples to pebble, and moisture to seep into her groin. Just a little more, and his urge to mate, to dominate her, make her submissive to his will would overpower him.

And she couldn't wait for it to happen.

Flattening her palms against his chest, she pushed. It was like trying to move a brick wall.

Leaning down, he nipped her shoulder. "Submit to me."

"Let me up." She pushed against his chest again.

Nostrils flaring, he stared into her eyes.

Feral, yellow flecks danced amongst the gray mist in his.

"Sub—mit."

"Make me."

Howling with frustration, he rose off her body, ripped her blouse and bra to shreds then tore her jeans in half along the seams. Her panties disintegrated in his fist. Then he grabbed her around the waist and rolled her over. Lifting her hips, he forced his hairy thigh between her naked legs.

She pushed back. Oh, to ride the hard muscles of that thigh.

Eileen gasped as he slid his thick cock back and forth between her legs. Gods, but she wanted it inside her.

Leaning over her back, he pushed her shoulders down, nipped the side of her neck. Need mixed with the command in his voice. "Say it. Say you're mine." Burying his face against her, he raked his teeth along the line of her shoulder. "Eileen! Please!" Then he kissed the back of her neck.

Beneath him, Eileen relaxed. Now. He was ready to take her now. "Yours, Garth. Always yours. I love you."

"Eileen, my Eileen," he whispered into her hair. Rising up, he dragged his hands lightly down her sides, cupped her ass cheeks and squeezed.

Goose bumps followed and she shivered. "Please, Garth. I need you inside." She pushed her ass back against his hips.

He growled and grabbed her hips and spread her legs farther apart. Swiveling his hips, he rubbed his cock against her clit.

"Damn it, Garth! Fuck me now!"

"Now?"

She pounded her fist into a pillow. "Yes! Now!"

With a deep growl, he plunged his cock into her.

Immediately, she tightened her internal muscles and sucked him deeper.

His breath hissed from his lungs.

Eileen shimmied her hips and leaned forward as he slid his

cock out. She pushed back as he plunged in again. "Yes, oh yes. More, harder."

His wiry pubic hairs tickled her ass. His breath was hot against her neck. "Harder? You want it harder?" He swiveled his hips.

"Yes, and deep, as deep as you can go." She tightened her muscles as he pulled his cock out.

"Christ, you're wet." He thrust again.

Eileen moaned into the pillow beneath her.

A deeper thrust. "More?"

"More!"

Another twist of his hips. "Are you mine?"

"Always."

He stopped talking and began to ride her in earnest. In and out, in and out, his sliding cock building friction and heat

Burying her face in a pillow, Eileen screamed. His cock was stretching and filling her completely. He lifted her knees from the bed with each powerful thrust. Her stomach muscles clenched. The friction of her nipples rubbing against the quilt beneath them pebbled them more and more tightly until they were two delicate points of pleasure-pain. Her clit ached. Pressure built deep inside her.

He thrust harder, plunged deeper.

Eileen screamed again.

Behind her, Garth thrust his cock into her faster and faster. His fingers bit into her hips as he held her motionless. A snarl was ripped from his throat. "Mine! You are mine!"

Roaring filled her ears and sparks of light danced behind her eyelids as heat exploded outward from her groin and enveloped her. Her internal muscles clenched and unclenched involuntarily; her entire body shook while she sobbed into the pillow.

Throwing back his head, Garth howled long and loud. Then, with a deep groan, he rolled off her and flopped onto his back.

She fell to her side and snuggled against him.

Sliding a finger under her chin, he lifted her head until she looked into his eyes. "By all the gods, Eileen, I love you."

* * * * *

Alex glared at his brother-in-law, the one he really, really didn't like. "What the fuck do you want?"

Still grinning, Brendan sauntered into the room. "I brought some things for Garth. Clothes mostly."

"How the fuck did you know he was here?"

"Dad always knows where we are." Brendan winked at Belle. "Well, almost always. Took him almost a week to figure out where Belle was when she disappeared." He looked around. "So where's Garth?"

Smiling, Belle hugged her brother. "Upstairs."

Brendan cocked an eyebrow. "Garth usually isn't so impulsive. Who?"

"Eileen. He just fought for her."

Honest happiness appeared on his face. "Eileen's here? Really? And who's stupid enough to fight Garth?"

Tucking her arm through Brendan's, Belle chuckled and led him back towards the door. "It's a long story. Come on, I'll tell you all about it back at the house. Let Alex do his Alpha stuff."

Brendan looked back over his shoulder. "Like I said, I'd be happy to take care of that bitch for you."

"Please, Alex," Tabitha whimpered, "give me to him." She'd stopped struggling and sagged in Richard's arms. Still, the glance she flashed Brendan's way was calculating.

Brendan grinned at her. "Oh, I heard what you said about my sister—'puling New York bitch'? Take my word for it, what I'd do to you would satisfy me—but not you."

Bowing her head, Tabitha sobbed as a heat spasm gripped

her.

Alex glared at Brendan. "I can handle my own pack. Get the hell out of here."

Belle strode across the room and grabbed Brendan's arm. "Come on. There's been enough fighting today."

Brendan's laughter floated through the door after him.

Snarling another curse, Alex looked to Richard. "Need any help getting her to the cage?"

Richard shifted Tabitha's unresisting body. "I don't think there's any fight left in her. I'll holler if I need help." Tightening his arms around her waist, he dragged her from the room.

Alex stepped over to Jill and helped her up from where she was still sitting on the floor. "Are you okay?"

Gingerly, she rubbed her hip. "I'll be fine, though explaining my bruises to Dave will be interesting."

Finally, Alex had something to chuckle about. "Good thing that asshole is gone. Dave's a lot tougher than he looks." He followed Jill's gaze as she looked around the room. A leg was broken off the table she'd been thrown into, and two of the chairs would have to be repaired. Deep gouges were scraped into the hardwood floor. Shattered glass lay along the wall, and the curtain that had fallen had dirty smudges.

Jill finger-combed her hair back off her face and looked around. "What a mess."

Putting his arm around her shoulder, Alex hugged her. "It won't take long to clean up. Then the guests will start arriving, and you'll be busier than you want to be. Today will just be a bad memory."

After a long sigh, she looked up at him. "You're a wonderful Alpha, Alex. The pack will prosper with you and Belle as leaders. Thanks for taking me and Eileen in."

Alex grinned. As if Belle had ever given him a choice.

* * * * *

"I don't think your mate likes me," Brendan said with a grin as he followed Belle into her kitchen. The hour she'd spent telling him about Garth and Eileen and what was new with her pack had been entertaining, even after Alex and his Betas had joined them. Now, though, he was hungry, and, when she put her mind to it, Belle was a hell of a cook. Nor did she want him to stay in the living room with the other men. Brendan grinned to himself. They were so easy to rile.

Snorting, she tossed a glare back over her shoulder as she reached for the coffeepot. "You don't have to be quite so antagonistic."

Still grinning, he shrugged. "Wait until he meets Dad if you think I'm bad."

"I can handle Dad. There's a peach cobbler in the fridge. Get it for me."

"Quite a story about Eileen. I'm glad Garth and she finally found each other. Dad's been looking for her, but it was like her family fell off the face of the earth." He set the cobbler on the kitchen counter. "So, what happened to your table?"

Chuckling, she scooped coffee into the pot. "Garth."

Shaking his head, Brendan stared at the two pieces of table. "He never did know his own strength. What are his plans?"

The sounds of voices and stomping drifted in from the living room.

"Garth and Eileen are finally here. Cups are in that cupboard on the second shelf. Get them for me, please."

"What do you do when you don't have a brother to order around?"

She orders her mate to get what she needs, of course. What else would she do?

Shaking his head, Brendan stared down at the cat now sitting in the middle of the kitchen floor. "Dad and Moira didn't believe me when I told them you had a cat."

She doesn't "have" me. I like living here.

"Stop arguing with Callie. I'll carry the cobbler. You bring the tray with the coffee and cups. And don't drop it!"

After picking up the tray, Brendan followed his sister back into the living room. "What's Garth going to do now?"

"He's staying here with Eileen. They are mated, you know."

"What about this CIA agent who's hunting him?"

"You could ask me," Garth said from next to the fireplace.

Setting the tray down, Brendan ignored his brother to smile at the woman standing next to him. "Hello, Eileen. It's really good to see you again. You sure you want to stay with a clumsy oaf like Garth? I'm still available."

Snorting, Eileen strolled across the room, stood on her tiptoes, and kissed Brendan's cheek. "I prefer an oaf to a ladies' man any day."

Brendan grinned. "Well then, welcome to the family." He grabbed her, lifted her off her feet, hugged her tight, and planted a long, deep kiss on her mouth.

Josh looked from Brendan to Garth. "Are you going to let him get away with that?"

Garth chuckled. "Just wait."

As soon as Brendan set Eileen back down, her palm connected with the side of his head.

His head snapped to the left.

"That was not a brotherly kiss. Next time, I'll let Garth hit you. Then see how pretty you are for the ladies."

After shaking his head, Brendan chuckled. "The bruises he'd give me would have all the ladies wanting to console me."

Throwing up her hands, Eileen glared at Brendan. "Someday, somewhere, a woman is going to rock your world and leave you chasing your tail. I just hope I'm there to see it." Whirling, she stomped back to her mate's side.

Brendan blew a kiss after her. "That's what everybody keeps telling me."

Epilogue

෨

Clad in camouflage pants and a tight, black tee shirt, he swaggered into her inner office like he owned the place.

Trying to focus her exhausted brain on the man glaring down at her, Melody fought to keep her upper lip from curling. Arrogance in a human was hard to stomach. None of them were as tough as they thought they were. And why wasn't John back from lunch yet to keep jerks like this out of her office? She needed to get some sleep. Oh well, she had to be nice to potential customers no matter how much she didn't like them. She blinked again. She was pretty sure she wasn't going to like this one at all.

Pushing herself to her feet, she held out her hand. "What can I do for you, Mr…"

He ignored it. "Nick Price, CIA. You look like hell."

Anger flared as Melody stared at his coffee-colored face. This guy wasn't just an arrogant jerk. He was a bona fide asshole. "Listen, Nick Price of the fucking CIA—if you're telling me the truth—I just spent the last forty-eight hours with very little sleep searching for a twelve-year-old runaway who thought she could survive in the wilds of Nevada. So, fuck you, shithead, and don't let the door hit you in the ass on the way out."

"Do you kiss your mother with that mouth?" He flashed his badge at her then tossed a picture onto her desk. "I'm looking for this man."

Blinking as she tried to focus, that *was* a real fucking CIA badge he just flashed at her, wasn't it? Melody picked up the picture, blinked some more to focus, and stared at it. "Yeah, I've seen him. What do you want him for?"

She glanced up in time to see the surprise flash in his eyes.

Grinning to herself, she dropped the picture on her desk. Ha! He didn't expect her to admit it. "Said his name was Jake Fields. He came in wanting to hire us to find his wife. Said she took off with a pile of his money."

The CIA spook pressed his palms against her desk and leaned forward. "His real name is Jake Hurley, and he's embezzled government money. Any idea where he is now?"

His scent was completely masculine. No fruity cologne for him.

The werewolf in her soul stirred for a moment.

Melody blinked again. Exhaustion settled more firmly around her shoulders, weighing her down.

Her werewolf soul sighed and fell into a deep slumber.

"You gonna help me or not?" His voice was terse, and he didn't bother hiding his irritation.

Looking up into his shuttered gaze, she pushed the picture back across her desk. "My assistant worked with him. When John gets back from lunch, I'll see what he remembers. Come back tomorrow, and we'll give you everything we have on him." *After I've had some sleep and am able to think again.*

Price picked up the photo, stared at her a moment, and nodded. "I'll be in touch." Spinning on his heel, he sauntered out of her office.

Melody didn't move until he'd cleared the outer office and disappeared through the door to the street.

Flopping into her chair, she stared at the opposite wall though she didn't see the pictures hanging there. As soon as she was able to think clearly, she'd contact her father. Garth's spook had traced him to her.

Enjoy An Excerpt From:

SHEALA

Copyright © JUDY MAYS, 2006.

so

"Brianna, I'd like you to meet my sex instructor, Bogarton don al' Chevin."

Immediately, Sheala slapped her hand to her mouth to cover her giggle as her sister-in-law halted in mid-waddle—she was so very pregnant—and gaped at her for a full thirty seconds before snapping her mouth shut.

"Your what!"

Sheala grinned. Brianna's reactions to the relaxed attitude about sex here on Drakan were priceless. "My sex instructor."

Brianna blinked then slowly lifted her hand to the…man—he was actually a hermaphrodite—at Sheala's side.

Chevin slid his knuckles under her fingertips and lifted her hand to his lips. "I'm honored to make your acquaintance, Alalakan dem al' Brianna. Sheala told me you were beautiful but her words pale next to the reality of your breathtaking personage. Are you, perhaps, interested in instruction of various Drakian sexual techniques?"

Another hand appeared and lifted Brianna's from Chevin's. "I'm quite capable of providing all the instruction my wife needs," Char said in an amused tone as he pulled Brianna to his side.

The older man smiled and nodded his head. "I understand completely." Turning, he held his arm out for Sheala. "Walk me to my transport, Sheala. I want to discuss how you used your tongue on my penis."

Char's laughter at his wife's bright red complexion followed his sister and her companion down the hallway.

"I can't believe you hired a man to teach Sheala how to have sex!" Brianna exclaimed as Char guided her into his study. "She's only seventeen!"

Still grinning broadly, Char kissed the top of his wife's fiery head. "Sheala will be eighteen soon, and we want her to be prepared and educated when she finally has sex. I warned you about our ways. Sex is very important to Drakians."

"Important my ass. You people are fixated on it."

"On your ass?" Char asked with an even wider grin. "I admit to my guilt. You have such a lovely ass."

Huffing with exasperation, Brianna settled into a comfortable chair next to a small table and shuffled some papers.

Char sauntered to his wife's side and looked down. "What are you working on now? You've managed to align Drakan's alphabet with Earth's."

Brianna glanced up.

His gaze was fixed on her breasts, not on the papers in her hands.

"You have a one-track mind."

His grin became lascivious. "You have beautiful breasts."

She smiled slowly. "My ass or my breasts. Make up your mind."

He bent and kissed the exact spot where her neck and shoulder met. "All of you."

Shivering, Brianna stared unseeing as he cupped her right breast and squeezed

Then she blinked—and blinked again. Leaning forward, she stared at the numbers on the paper in front of her. "Drakan takes four hundred and twelve days to go around your sun."

"So?" Char kissed the other side of her neck.

"Earth only takes three hundred and sixty-five days to go around our sun."

"So?" He cupped both breasts.

"In Earth years, Sheala's over twenty."

Char lifted his head and looked into his wife's face. "This matters to you?"

She shrugged. "Seventeen just seemed so young…"

"To have a sex instructor?" Char grinned. "I thought you were losing your prudish ways."

She elbowed his hard stomach. "I'm not a prude."

He chuckled and pulled her to her feet. "No, you aren't—only some of your ideas are."

"My ideas are—"

He silenced her with long, hard kiss then lifted his head. "We're alone."

Brianna looked down at her stomach. "No, we aren't."

Char spread his hand over her swollen abdomen, smiling as a small foot kicked it. How had he gotten so lucky?

Why an electronic book?

We live in the Information Age—an exciting time in the history of human civilization, in which technology rules supreme and continues to progress in leaps and bounds every minute of every day. For a multitude of reasons, more and more avid literary fans are opting to purchase e-books instead of paper books. The question from those not yet initiated into the world of electronic reading is simply: *Why?*

1. *Price.* An electronic title at Ellora's Cave Publishing and Cerridwen Press runs anywhere from 40% to 75% less than the cover price of the exact same title in paperback format. Why? Basic mathematics and cost. It is less expensive to publish an e-book (no paper and printing, no warehousing and shipping) than it is to publish a paperback, so the savings are passed along to the consumer.

2. *Space.* Running out of room in your house for your books? That is one worry you will never have with electronic books. For a low one-time c ost, you can purchase a handheld device specifically designed for e-reading. Many e-readers have large, convenient screens for viewing. Better yet, hundreds of titles can be stored within your new library—on a single microchip. There are a variety of e-readers from different manufacturers. You can also read e-books on your PC or laptop computer. (Please note that Ellora's

Cave does not endorse any specific brands. You can check our websites at www.ellorascave.com or www.cerridwenpress.com for information we make available to new consumers.)

3. *Mobility.* Because your new e-library consists of only a microchip within a small, easily transportable e-reader, your entire cache of books can be taken with you wherever you go.

4. ***Personal Viewing Preferences.*** Are the words you are currently reading too small? Too large? Too... ANNOYING? Paperback books cannot be modified according to personal preferences, but e-books can.

5. ***Instant Gratification.*** Is it the middle of the night and all the bookstores near you are closed? Are you tired of waiting days, sometimes weeks, for bookstores to ship the novels you bought? Ellora's Cave Publishing sells instantaneous downloads twenty-four hours a day, seven days a week, every day of the year. Our webstore is never closed. Our e-book delivery system is 100% automated, meaning your order is filled as soon as you pay for it.

Those are a few of the top reasons why electronic books are replacing paperbacks for many avid readers.

As always, Ellora's Cave and Cerridwen Press welcome your questions and comments. We invite you to email us at Comments@ellorascave.com or write to us directly at Ellora's Cave Publishing Inc., 1056 Home Avenue, Akron, OH 44310-3502.

THE
✟ ELLORA'S CAVE ✟
LIBRARY

Stay up to date with Ellora's Cave Titles in
Print with our Quarterly Catalog.

TO RECIEVE A CATALOG,
SEND AN EMAIL WITH YOUR NAME
AND MAILING ADDRESS TO:

CATALOG@ELLORASCAVE.COM

OR SEND A LETTER OR POSTCARD
WITH YOUR MAILING ADDRESS TO:

CATALOG REQUEST
c/o ELLORA'S CAVE PUBLISHING, INC.
1056 HOME AVENUE
AKRON, OHIO 44310-3502

ELLORA'S CAVEMEN
LEGENDARY TAILS

Try an e-book for your immediate
reading pleasure or order these titles in print from

WWW.ELLORASCAVE.COM

erridwen, the Celtic Goddess of wisdom, was the muse who brought inspiration to story-tellers and those in the creative arts. Cerridwen Press encompasses the best and most innovative stories in all genres of today's fiction. Visit our site and discover the newest titles by talented authors who still get inspired - much like the ancient storytellers did, once upon a time.